# SUMMONED BY

# DRAGONS

# SUMMONED BY DRAGONS

JOAN MARIE VERBA

FTL Publications
Minneapolis, Minnesota

FTL Publications
P O Box 22693
Minneapolis, MN 55422-0693
www.ftlpublications.com
mail@ftlpublications.com

Cover design by GetCovers

ISBN 978-1-936881-74-1

# CHAPTER 1

Rhea Monroe sat on her favorite stone bench on the University quadrangle and looked up, searching the sky for dragons. She saw a brilliant blue sky with scattered clouds, but no sign of her dragon friend, Wondry, who had flown away six years before.

Every day since then, Rhea had started her morning by scanning the heavens, hoping that Wondry would come back for her. But just as with all those other days, there was no sign of her friend this day. She sighed.

Her boyfriend, Nick Grant, appeared between the library and the administration building. He walked toward her and put a hand on her shoulder. "One more final and we're done. Ready?"

Rhea turned to him, smiled, and nodded. "Let's go."

After the exam, free of the obligation of going to classes and taking tests, Rhea felt as if a burden had been lifted from her. Smiling, she took Nick's hand. They strolled through the quadrangle again, unhurried. Only a few students lingered there, with finals over, sitting in the grass or on the stone benches.

Nick turned to Rhea. "Do you want to check out the farm display in the agriculture department, so you can tell them everything they did wrong in the dragon exhibit?"

Rhea chuckled. "I'm not the only one with dragon knowledge. Dragons have been appearing at farms regularly since the 1890s. The Dragon Appreciation Society has an entire library of accumulated knowledge."

"But you're the only one I know of who grew up with a dragon in her home."

"Only because a farmer sold his land to a developer and placed his dragon in an animal shelter for someone to adopt."

"Still, you probably have more knowledge than most."

Rhea took out her smartphone and checked the screen. "That's probably why they invited me to check out the preview. My pass says I can bring a guest."

"I'm game if you are."

Rhea nodded.

They found the building easily, which had a banner at the front announcing their official opening on Saturday. At the entrance, a security guard checked Rhea's electronic pass before letting her and Nick through.

They walked past the displays of cows, chickens, hogs, and other farm animals until they reached the dragon display. There they saw a figure of a dragon standing in a diorama behind a descriptive plaque.

"Until 1891, dragons were thought to only be legendary," Rhea read. "But that year, mother dragons began appearing on our world to lay their eggs on farms before disappearing again. At the farms, the dragons hatched, grew, and became part of the farm family by keeping away predators, eating pests, and fertilizing land with their droppings. Farmers welcomed them eagerly, even though when the dragons reached 15 or 16 years of age, they would grow wings and disappear, presumably to their world of origin. Dragons continue to come here to lay eggs regularly and can still be seen in farm country."

Rhea turned to Nick. "So far, so good." She leaned forward to inspect the dragon figure. "It looks accurate. It has the scales and spine ridges. I can't tell what the model is made out of, though."

"Did they stuff a real dragon?" Nick speculated.

Behind them, they heard a laugh. "No. Oh, no. Dragons are a protected species. We wouldn't do it if we could, and we couldn't because there's no known way to kill a dragon. No dragon appearing here has ever been known to die. They all grow up and fly off."

Rhea and Nick turned to see a slim, black-haired man in his late-20s standing behind them.

He smiled and extended a hand. "Daniel Yang, DVM."

"Rhea Monroe," she said, taking his hand and shaking it. She indicated Nick. "My boyfriend, Nicholas Grant."

"Call me Nick." He shook hands with the man. "Pleased to meet you, Dr. Yang."

"Oh, call me Dan. Dr. Yang is what they call me when someone needs a veterinarian."

"You practice on dragons?" Nick asked.

"Not exactly," Dan said. "Since dragons don't get sick, I haven't treated any, but I do study them. I did a lot of my veterinary training at farms and started gathering all the information on dragons that I could. I did a lot of searching in the literature and found out there was nothing in the veterinary journals about them. Nothing. About the only information I could get was published online by the International Dragon Appreciation Society, but that wasn't very comprehensive. I read articles about dragon habits, but nothing about dragon anatomy or cellular structure, for instance. I did whatever research I could and published some papers myself, hoping that others would add to the research, but no one did. I got a reputation as being the world's foremost expert on dragons, even though I felt I really didn't know that much about them. That's why my husband, who graduated from the School of Agriculture here, recommended me to consult on this exhibit."

Rhea nodded at the model. "I think you did a good job."

Dan turned toward the model. "The artist made a good copy, after going out to a farm and studying a dragon. By the way, this is a female dragon. Their scales are golden. The male dragons are silvery."

Nick motioned toward Rhea. "Rhea grew up with a dragon."

"I know," Dan said. "I read interviews with her in the Dragon Appreciation Society newsletter and saw her picture there. When I noticed her name on the Dean's list, I asked the exhibition managers to send her an invitation. I was hoping you would come."

Rhea smiled. "Thank you for that."

"My pleasure. I'm always happy to meet another friend of dragons."

"I've never seen a dragon," Nick said. "Rhea's dragon companion, Wondry, grew wings and flew off before we met. But she's told me some amazing stories."

Dan nodded. "Probably much more than I read in the newsletter interviews."

"Oh, yes," Rhea said. "At first all we knew was what the lady at the animal shelter told us. But as the years went on, we learned a lot."

"I bet you've seen amazing things yourself," Nick said to Dan.

Dan nodded. "I saw a dragon mother lay an egg once. She appeared out of nowhere in the sky, landed next to the barn, laid the egg, flew back into the sky, and disappeared."

"Must have been quite a sight," Nick said.

"It was. The farm family was delighted. They had always wanted a dragon, since the next farm over had a dragon and it kept the pests under control. They told me that they had relatives who were cattle ranchers out west and they were always happy to have a dragon since it scared the wolves away."

"Didn't the dragon eat the cattle?" Nick asked.

Dan shook his head. "The dragons I observed treated the farm animals as family and protected them. They ate the intruders. The cattle ranchers reported that the dragon would largely eat deer and foxes and such."

"They'll eat anything," Rhea said. "They love flowers, it's like candy to them."

Dan nodded. "They'll eat rocks, too. Helps the digestion, as far as I can tell."

"You said earlier that there's no known way to kill a dragon," Nick said. "Not that I endorse the idea, but has anyone tried?"

"They have," Dan said. "People with guns have tried to shoot them, others have tried to stab them, a couple of times someone has tried to use explosives. Nothing has worked. Farmers and others organized and got laws passed to protect them."

"Has a dragon ever attacked a human?" Nick asked.

Dan shook his head. "Though they'll get angry if someone harasses them. They can let out a roar that has the power of a sonic boom."

Rhea lifted her head slightly. "Wondry did that once. It was heard for miles around."

"I'm not surprised," Dan said.

"What about breathing fire?" Nick asked.

"Hasn't been observed in the young dragons," Dan said. "Some who have seen the mothers come to lay eggs say they've seen them breathe fire."

Nick waved at the dragon model. "Is this as big as they get?"

Dan turned in that direction. "The model is between four and five feet high. I'd say maybe six or seven years old. Older dragons are significantly larger."

Rhea nodded. "The model is about the size Wondry was when she joined us. At first, she was small enough to fit in my double bed. Eventually, she became too large to fit through a door. My dad built a shed for her in the back yard. Then she started to grow wings. When those were large enough, one day she just flew into the sky and disappeared." Her voice broke at the end. She rubbed her face with a hand.

Nick put an arm around her shoulder and gave her a brief hug.

"Did she ever talk to you?" Dan asked.

Rhea sobered quickly and turned to him. "Talk?"

"Yes. They have vocal cords."

"I didn't know that. No, she only made sounds. Trilling, like a bird."

"How do you know they have vocal cords?" Nick asked.

Dan smiled. "Well, it's difficult to get a dragon to hold its mouth open long enough for me to look at its throat, but I have managed to coax a dragon to do that once or twice, and there are definitely vocal cords there. I have pictures."

"Did any dragon ever talk to you?" Nick asked.

"No. I was hoping one would, but none ever did. I'm sure that if any of them talked, someone would have reported it."

Rhea shook her head. "I wish she had talked. We did communicate, in a way. She'd nudge me if she wanted me to go in a certain direction. She'd nuzzle me if I was feeling sad. Sometimes, when she was smaller, she'd cuddle. The day she left, she rubbed her head against me and gave me a sort of hug with her forepaws. After she had gone, I wondered if that was her way of saying goodbye. Ever since, I've been watching for her. I thought she might come back, if for no other reason to lay an egg."

Dan lifted his phone. "I wondered if I could give you my number, in case she comes back. I'd like to see her."

Rhea faced Dan but did not answer immediately.

Dan put the phone down. "It's entirely up to you, of course. I don't want to be intrusive."

Rhea waved a hand. "Uh, no, it's not that. Of course, you can give me your number. It's just that...well, I hoped she'd come back, but it's been so long. I can't guarantee anything."

"I'm not asking you to." Dan tapped his phone against Rhea's when she reached over with it in her hand. "Thanks."

His phone beeped and he checked the screen. "Oh, gotta go. It seems I have a consult."

"Are you assigned here?" Nick asked.

Dan nodded. "The university veterinary clinic is my home base, though I go out to farms and other places when called. I live close to campus, at least until my husband returns. He's doing a land reclamation project for a few months."

After they had said their farewells and Dan had walked away, Rhea and Nick went to the college cafeteria. The area stood largely open since most students only came to campus on the last day of finals if they had a test. Rhea and Nick took their trays and sat side-by-side at a long, empty table.

They ate in silence at first. After a few minutes, Nick turned to Rhea. "Can we talk about our relationship, now that we've almost graduated?"

Rhea nodded.

"I was hoping we could start making some plans," Nick said. "Jobs, living arrangements, that sort of thing."

Rhea sighed. "I know. It's not fair to you, really. I realize I've held off on our being intimate...."

Nick waved a hand. "I can wait until you're comfortable with the idea. I just want to know where our relationship is going."

"I told my parents that if Wondry ever comes back for me, I'm going with her. I didn't want to make a commitment to you until I was sure."

"And?"

"I don't know, Nick. I just have this feeling, this strong feeling, that I'll see her again."

Nick reached over and took Rhea's hand. "If you go, I'll go with you. We've been seeing each other ever since freshman year, and we did fine going on the Engineers Beyond Borders projects."

"That was with a large group, Nick."

"Still. You're my one and only girlfriend and I was sorta hoping that would continue."

"You talked about plans, but I haven't made any plans, Nick. I don't have a job lined up. I kept hoping I'd see Wondry before that."

"Well, I came into my inheritance at my 21st birthday last month. Uncle Jack told me I needed to get out and make my own way in the world, so I have no attachments and more than enough to support both of us, if you want to wait."

Rhea considered for a moment. "No. I guess it's unrealistic of me to wait forever for Wondry. I'll just have to go back to my parents and start looking for a job."

"Why not stay together? Engineers Beyond Borders can still use us, and we can apply for jobs while working with them."

Rhea nodded. "That sounds like a plan."

Nick squeezed her hand. "I love you, Rhea."

She smiled. "I love you, too, Nick."

They exchanged a kiss and turned back to their lunches.


On graduation day, Rhea's parents, Heather and Steve, and her younger sister, Lynn, came over to campus for the ceremony. Nick had already helped Rhea move her things from her dormitory to her car, which was fully packed. After the ceremony, Rhea's family went to a fancy restaurant and had dinner with Nick and his Uncle Jack. Nick's Uncle gave Nick a hearty congratulations and warm farewell before leaving. Rhea's parents said they'd meet Rhea at home.

Hand in hand, Rhea and Nick walked across the empty quadrangle toward the place where Rhea's car was parked.

A strong sudden wind hit them in the face. Rhea looked up to see an enormous golden dragon in the sky, wings beating the air.

"Rhea Monroe! Come with me!" the dragon's voice thundered.

# CHAPTER 2

The dragon settled on the grass near them. Rhea ran to her. Wondry lowered her neck, giving her human friend the opportunity to put her arms around it for a hug. When Rhea stepped back, Wondry bent her legs, folded her wings, and lay with her belly on the ground. She took up a significant part of the northwest section of the quadrangle, an area comparable to a large commuter bus.

"Wondry! I'm so happy to see you!" Rhea said.

In a more conversational tone, the dragon said, "You gave me that name. Wondry. I liked it. It's a nice name. Now that I'm grown up, I gave myself another name, one that I heard when I was growing up here. I'm Zinnia now."

Rhea smiled. "Zinnia! Yes, I'll come with you. I'm so glad we can talk to each other."

"I wanted to talk to you when I was small, but I wasn't grown up enough to speak human languages then."

Nick stepped forward and looked Zinnia in the eye...which was a huge eye. "Can I ask some questions?"

Zinnia turned to Rhea. "Who is this?"

"This is Nick, my boyfriend."

"Future mate?"

Rhea turned from Nick to Zinnia. "Yes."

Zinnia's head bobbed up and down in a nod. "I have one of those, too."

Meanwhile, people began to rush into the quadrangle, staying at a respectful, wary distance away from the dragon. A campus police officer walked up to Rhea. "What's going on?"

Rhea turned to the officer. "We're just talking. We shouldn't be here long."

"I'll set a perimeter, then, so that you won't get crowded."

Rhea looked around. People were taking pictures with their smartphones. She turned back to Zinnia. "We probably shouldn't stay here too long."

"There are some things I need to tell you before I take you to my world," Zinnia said.

"Yes!" Nick said. "I have some questions, if you don't mind."

"What are your questions?" Zinnia asked.

"Well, first of all, are you sure that humans can live were you come from? Is there enough oxygen? Is the climate moderate? For starters."

Rhea turned to Nick. "Of course humans can live there. Dragons breathe, just the same as we do. They're structurally built to move around in our gravity. If their world was significantly different, they couldn't exist here."

Zinnia turned to Rhea. "He is concerned for your safety. A good future mate." She turned to Nick. "Yes, humans can live where I come from. Humans have come occasionally. One came to live on my world for a long time. He grew up with a dragon here and they couldn't bear to part with each other when the dragon became old enough to return to our world."

"Can we meet him?" Nick asked.

"This was many, many years ago. He died and the dragon stacked rocks over him. I can take you to where he lived."

"Is the dragon still alive?" Nick asked.

"No," Zinnia said. "We dragons live a long time, but the dragon died well before I was born. The human left a book. We dragons can't read. You can see it."

"I would very much like to," Nick said. "Next question: Where would we live?"

"There are large insects on our world," Zinnia said. "Every year they swarm and make large houses with openings. Once their young have hatched and grown, they leave the houses behind. They never go back to them but build a new one every year. The man who lived on our world lived in one of these abandoned houses. We cleaned one for you. It's near to where my family lives."

"How many in your family?" Rhea asked.

"My father, my mother, our brother dragon, me, and my future mate. I have older brothers and sisters, but they live apart from us in their own homes. My grandparents have hibernated."

"Hibernated?" Nick asked.

"You'll see."

A voice came from the crowd. "Rhea! Nick!"

Rhea turned to see Dan waving at them. She swung around to Zinnia again. "That's Dan. He's a veterinarian, an animal doctor. He knows dragons, at least here. I think he just wants to see you."

"We may need him," Zinnia said. "It's part of what I want to tell you."

Rhea waved Dan over and the campus police let him through. When Dan reached them, Rhea said, "This is Zinnia, who was Wondry when I was a child."

Dan nodded to Zinnia. "Pleased to meet you. I'm Dan."

"Good," Zinnia said. "I need all of you to listen to me."

"We're listening," Rhea said.

"We dragons got together and sent me to bring humans back. We need humans who can do things, build things, figure out things. I said that I knew of a human who could do that. When I was with Rhea, she built things and was planning to go to college to learn even more."

"I remember you watched me when I built robots for the high school robotics team," Rhea said.

Zinnia continued, "You know that dragon mothers lay eggs here and have been for many mating cycles. Before The Terror, dragons only came to this world occasionally, and not in large numbers."

Nick cautiously raised a hand. "The Terror?"

"It devours our eggs, shells and all. It kills dragons. As you know, we are hard to kill, either here or in our own world. That's why dragon mothers come here to lay eggs. The eggs are safe. The young dragons can grow up. But it's hard to find farms now. Those are the best place for dragons to grow up."

"I know," Rhea said. "Fewer family farms, more corporate farms."

"My mother and father are afraid that when I mate, there won't be a safe place for me to lay my eggs. Other older dragon parents said the same. That's why we got together and talked. We thought maybe humans could help us. Find a way to protect us against The Terror."

"Any idea what it looks like?" Nick asked.

"I have never seen it. Other dragons say it's a sound in the night or a dark cloud in the air. But the eggs, if they're left out, they're gone. Dragons who try to protect the eggs, they're eaten."

"Would they attack us?" Nick asked.

"I don't know. We don't know that The Terror has attacked any creature on our world except dragons. Perhaps they have. Perhaps they haven't."

"But it sounds as if they're mostly interested in eggs," Rhea said.

"Yes. Dragons who don't stay around eggs aren't attacked."

Nick turned to Rhea. "Do you still want to go?"

"Yes," Rhea said. "Do you?"

"If you go, I'll go."

"I'll sure as hell go, if you want me," Dan said.

Nick turned to Dan. "Let us go first and scout around. Make sure that it's safe enough to stay awhile."

Dan opened his mouth as if to speak, then closed it again and nodded. "Yes. I'd like to go now, but if I'm going to set up a veterinary clinic there, I have to gather supplies first."

"Need some funds for that?" Nick asked.

"Um...yes, that would help."

"Do you have a money transfer app?"

Dan took out his phone and showed it to Nick. Nick brought out his own phone and entered something on the touchpad.

"I don't know how much you might need," Nick said to Dan. "Would this be enough?" He showed Dan his phone.

Dan's expression showed pleasant surprise. "Yes, that would work. Can you afford it?"

Nick again manipulated the touchpad and pocketed the phone. "I have more than enough in my account."

"My app shows the transfer went through. Thank you!" Dan said.

Nick nodded and turned to Zinnia. "Can you go back and forth?"

"Yes," Zinnia said. "Anytime I want. We dragons can see this world from our world. That is how I knew Rhea was here."

"Wow," Dan said. "How do you do that?"

"I don't know," Zinnia said. "We just do."

Nick turned to Rhea. "We should probably take some stuff with us. My 'go' bag for Engineers Beyond Borders is always packed. Is yours?"

Rhea nodded.

"There's another thing I have to tell you," Zinnia said. "It's about our brother dragon, Evvin. My parents took him in when he was orphaned by The Terror. His birth mother laid her egg in our world and she died protecting the egg. Then his birth father died protecting the hatchling. He grew up with my parents on my world while I grew up with Rhea on this world. Evvin is a nice, polite dragon, but he is awkward and can do harm sometimes without meaning to. We will watch him, but you needed to know about him."

Rhea turned to Nick. "I think we can handle it."

Nick nodded.

"You can bring things with you," Zinnia said. "As long as they're within reach of me, they will come with me when I make the journey to my world. You should bring a harness. When Rhea and I were young and small, she could ride on my back. If she slipped off, it was not far to the ground. Now it would be, especially if I were flying. Humans slip off."

"Have you had humans slip off when you were flying?" Nick asked.

"Not me. We haven't seen humans in our country for a long time. It's part of dragon lore."

Rhea turned to Nick. "Oral tradition."

"Yes, so I gather. I was thinking of going to the depot where we get our things for the Engineers Beyond Borders projects. I can buy two supply carts, one for you and one for me. They have rock climbing equipment, too. We can adapt those harnesses for us."

"Do you think they'll be open?" Rhea asked.

"Oh, yes. They keep regular business hours no matter what time of year it is."

"Tell you what," Rhea said. "I'll stay here with Zinnia while you get the carts. I need to call my Mom and Dad to pick up my car." She reached into her pocket. "Here are my keys. My go bag is in there. Leave my keys off with campus security for them to pick up."

"I'll have to do the same with my car, and call Uncle Jack." He nodded at Rhea and started to walk away.

"Need some help with the carts?" Dan asked.

"Sure," Nick said.

Arrangements took about another hour. In the meantime, news organizations had set up cameras at the perimeter. Some reporters shouted questions to Rhea. She answered a couple of them before saying she had no further comment.

Zinnia, meanwhile, waited patiently until Nick and Dan came back. Each of them rolled a cart about the length and width of a golf cart piled with equipment. Nick's and Rhea's bags had been perched on top.

"We're ready to go," Rhea said to Zinnia. "How does this work?"

"Put the carts against my body," Zinnia said. "I'll wrap my tail around them. You and Nick grab on to me."

"Where?" Nick asked.

"Anywhere," Zinnia said.

Dan backed up. "I'll be at the campus veterinary clinic whenever you need me. Good luck."

"Thanks!" Rhea and Nick said.

Zinnia lifted her head and body and spread her wings, though she did not fly. The surrounding crowd gave an "aah" of appreciation. Rhea and Nick grabbed Zinnia's tail ridges.

Then they were moving. Zinnia walked on all fours while Rhea and Nick held on to her and walked next to her. Rhea did not feel has if she were being dragged, but she felt air circulating around her. The campus disappeared as if shrouded in a thick fog. Zinnia made huffing noises, though she did not seem to be in distress.

The scene cleared. Above them was blue sky and fluffy white clouds. Sunlight streamed down. Rhea easily located the sun, shading her eyes, since it was as bright as the sun on Earth. She took a deep breath and tasted sweet, warm air. She turned to Nick, who also was looking around.

Zinnia folded her wings and sat up, neck outstretched. "We're home."

# CHAPTER 3

"There must be a lot of birds here," Nick said. "I hear warbling."

"Those are dragons," Zinnia and Rhea said at the same time.

"That's dragon language," Rhea added.

Nick stepped next to the carts and put a hand on one. "The carts made it."

"Yes, they did," Rhea said.

Zinnia moved to one side. Rhea saw that she had been blocking the view of four other dragons, all seated on their haunches with wings folded and heads up. Two, one gold and one silver, were tremendously large, half again as large as Zinnia. Another silver dragon about Zinnia's size sat next to them. The fourth dragon, a silver one, sat a short distance away. He craned his head to look at them curiously. Still watching the newcomers, he lowered himself so that his belly and neck rested on the ground. All turned to the humans.

"This is my family." Zinnia indicated the other dragons by craning her neck in their direction. "My mother, Thalia," Zinnia began, indicating the large gold dragon, "and my father, Kieran," the larger silver dragon, "my future mate, Morran," the next silver dragon, "and Evvin," she said, gesturing to the dragon on the ground. Evvin was slightly smaller than Morran, and his silvery scales less brilliant. Rhea thought that perhaps Evvin was younger. She had already noticed that Zinnia's golden scales were brighter than they were when she was younger.

Zinnia then turned to indicate Rhea. "This is Rhea, and her future mate, Nick."

Morran raised his head. "You brought a human for me. Good." He placed his forelegs on the ground and walked toward Nick. Thrusting his head toward Nick, he added, "A smart human, too, finding someone before mating season."

Rhea turned to Nick. His brow furrowed and his eyebrows went up and down as if he were wondering whether to respond.

Thalia bent her neck and moved her head closer to the humans. "Welcome. We are glad that you were able to come. Let us take you to your new home." She turned to the carts. "You can take your human things there."

Evvin lunged in their direction, causing Rhea and Nick to jump back. "I'll help!"

Thalia put a foreleg on Evvin's shoulder. "Evvin, just stay back and watch for now. The humans just got here. We don't want to scare them."

Evvin lowered his head as if chastised and moved back a couple of steps.

"Zinnia, you lead the way," Thalia said.

The place they had landed in was a large gray flat area, surrounded by boulders of jagged stone. There was an opening at one side. Zinnia placed all fours on the ground and started walking. Rhea and Nick followed, each guiding a cart. There was no road, but a path of compacted ground with vegetation on either side. Rhea noted that the grasses were green. She also saw trees, with green leaves, though some trees had unusual shapes. One in particular had branches spiraling upward around the trunk.

Glancing behind, she saw the other dragons following. Thalia walked directly behind her and Nick, followed by Morran, then Kieran, and Evvin last of all. Despite their bulk, they all moved smoothly, and the ground only vibrated slightly from their gait.

Everyone moved at an easy pace, and within a few minutes, they reached a dark red dome with openings on the sides, set in the middle of a clearing.

"This is the house we picked for you," Zinnia said. "We hope it's all right."

Rhea and Nick let go of the carts and walked up to the dome. It was shaped like half an egg. The topmost part had to be two stories high.

Nick put a hand on the outside wall. "How much weight can it bear?"

"We sometimes sit on the roof to watch the stars at night," Thalia said. "We can fit three dragons there."

Nick's eyebrows went up. "That should be solid enough."

Rhea felt the wall. It was smooth and cool.

Zinnia walked to an opening on the side. "This is where we go in."

Rhea and Nick walked through the opening to the center of the room and looked around. Sunlight streamed through the holes...or perhaps they should think of them as windows? Rhea counted six of them. They were about evenly spaced around the dome and were about four feet up from the foundation. Each window was shaped like a square with rounded corners. There was only one door, the single opening which stood about seven feet high and five feet wide and reached to the foundation.

Zinnia and Thalia came in next. Even with the dragons there, the place seemed quite roomy.

"We cleaned it up for you," Thalia said. "I hope it will do."

Rhea looked around. The floor was flat and smooth, and the same color as the walls and ceiling. Everything was immaculate.

"I take it you didn't use a broom," Nick said.

"No, we burned all the debris," Thalia said, "and blew out the ash."

"No scorch marks," Rhea said.

"No smell of smoke, either," Nick said. "Everything smells fresh. You dragons must have some lung power."

"We do," Zinnia said, "but we used our wings to create a wind."

"Can you live here?" Thalia asked.

Rhea and Nick exchanged a nod before turning to the dragons. "Yes. It's perfect. Thank you," Rhea said.

"Survival comes first. Let's unpack the necessities." Nick turned to Rhea. "I'll set up the composting toilet. You get the solar panels."

The carts had been stacked so that the most vital equipment was on top. Morran shadowed Nick and helped him lift the box with the composing toilet off the top. Rhea noted that their forelegs doubled as arms and their forefeet were more like hands with flexible fingers. Zinnia had showed this potential when she was a younger dragon living with Rhea, but this dexterity was more noticeable in the mature dragons.

"Thanks." Nick paused, put a hand on the box, and looked Morran in the eye. "So I'm your human?"

"Like Rhea is Zinnia's human."

"I guess I can live with that."

While Nick and Morran moved the toilet indoors, Rhea pulled out the light meter. She walked next to a window and called to Nick. "We have more than enough light for the solar collectors."

"Good," Nick called.

Rhea retrieved the meteorological box and took readings. "Temperature is 78 degrees Fahrenheit or roughly 25 degrees Celsius, the UV index is low, and the humidity and dew point are high enough for us to be able to use the condenser to collect water."

"That will work," Nick called again.

"We have water," Evvin called.

Rhea glanced in the direction of his voice. He sat a bit farther from the house than the other dragons but appeared to be observing.

"We humans need water that's free of bacteria, lead, and other elements," Rhea explained. "We'd have to analyze your water before drinking it."

Evvin dipped his head but said nothing.

Rhea reached for the box with the solar panels. Zinnia helped her take it off the cart and lower it to the ground. Rhea found the toolbox, opened it, and used a screwdriver to open the box. She peered inside to be sure the solar panels were there.

She turned to Zinnia. "We can set these on the ground, though it would be better if we can put them on the roof."

"We can fly them to the top," Kieran offered.

"I need to see if I can drive a nail or screws in this material first. We can secure the panels with a strong glue or caulk, but screws are better."

"We don't know what some of those human words you've been using mean," Thalia said, "but we'll help wherever we can."

"Sorry," Rhea said. "Nick and I are used to talking in technical terms. We'll try to be more understandable."

"Use whatever words you need to get your work done," Kieran said. "If we need to know something, we'll ask."

"Thanks." Rhea took up a hammer and nail. She attempted to pound the nail into the side of the house. It was possible, but it took some strength. Taking out the battery-operated drill, she had better luck. She drilled only a fraction of an inch so as to not make too much of a hole. Reaching over, she put a hand on a window opening and examined it. "The walls seem to be maybe three or four inches thick."

"That should work," Nick called. "Any luck with the drill?"

"Yes, we can use it." Rhea turned to Zinnia. "Can you get me and the solar panels up on the roof?"

"Yes." Zinnia enfolded Rhea with her forearms and held her close. "Ready?"

"Oh, yes." Rhea could feel Zinnia spring up and heard the beating of her wings. They were flying! It was exhilarating, even better when she rode on Zinnia's back as a child.

Zinnia landed on the rooftop and set Rhea there carefully. Rhea slid to a sitting position with her legs out in front of her. The curvature at the top was almost flat. Rhea felt secure there and in no danger of sliding off. Zinnia sat behind her and held Rhea gently at the waist with one hand.

Rhea looked down. "I need the box with the solar panels."

Thalia put a hand on the box. "This one?"

"Yes. And the toolbox beside it."

Thalia flew up with the boxes and set them next to Rhea. Thalia, too, remained there as Rhea set up the solar panels. Once they were firmly in place and Rhea had drilled a hole to thread the wires through the ceiling, the dragons flew Rhea and the boxes back to the ground.

In this way, with the help of the dragons, Rhea and Nick set up two sleeping areas, a kitchen area, a bathroom, and an area with a couple of desks. Nothing was wasted in the cart equipment: the box sides were taken apart and used as room dividers.

By the time the sun neared the horizon, one of the carts had been nearly unloaded. Rhea and Nick decided to save the other cart to set up a domicile for Dan later.

Suddenly, they heard a cacophony of sound.

"What the heck is that?" Nick said.

"Sounds as if there's a giant flock of geese and ducks passing by." Rhea looked up but saw nothing in the sky but clouds.

"Those are swimmers," Thalia said. "They come from the lake to their nesting grounds at sunset. At sunrise, they go back to the lake and eat fish and water weeds during the day."

"They're tasty, too," Morran said.

"Do they fly?" Rhea asked.

"They can fly," Thalia said, "but they spend most of their time on the ground. They walk to and from their nesting grounds as a group."

"How many are there?" Nick asked.

"Too many to count," Kieran said. "They multiply quickly, which is good since we eat a lot of them."

"You'll have to take us to see them," Nick said.

"At a distance," Thalia said. "You wouldn't want to get in their path in the morning or evening. They would run over you and maybe crush you."

"They wouldn't crush dragons," Morran added. "You're smaller."

"How large are they?" Rhea asked.

The dragons spread their hands vertically and horizontally.

"About three feet high and two feet wide," Nick observed.

"Tomorrow you'll have to show us around," Rhea said.

"We planned to take you to where the human lived to see his book," Zinnia said.

"Yes! That's an excellent idea," Rhea said.

Nick turned to the dragons. "Rhea and I need to make supper for ourselves and then get ready to sleep."

"Shall we get a swimmer for you?" Morran asked.

"Uh, no, but thanks," Nick said. "We bought some human food with us, though you're right, eventually we'll have to start eating food that comes from here."

Rhea turned to Nick. "Which is why we need to see that book. Maybe the man wrote down what he ate."

Nick nodded.

Rhea looked at the windows and entrance to the dwelling. "We covered the windows on the inside with some flexible plastic that we can open if we wish and set up a sliding door inside the entrance. Before we do any more than that, I wanted to ask if there are insects, birds, or other animals that might come in? Is there anything that might hurt us?"

"Scavengers have sharp teeth and claws, but they'd only be interested in you if you're dead," Morran said.

"Birds stay away from dragon country," Thalia said.

"Competition," Kieran explained.

"The insects that make the houses go away and never come back," Zinnia said. "Other insects and animals stay away from the houses. They think the insects that made them are still there and will attack them."

"Don't worry," Morran said. "The insects that build these houses only come out during birthing season when they put together new houses far away from the old ones. You may never see them."

"Sounds safe enough." Nick turned to Rhea, who nodded.

"We can sleep outside your home tonight," Thalia said.

"Is that inconvenient or uncomfortable for you?" Rhea asked.

"No, not at all," Zinnia said. "It will make us feel better if we're here if you need something."

"We can come inside if you want," Morran offered.

"Um, no, but thanks," Nick said. "I don't think that will be necessary. We can leave the door open, though."

Rhea turned to the second cart. "Shall we leave this here, or take it inside?"

"Does it rain here?" Nick asked.

"Sometimes," Thalia said.

"We'd better take it in, then." Rhea walked around to the other side of the cart, intending to push it, and found herself looking at a dragon tail.

"A wheel broke," Evvin explained, "and it began to tip over, so I steadied it."

Rhea bent down and checked the wheel, which had come off its axle. "Thanks, Evvin."

Morran stepped up and lifted the cart. Rhea replaced the wheel, and Evvin withdrew his tail. Rhea and Nick pushed the cart inside the house and set it against a wall.

By the time they had made themselves supper from the food they brought with them, the sun had set. The solar collectors had not been up long enough to provide much power, but they had enough battery-operated lights and devices to provide illumination until the batteries were charged.

As they ate at the table, Nick turned briefly to the doorway. "Trilling. That's the dragons talking among themselves?"

Rhea nodded.

"Do you understand any of that?"

"No. I wish I did, but no."

After they cleaned the dishes, they walked out of the house. The air remained warm, with a slight, pleasant spicy scent.

Rhea looked up. "Nice stars, and there's a Milky Way." She pointed.

"Can you tell if the stars are the same? I never paid much attention to constellations."

Rhea shook her head. "Neither did I. We'd probably have to get someone from the astronomy department to tell exactly."

The dragons had bedded down on the hardened ground surrounding the house. All were on their stomachs. Kieran and Thalia slept side-by-side, as did Zinnia and Morran. Evvin was off by himself, though still within sight of the door.

When they went back inside, Nick turned to Rhea. "Did you make a note of when sunset was, so we can tell how long the nights are?"

"Yes, I entered it on the tablet app."

Nick checked the battery-operated timepiece he brought with them. "It's about 11 pm back home, though I'm not sure how that translates here."

Rhea drew a long breath and let it out. "I suppose we'll find out. I'm ready to go to bed after all that work. You can stay up if you want to."

"No, I'm tired out as well. Might as well sleep when the dragons sleep."

They had sectioned off a bedroom area, with a divider between Rhea's and Nick's beds. To save on laundry, they simply changed to clean t-shirts and pants to sleep in, which they would wear the next day.

Rhea slept peacefully until she was awakened by a light coming in through the windows.

"Rhea?" Nick whispered. "You awake?"

Rhea propped herself up on an elbow. "Yes."

"What is that, a searchlight?"

"I don't know. Let's go out and check."

Rhea met Nick at the door. They stopped just outside the house and looked up and around.

"Look at that moon!" Nick whispered.

"Well, we're not on Earth anymore. It's huge."

"Not quite a full moon," Nick said. "There's a crescent shadow at the side."

"I think they call that a gibbous moon," Rhea said.

"I'm getting my phone and taking a picture." Nick went inside.

Rhea kept looking at the moon. It was maybe four times the size of Earth's moon. No evidence of an atmosphere. The surface seemed relatively smooth, with craters here and there plus a couple of mountain ranges. The surface seemed to be a yellow-golden color.

Nick came out and got a shot. "I suppose we'll eventually go home and then I can show this to someone."

"Do you need something, humans?" a low voice said.

Rhea and Nick started at the unexpected voice. They turned to Evvin, who had one eye open.

"Um...no," Rhea said. "Just looking at the moon. It's different from the one where we came from."

Evvin closed his eye.

Nick and Rhea went back inside and settled into their beds.

They could tell when the sun rose. The swimmers woke them with their quacking and honking, just as loud as the night before. Outside, they could hear the dragons trilling and moving around.

Rhea and Nick got out of bed, took turns in the bathroom, and headed to the kitchen area.

As he opened the orange juice container, Nick said, "How long was the night? Were you able to check?"

"Eleven hours, fourteen minutes." Rhea said as she warmed the bread.

Nick nodded. "About how long it is in the equatorial regions."

"We can see how long the day is at sunset."

They brought the food to the table and sat down to eat.

"Although we have the basics set up," Rhea said as she buttered her roll, "I've started to make a mental list of other things that I'd like to bring here from home."

"Me, too," Nick said. "Do you think we can get Zinnia to take us back and drop us off briefly at a hardware store?"

"We can ask," Rhea said.

"There's nothing that I urgently need, though," Nick said.

"Same here. Maybe we could give it a week and see if we need anything else."

"At least a few days," Nick agreed.

After they had eaten and cleaned up, they walked outside. The dragons faced them.

"How did you sleep?" Morran asked.

"Very well," Nick said.

"We all need to go and hunt," Thalia said. "We'll return when we're done eating. You humans should be all right by yourselves. Don't wander too far and keep to the paths."

"I was wondering about that," Nick said. "Who made the paths?"

"Just dragons and other animals going back and forth," Kieran said.

Without another word, the dragons launched themselves in the air, spread their wings, and flew away. They quickly disappeared from view.

Nick turned to Rhea. "What next? Any ideas?"

"Set up the wi-fi? We probably can't connect back home, but we can at least text each other if we're separated."

"Good idea."

The dragons still had not returned when they had finished setting up and testing the wi-fi.

"Shall we explore a little?" Nick suggested.

"Yes, but let's not go too far."

"I'm sure the dragons can spot us easily from the air," Nick said.

They each pocketed their phones, and selected a walking stick before setting out on a path that took them away from the house and the dragons' home. Their surroundings consisted of a forest with widely-spaced trees and short grasses.

"The leaves are pretty much the same," Nick said. "Narrow on some trees, wide on others."

"I don't see anything like pine, with needles and cones."

"Me, neither."

They had walked for a while when they came to a hill, which had a cave entrance near them.

"Want to explore?" Nick suggested.

"We'll need to be cautious in case there are animals in there."

"Haven't seen any so far. You?"

"No, that's why I'd say we need to be cautious."

Nick took out his phone. "We can turn on the lights on our phones and check."

Rhea looked up, seeing movement in the distant sky. "That's Evvin."

"Coming back?"

"I don't know."

"Do you think he sees us?"

"No sign of it, but from what Zinnia said, I don't think it's a good idea to be alone with him, at least until we have more experience with the dragons."

Nick indicated the cave. "Well, we have a place to hide."

They scrambled to a place just inside the cave entrance and turned on their phone lights. They could see the back of the cave, and it was empty. The cave floor was a little dusty, but otherwise free of debris.

Nick led the way and found a couple of large, smooth rocks. "We could sit here."

"Good idea."

When they had settled themselves, Rhea turned to Nick. "How are you holding up?"

"Okay so far. I was startled when Morran referred to me as 'his' human."

"When Zinnia lived with us, I referred to her as 'my' dragon. So I suppose I shouldn't be surprised if she thinks of me as 'her' human."

"I hadn't thought of that. Now that you mention it, dogs and cats seem to think of their caretakers as 'their' humans."

Rhea nodded. "So far, this seems to be a nice place. Livable. Comfortable."

"Yes. One of the reasons I joined Engineers Beyond Borders was to see places I'd never been to before and meet others with different customs and practices. To have new experiences and see new things."

"Same here. A completely different world with completely different species is even more exciting."

"Exciting doesn't even begin to describe it. The hardest part is the setting up, which we have to do first because we have to eat and sleep. But I would rather be out exploring."

"Me, too. I'm looking forward to Zinnia and Morran taking us to the place where the human lived."

Nick checked his timepiece. "Speaking of dragons, Evvin must have flown off by now. Let's go out again."

Rhea nodded. She dusted herself off and picked up her walking stick. Nick did the same.

They took a couple of steps outside the cave entrance. Looking toward the horizon, they saw no sign of any dragon.

"Seems like the coast is clear," Nick said.

"Hello, humans!"

Rhea and Nick both jumped, startled. They turned around. There was Evvin, perched on the hill behind them.

# CHAPTER 4

Evvin flew from the top of the hill and to the ground directly in front of Rhea and Nick. He lowered himself and faced Rhea.

"Can you get a human for me?"

Rhea felt too stunned to answer immediately.

Nick said, "It doesn't work that way, Evvin. I came with Rhea because I'm Rhea's future mate."

Undaunted, Evvin said, "But there are humans where you were. Can you find one for me?"

"We can't just grab a human, Evvin," Rhea explained. "We don't even know how we're going to live here yet."

"But there was a human who lived here for a long time," Evvin said.

"Yes, Zinnia told us," Nick said. "But we need to know how he lived here. Not every human could survive here."

"And the human would have to be willing to come," Rhea said. "The other human came because he was friends with a dragon in our world. I came because I am Zinnia's friend."

"I would be the human's friend," Evvin said. "I would take very good care of the human and make sure that the human had everything a human needs."

Out of the corner of her eye, Rhea saw motion and looked up. Zinnia descended and landed next to Evvin.

"Evvin," Zinnia said, "our human friends need to go home now. They have to get ready for Morran and I to take them to the old human's house."

"I can come with you," Evvin said.

"This will be the first time that the humans will sit on our backs while we fly. Morran and I need to do this ourselves."

Evvin said nothing in reply. He dipped his head and flew off.

Zinnia turned to Rhea and Nick. "Sorry. I should have come around sooner."

"No harm done," Rhea said.

"He wants a human of his own," Nick said.

"He would," Zinnia said. "But I don't think he has any idea what it really means to share space with a human. The rest of us, the ones who grew up on your world, have had years of experience that he hasn't had."

Rhea turned to Nick. "Let's start back, then."

"I'll walk with you," Zinnia said. "Do you have what you need to make sure you won't fall off our backs?"

"I think I have it," Nick said. "I have safety harnesses for Rhea and me, as well as adjustable straps to put around you and Morran. I brought helmets for Rhea and I, which have microphones in them so we can talk to each other, and Bluetooth devices I can clip to your and Morran's ears."

"What are those for? Those Bluetooths?" Zinnia asked.

"That's so you can hear Rhea and I while we're flying."

"We can hear each other when we're flying. We should be able to hear you, too."

"Would you be willing to try it in the first flight?" Rhea asked. "If we find it isn't necessary, we can leave them off afterwards."

"Yes, I'm willing to try," Zinnia said.

"When do you want to start?" Rhea said.

"It's a long flight. We wanted to start as soon as we were finished hunting. Morran is waiting at your home."

"How long?" Nick asked.

"Longer than a usual flight. Outside our territory. I can't put it in hours and minutes, if that's what you're asking."

"Fair enough," Nick said.

"Can we get there and back before sunset?" Rhea asked.

"Yes," Zinnia said. "The sun will move a few widths, but not a great many."

"When we get to the house," Nick said, "Rhea and I will grab a quick lunch and then join you and Morran."

They found Morran waiting at the house, as Zinnia had said. Zinnia told him they needed to wait briefly while the humans had a meal.

When they had finished eating, Rhea and Nick put on the helmets, as well as elbow and knee pads, before gathering their equipment and going outside.

Nick approached Morran and held up the Bluetooth. "If it's all right with you, I'll attach this to your ear. You'll be able to hear me and talk with me at a distance."

"Is this the same as I saw humans wearing when I was a young dragon on Earth?" Morran said excitedly.

"Yes," Nick said.

"That's great! If we're apart, I won't have to fly to you in order to talk. Put it on."

Morran dipped his head so that Nick could reach his ear. Nick clipped the Bluetooth at the side of an ear. "Does that hurt?"

"No, I can barely feel it."

"Let me turn the helmet microphone on. Testing, testing...."

"Yes, I can hear you, though it's not exactly your voice when you talk without it."

"There's some filtering." Nick approached Zinnia. "Can I clip one on you, now?"

Zinnia lowered her head and Nick clipped it on. "Is it comfortable?" he asked.

"Yes," Zinnia said.

"Good." Nick gathered the straps and harnesses. He stood next to Morran and looked him over.

"Something wrong?" Rhea said, when Nick did nothing for a while.

Nick scratched his head. "Um, I'm not sure where to start."

"Let me," Rhea said. "I've put harnesses on Zinnia before."

"She was a lot smaller then," Nick said.

"Still." Rhea gathered her own set of straps and harnesses. She approached Zinnia. "I think the best place for us to sit would be behind the first ridge. It's where the back and neck join."

"That is what I was thinking," Zinnia said.

Rhea threw one strap over Zinnia's back, and another underneath her. Working together, with Zinnia using her forearms and hands to help position the straps and Rhea making adjustments, they worked quickly.

Meanwhile, Morran and Nick edged closer to get a clear view. At one point, Zinnia said, "Step back. We need to work."

They did.

At last, they had straps encircling Zinnia's body on either side of her forelegs. Rhea made cross connections, then attached her body harness to the straps. She made one loop to use as a foothold, another loop to use as a handhold, and with those, climbed onto Zinnia's back between the first and second ridges, sitting as if she were on a horse. She put a leg in and around a strap on either side.

Once secure, she turned to Nick. "This should work." She leaned forward. "Zinnia, is any of this squeezing you at all?"

"No, it's firm. I don't feel as if you would slide off my back." Zinnia turned to Morran and Nick. "Now, you do it."

With instructions and encouragement from Rhea and Zinnia, Nick and Morran got everything in place, and Nick climbed onto Morran's back.

Nick sat up straight. "I can see over the ridge."

"The first one is small enough to do that, yes," Rhea said.

"Is he secure?" Zinnia asked Morran.

"Feels firm," Morran said.

"Ready to go?" Zinnia asked.

"Yes," Rhea and Nick said.

"Let's go." Zinnia spread her wings behind Rhea and jumped into the air. Her wings started beating, and they began to ascend.

"Whoo!" Nick shouted as Morran ascended.

"I hope that means you're doing fine," Morran said.

"This is awesome!" Nick replied. "How are you doing, Rhea?"

"Great!" Rhea said. "The view is stunning."

"Yes, seeing everything from above is wonderful." Zinnia said.

Rhea had put a strap around the ridge for her to hold on to, or she could hold on to the ridge in front of her directly, but she also felt secure enough to let go and take a measuring instrument from a pocket.

"We're about 100 meters up," she said to Nick. "And the temperature is only a few degrees lower than the ground."

"We won't go too much higher," Zinnia said. "Otherwise it gets too cold, even for us, and it's harder to fly."

"Air is thinner," Rhea said.

"Yes," Zinnia said.

"We've reached an airspeed of about 40 mph relative to the ground, and slowly accelerating," Rhea said.

"We'll go a little faster, but not too much," Zinnia said. "It's a long way, and we don't want to get too tired."

"How fast can you go?" Nick asked.

"If we're really trying, much faster than this," Morran said. "We go fastest when we fly high up in the air, and then dive down."

"We often do it just for fun, or if playing with other dragons," Zinnia added.

Rhea looked around and down. She could see treetops for quite a distance. If the sun here rose in the east and set in the west, then they were traveling northwest. Due north she could see mountains. To the east of them, a river. Farther north, what seemed to be a large body of water. A sea or ocean? Turning around, to the south, she saw a large lake. Lowering the distance lenses on the helmet, she could see what she guessed were the swimmers on the lake.

Still looking south, she saw silvery dragons rising up from the ground, flying in their direction.

"Company," Rhea said.

"Company?" Zinnia queried.

"Dragons behind us, flying toward us," Rhea clarified.

Morran turned his head.

"Were you expecting them?" Nick asked.

"No." Morran turned to Zinnia. "Let's go on. If we ignore them, they may go away."

"They're closing fast," Rhea said.

The dragons—Rhea counted seven of them—soon caught up to them. Some breathed fire.

"Wow!" Nick exclaimed. "Fire!"

"Not necessarily a good thing right now, Nick," Rhea said into the microphone, using a low voice.

Morran swerved to get more distance between them and the group of dragons.

"Humans!" a dragon called. "Are they fireproof?" The dragon exhaled a stream of fire.

"Why don't all of you go chase some swimmers?" Morran said.

Zinnia also swerved to put more distance between them. "Go find something else to do."

"But this is so much fun!" said another silvery dragon.

Rhea hung on to the ridge in front of her as Zinnia maneuvered away from the newcomers. She admired Zinnia's flight skills.

Across from her, Nick also hung on to Morran's first ridge as Morran dipped and soared. Neither human said anything. Rhea guessed that Nick also remembered the lecture they had been given at Engineers Beyond Borders: when your pilot or driver is avoiding hazards, shut up and let them to their jobs.

RRROOOAAARRRRR!!!

Rhea had heard Zinnia roar as a younger dragon. Just as then, the air shook as if they were in the middle of a sonic boom. Rhea was glad that the sound system within the helmet had a decibel limit. The roar was loud enough coming through earphones.

All the dragons stayed airborne, but they all quavered a little with the force. They turned their heads to look behind them, in the direction of the sound.

Rhea turned too and saw Evvin flying behind them all.

"Leave those humans alone!" Evvin thundered. "Go away!" He began to chase the silvery dragons.

They evaded him and circled around him. "Look who's here," one of the dragons remarked.

"Yes, it's me. And I say leave the humans alone."

Out of the corner of her eye, Rhea saw a dragon zipping through the air toward them, amazingly fast. This dragon went under and ahead of them, and when the dragon slowed enough for her to make out identifying features, she saw Kieran hovering just ahead of them, facing all of them.

"It looks like some of you are lost. Home is that way." Kieran gestured with his head and neck. "You turn around. I'll follow and make sure you get there."

Without saying a word, or issuing a trill, the seven silvery dragons changed course and began to fly away. Kieran flew behind him.

Morran, still hovering, turned to Zinnia. "We need to land."

"We're fine," Nick said. "We can go on."

"Nick," Rhea said. "They're the flight experts. If they say we need to land, we need to land."

"Oh. Right. Sorry," Nick said.

Silently, the dragons circled and came to rest in a forest clearing. Rhea found the landing amazingly soft.

"Shall we get off?" Nick asked.

"No," Zinnia said. "Are you sure you're both all right?"

"Fine," Rhea said.

"Fine here," Nick said.

Evvin landed and faced the two other dragons. "They're not supposed to do that!"

"We know, Evvin," Zinnia said gently.

"Who were those guys? Those other dragons?" Nick asked Morran.

"Bachelor dragons," Morran said, "ones without the smarts to find a future mate before mating season. They live, play, and hunt together."

"And flirt with the unattached female dragons," Zinnia added.

"They'll wait until the last minute and just mate with whoever is available," Morran said. "Not a good plan."

"Though a number of dragons get along just fine doing that," Zinnia said.

"Not the way I want to mate," Morran said.

"I don't, either," Zinnia said.

"What happens now?" Nick asked.

Morran turned to Zinnia. "We take the humans home."

"Yes." Zinnia craned her neck to face Nick and Rhea. "We can go to the other human's house another day."

"You're the experts," Nick said.

The dragons took off again. When they landed at the house, Zinnia said, "You can get off now. But leave the harnesses on us."

Once Rhea and Nick were on the ground again, Morran said, "You know, I always wondered about you humans wearing clothes, why you would want to cover yourselves. But the harness you put on me makes me feel...impressive, somehow."

"I always felt that the harness I wore on the human world was something Rhea had just for me, and showed that we were friends," Zinnia said. "I didn't mind it at all."

"We humans often wear special clothes to show off," Nick said.

"Leave the Bluetooth on, too," Morran said. "I can call you and you can call me without our having to be within sight of each other."

Rhea heard a keening sound. She looked up and around to see if she could determine where it came from.

Nick was turning around, too. "What is that?"

The dragons had stretched their necks upward as if listening. Zinnia turned to Morran briefly before answering. "Dragon talk."

"What does it mean?" Rhea asked.

"Dragons getting together," Evvin said.

"We need to go," Zinnia said. "We'll return later."

"Can we go with you?" Nick asked.

"Not now," Morran said. "Stay within sight of the house and do human things."

The three dragons took flight.

Rhea turned to Nick. "When Zinnia first appeared on campus, she said that the dragons got together and talked about us before sending her to us."

"I have a feeling they're going to talk about us again."

"Or the other dragons."

"Or both."

Rhea nodded.

"I have a feeling those other dragons are being taken to the woodshed," Nick said. "Evvin said they weren't supposed to do that, and Zinnia agreed. When Kieran appeared, they did as he said without talking back."

"Apparently, they respect their elders."

"I noticed that their elders are considerably larger, too."

"They are," Rhea said. "I'm glad you said you were willing to go on."

"Of course," Nick said. "I'm not going to be discouraged by a few bad actors."

"They all have the ability to kill us, you know."

"Oh, I know. But we humans live among other humans, and any of us could kill each other, too."

"Not to mention all the animals at home that can kill us."

Rhea took a long breath and let it out. "Well, I guess we just wait and see what develops. I'm sure Zinnia and Morran will tell us."

"If they don't, I'm going to ask!"

Rhea and Nick had been inside the house, continuing the process of unpacking and organizing, when they heard the whooshing of air outside. They stepped outside the door and saw Zinnia and Morran landing.

"We're here to ask you to come with us to a dragon gathering," Zinnia said.

"You'll see the dragons that followed us earlier," Morran said. "Don't worry, they won't hurt you."

Nick turned to Rhea and back to Morran. "We're not worried."

"We trust you," Rhea said.

"That's good," Morran said. "But you should be cautious around any of us. We can injure you easily, you know, and without much effort."

"We know," Rhea said.

"That's why we warned you about Evvin," Zinnia said. "He means well, but he's still awkward in many ways."

"Evvin did, however, try to protect us from those other dragons," Rhea said.

Zinnia nodded her head. "He did, but you should still be cautious."

Morran turned to Rhea and Nick. "Climb on, we'll fly you there."

"Where's 'there?'" Nick asked.

"The place the bachelors live," Morran said. "They'll be properly supervised and won't harm you."

Rhea and Nick ducked into the house, grabbed their helmets and padding, and got into their respective harnesses.

"Is it a long flight?" Rhea asked.

"Short flight, long walk," Zinnia said.

Once they were airborne, Rhea saw a group of dragons not far away circling above a large ring of jagged boulders. As Zinnia flew closer, Rhea could see elder dragons, gold and silver, perched on the boulders. Zinnia and Morran flew over the boulders and into the ring. The area resembled Zinnia's family home: flat, smooth, rocky surface, but significantly larger.

When Zinnia landed, Rhea climbed down and looked around again. There were a great many dragons sitting in the area. A group of golden dragons around Zinnia's size caught her eye. Other silver and gold dragons of various sizes stood watching as Zinnia and Morran stepped back, leaving Rhea and Nick standing facing the middle of the circle. Rhea, however, noticed that Zinnia and Morran stood close behind them.

A silver dragon stepped forward and dipped his head. "We want to say how sorry we are. We didn't mean any harm. We wouldn't have hurt you. We were just having a little fun. But it was wrong to approach you like that. We won't do it again. If there's anything you need, we'd be glad to help you. Just ask."

The six other silver dragons with him murmured assent.

Rhea turned to Nick and then to the dragons. "We understand. We accept your apology."

"We want to be friends with all dragons," Nick said.

The group of seven turned to Kieran, who had strolled up to them as they talked.

Kieran turned to Rhea and Nick. "Are you still willing to stay and help us?"

"Yes, of course," Nick said.

"Absolutely," Rhea said.

"Thank you." Kieran lifted his head and looked around. "We are all here to demonstrate that we are in agreement and you can count on our good will."

"We're grateful for everything you've done," Rhea said.

"We will help you in any way we can," Kieran said. He turned back to the assembly. In singles or in groups, they began to fly away.

"We can go back home now," Zinnia said.

# CHAPTER 5

When they returned to the house, and had dismounted, Nick stood by Morran. "Be sure to turn off the Bluetooth, to save the battery."

"I...only understand a little of that."

Rhea, standing next to Zinnia, turned to Morran. "Let me show you." She reached up and touched Zinnia's Bluetooth, still attached to her ear. "There's a button here that you press when you're not using it."

Morran had stepped closer. "But I can't see my ear."

"Can you scratch it?" Nick asked.

"Of course."

"Then you can do it by touch," Nick said. "Humans do."

Rhea looked Zinnia in the eye. "Here, Zinnia, give me your hand."

Zinnia settled down and reached up. Rhea took Zinnia's hand. It was much larger than she remembered as a child. Rhea needed both her hands to hold one of Zinnia's. She brought Zinnia's hand up and separated a finger.

"Can you retract the claw?" Rhea asked.

Zinnia did so.

Rhea took Zinnia's fingertip and pressed the power button.

"Oh, that was easy," Zinnia said. "Let me try it by myself." She did.

"You turned it off," Rhea said. "Now press it again to turn it on, and then turn it off again."

Morran reached up and felt for the power button on his Bluetooth. He found it within a few seconds and turned it off.

Nick nodded. "Now, if you need to call us, press the button."

"What if you need to call us?" Zinnia asked.

"You'll hear a chime," Rhea said. "Then press the button."

"This is good," Zinnia said. "Morran and I can sleep outside your house again tonight, but afterwards, we can sleep at our own place."

"Yes, of course," Rhea said.

"I'll tell Mother and Father and Evvin they can sleep at our place tonight."

The next day, after the dragons' daily hunt, Rhea, Zinnia, Nick, and Morran set off again. This time they had the sky to themselves as they traveled. Rhea again spotted low mountains to the north. Due east, even taller mountains—an entire range as far south as she could see—with steep cliffs. Beneath them, and to the west, she saw forest with occasional clearings, dotted with an occasional lake, sometimes with a stream running through. After about an hour of flight, she began to see a hilly area in front of them, with the forest thinning out in favor of more grassy areas. In another half hour, she saw a grassy plain to the west, and perhaps a herd of...cows? Bison? Even lowering the distance lenses, she could not make out the animals clearly.

At just under two hours, the dragons landed on a hill with a flat top. There were trees in the area, widely scattered, and short grasses. A reddish structure like theirs dominated the area. Close to it they saw a rectangular pile of rocks. Beyond that, what appeared to be a fire pit made of stone.

"This is the place," Zinnia said, as Rhea and Nick dismounted.

Nick immediately walked over to the house and put a hand on it. "This is impressive work. He built a door, the windows have awnings and shutters, and I think that's a chimney I see sticking through the top."

Morran walked over to the pile of rocks. "The human is underneath these rocks. He told his dragon friend to pile them on top when he died."

Zinna moved toward the door. "The book is inside. I have seen it. Dragons visit here from time to time. We open the door and shut it again when we leave."

The main entrance, wide and tall enough for a dragon to walk through, had a double door. Instead of a knob, there was a ring on a hinge attached to each door. Rhea pulled on a ring. The door opened easily. Zinnia pulled the other open.

They walked through. Sunlight streamed through the windows.

Nick walked over to one. "The shutters are open. These are actual glass windows." He reached up and touched one. "I doubt that he made these. Probably brought them with him, or had the dragon bring him back to our world to buy some."

Rhea noted the bed against a wall. The blanket had been pulled almost to the foot of the bed. A large space separated the bed from the rest of the room. Looking around, she saw what seemed to be a stone oven with a cast iron grill as a stovetop. "Here's where the chimney goes up. Draws smoke from the cooking fire."

Nick pointed. "Looks like a workshop over there. Bench, tools, even a pedal-driven buzzsaw."

Zinnia moved toward a desk. "Don't you want to see the book?"

Rhea and Nick walked to a table and chair. "Yes, we do."

On the table was a large, thick book. Upon closer inspection, Rhea saw two books stacked neatly on top of each other. A pen and inkwell lay nearby.

Nick moved the chair to get closer to the books.

Rhea lifted the top book and handed it to Nick. "You check this one, I'll check the other one."

Nick nodded, laid the book on the tabletop, and carefully opened the cover. "It's old, but at least it's not falling apart."

Rhea lifted the cover of the second book with equal care. "Yes, we should turn the pages gently."

"I will." Nick sat and turned a page. "There's a name on the inside front cover. Arthur Johnson. Then on the first page, there's a date. 'May 12, 1907. Rex found me this house, which is real nice, but needs fixing up. Don't know how he found me since I moved from the farm into the woods. Learned to talk, too, which he didn't when he grew wings and left. Said he missed me and I should come and live with him, seeing as how I didn't have family anymore. I thought that was a good deal since I missed him, too. We were real close. Never did get along well with people.'" Nick stopped reading and looked up at Rhea.

Rhea gingerly browsed through the volume she had and spoke as she turned from page to page. "This is what we want. He says the water is good to drink. There's a grain here that he says makes good bread. He has a sketch here to show what it looks like."

Nick turned and nodded to the other end of the room. "I thought I saw a hand mill over there."

"Swimmers are good eating, he says." Rhea glanced at Morran. "Agrees with Morran there. Apparently there's a leaf, which if you brush against it, your skin goes numb."

"Yes, we know about that," Zinnia said.

Rhea nodded. "He notes other leaves are good for healing, with more sketches. Has recipes. Other notes on what's good to eat. Sketches of more animals." She carefully closed the book and looked up. "We need to read this."

Nick lifted the book in front of him. "We need to read this, too. His experiences have to be valuable."

Both Rhea and Nick had brought messenger bags. Rhea carefully put the books in her messenger bags.

"Let's see if there's anything else we want to bring with us," Nick said.

Rhea nodded. She and Nick searched the rest of the house. Rhea was impressed by how neat and organized everything was. There was very little dust, and no musty smell.

Nick put a hand on a shelf. "More books."

Rhea turned to him. "Journals?"

"Yes. We'll take those. The books by Mark Twain and Jules Verne and others, I think, we can leave here. See anything else we can use?"

"Not now." Rhea turned to the dragons. "Could we come back if we need to?"

"Yes," Zinnia said. "But not today. We would have to rest first."

Rhea nodded. "I understand. Nick and I will want to take a look around outside before leaving."

The dragons preceded them out the door. Rhea and Nick closed the doors behind them. They began to walk around the house.

"Looks like a pen for animals," Nick said, indicating a small fenced-in area.

"Not for dragons," Rhea said. "Too small, and the fence is too low."

They walked to the edge of the hill and looked out over the grassland.

Nick pointed. "Could he have had one of those herd animals out there?" He turned to Morran. "Know anything about them?"

"They taste good," Morran said. "But I only eat them once or twice a year. It's a long way to fly."

"Do they give milk?" Rhea asked.

"Yes," Zinnia said. "They're like the cows we saw on the human farms. But smaller."

Nick turned to Rhea. "That could be it, then."

Rhea pointed. "Do you know what's beyond the grassland?"

"Another dragon community," Zinnia said.

"Do you ever go there?" Nick asked.

"I haven't," Morran said. "Long flight."

"Some dragons in our community have been there," Zinnia said. "But we dragons mostly stay in our own areas."

"Are they friendly?" Nick asked.

"All dragons are friends," Morran said. "We don't fight each other as humans do."

Rhea walked to another area of the hilltop and faced northeast. "There's a large body of water there. A lake?"

"Ocean," Zinnia said. "The water isn't good to drink, but it's safe to swim in."

"Do you go there?" Nick asked.

"Sometimes," Zinnia said. "It's closer. We play there, hunt the fish, swim."

Nick pointed southeast. "Those cliffs. That's quite a mountain range."

"Yes," Morran said. "We hunt and play there."

"Dragons go there to hibernate," Zinnia said.

"Or die," Morran said.

"It's a dragon graveyard?" Rhea asked.

"Part of it," Zinnia said.

"When a dragon feels death coming on," Morran said, "a dragon will go there and find a place among the rocks to rest. Eventually, we become one with the rock."

"Fossilized?" Nick asked.

"I don't know what that human word means," Morran said.

"Dragons don't decay like other animals do," Zinnia said. "Our bodies harden inside and out. We become like stone."

Nick nodded.

"What's beyond the mountains?" Rhea asked.

"Grassland. Nothing to see there," Morran said.

Rhea and Nick continued to walk around the house and found a ring of stones. Burnt wood lay in the middle.

"A fire pit?" Nick asked.

Rhea nodded. "Seems so. This reminds me: although we use up most of what we brought, we need waste disposal of some kind. If we had something like this, we could put the waste there and the dragons would burn it."

Nick turned to the dragons. "What do you think? There's a large patch of hard, rocky ground near the house. Could you put a ring of stones there and burn things we don't need anymore?"

"Just a little ring, like that one there?" Zinnia asked.

"Yes," Rhea said.

"That would be easy," Morran said.

"Thanks," Nick said.

Rhea turned to Nick. "Ready to go home?"

"Yes, we have what we came for," Nick said.

Once back home, Rhea and Nick spread the books out on the table and began to read. When they were students, they often read books together, sitting next to each other. Eventually, they became aware of a pattering on the clear plastic shields over the window openings.

"Rain," Nick said.

Zinnia stuck her head inside the door. "We're going to another shelter near here to stay dry."

"Are we living in your rain shelter?" Rhea asked.

"There are many places to shelter here. We're going to a double house not far from here. Dragons can stay out in the rain if they want. It won't hurt us. We just prefer to stay dry if we can."

"Your Bluetooth devices are waterproof," Nick said. "We'll call if we need anything."

"But we probably won't, we're reading," Rhea said.

"We'll come back when the rain stops." Zinnia withdrew her head.

Nick turned to Rhea. "I'll close the door."

When Nick returned to his seat, Rhea said, "The supply carts we brought with us have tarps and tent supports we aren't using. We can probably build the dragons a rain shelter at their home so they won't have to go somewhere else."

"I was thinking the same thing," Nick said.

They paused in their reading for supper. Rain still thrummed against the house.

"It's a good thing he didn't journal every day," Rhea said. "He lived a long life, and we would have been reading into the next week."

"I presume he died shortly after the last entry, which he reckoned was in 1956," Nick said. "Rex was cooking for him, helping him move around, and he figured he didn't have much time left."

"Yes, I thought it was nice that Rex slept on the floor next to his bed every night."

"That explains the space we saw."

"It probably wasn't exactly 1956," Rhea said. "The days here are one hour and twelve minutes longer, and Arthur said himself when Rex brought him back to our world every so often, the dates weren't what he thought they were."

"Besides, he stopped coming to our world after World War I," Nick said. "He wrote that when the shopkeeper he was buying from told him supplies were short because of the war, that was it for him."

"He had a good cover story...that he was living alone in the woods and didn't get into town a lot," Rhea said. "He said that's why he didn't know about the war."

"The description of 'the war to end all wars' seemed to disgust him."

"It was probably just as well," Rhea said. "He missed the 1918 Pandemic, which might have killed him. He missed the Great Depression and Dust Bowl, and World War II."

"I'm sure hearing about the dropping of the atomic bomb would have sealed it, if he'd heard," Nick said.

"The second book...the one with the descriptions of the plants and animals...we need to get that to Dan," Rhea said. "The first one, too, but especially the second."

"Yes, we need to talk to the dragons about taking us back home, at least for a couple of hours," Nick said.

The rain continued after they finished eating dinner and cleaning up afterwards. They spent the evening reading the other journals and writings.

Just before getting ready for bed, Rhea said, "There's a lot about this world in Arthur's journals that Zinnia and her family haven't told us."

"I suppose if they told us everything they knew, it would take weeks, if not months."

"Oh, yes, I agree. This is only our third day here and all they could do is give us highlights," Rhea said. "But I wondered why they didn't mention the clinging vines when we asked if there was anything dangerous around here, for instance."

"Maybe there aren't any clinging vines around here. Besides, I gathered that the vines just trap you. They don't kill their prey outright, they just hold on until the prey starves to death."

Rhea considered. "Yes, I suppose the dragons just presumed that if we were caught in one, there would be plenty of time to come and rescue us before that happened."

Nick nodded. "That sounds right. But I do agree with you that there are other things in Arthur's journals that I want to ask about."

"They need to go hunt in the morning," Rhea said, "but we could talk to them afterwards if there seems to be an opening to do so."

The next morning, the rain had stopped. After breakfast, the dragons returned. Rhea and Nick walked outside to meet them.

"Did you read the books?" Zinnia asked.

"Yes, they were very helpful," Rhea said. "We wanted to ask you questions about it."

"We wanted to ask you questions about it, too," Zinnia said.

"What questions did you have?" Rhea asked.

"Did they say anything about The Terror?" Thalia asked.

"Yes," Rhea said. "Rex told him about it."

"Rex was the name of the dragon?" Kieran asked.

"Yes, and Arthur was the name of the man," Nick said. "You didn't know the dragon's name?"

"The dragon's name was...," Morran let out a trill. "But we didn't know the human name."

"What did Rex tell him?" Thalia asked.

"That the dragons didn't lay eggs here anymore because The Terror ate them. Rex pointed out where dragons used to lay eggs. It was far away, but Arthur used his spyglass to look at it from the hilltop. One day, they saw a shadow pass over the area. Arthur wanted Rex to take him there, but Rex said no, that was The Terror and they weren't going anywhere near there until it passed. From then on, Arthur always checked the area with his spyglass before he and Rex flew in that direction."

"The Terror comes only during birthing season," Thalia said. "Not all the time."

Rhea nodded. "Arthur said that mating season is in the fall, and birthing season is in the spring."

"Fall and spring here, yes," Zinnia said. "Though the weather is almost the same here whatever the season. No snow, except for the mountain tops. No freezing cold. It's summer right now."

"Arthur said he saw the shadow elsewhere, too," Nick said. "Still only in birthing season, but in the northwest area near the ocean. He wrote there were two main herds of animals, the northern and southern herds. The shadow would go to the northern herd in the grasslands near the ocean, and they were visibly reduced afterwards. He and Rex never went there, though. The southern herd was the one close to them, and they didn't have a need to go north that far."

The dragons looked at each other.

"If we can go back to Arthur and Rex's house someday," Rhea said, "we can install a camera there with a long lens that can scan the area and we can keep watch."

"That sounds good," Kieran said.

"That gives us a starting point, at least," Rhea said, "and we had some questions we wanted to ask you, too."

"Zinnia and I thought we'd take you to see her grandparents in the mountains after we hunt today," Morran said. "Can we answer questions afterwards?"

"Of course," Rhea said. "We'd love to go with you to the mountains."

"Before you go hunting," Nick said. "Rhea and I thought we could make you a rain shelter at your home so you won't have to go somewhere else to stay dry."

"You can do that?" Kieran asked.

"I said they build things, Father," Zinnia said.

Rhea smiled. "Yes. We'll have to check the ground to see what sort of shelter is possible."

"And come up with a design," Nick said.

"With your permission, we'll go to your home while you're hunting and look it over," Rhea said.

"You're welcome at our home anytime," Thalia said.

The dragons flew away.

Nick and Rhea got a tablet and some measuring instruments and walked to the dragons' home.

When the dragons returned, Rhea and Nick approached them.

Nick held out the tablet and the dragons huddled together to look at the screen.

"We came up with a couple of designs," he said. "We wanted the shelter to be tall enough for you to comfortably sit with your heads up, and wide enough so that all of you could lie down within it. This is three-sided with an opening." Nick swiped right. "This is a little smaller, top to bottom, but it has a flap you can close."

"There's also a difference in the supports," Rhea said. "The ground seems hard here. The smaller design doesn't use stakes, so we would need to use some of the support poles as a base. The larger one depends on anchoring the support poles so they go straight up and down. We weren't able to drive a test stake in the ground with a mallet, but you dragons are stronger, so you may be able to."

Morran moved toward Rhea. "Give me a stake."

Rhea did so.

Morran took the stake in two hands and shoved it easily into the ground. "You mean like that?"

Nick and Rhea exchanged a smile. "Yes, like that," Rhea said.

"I like the three-sided one better," Thalia said. The other dragons trilled in a tone that sounded like approval.

"The shelter will be a tarp supported by poles," Nick said. "The tarp is waterproof, but not fireproof, so keep that in mind."

"Though you could build a fire at the entrance at ground level. We can show you if you wish," Rhea said.

"I don't think we need a fire," Kieran said. "We just want to stay dry. We would be warm enough."

"If that's settled, let's go back to our house, gather the materials, and start working," Rhea said.

The shelter went up fairly quickly. The dragons pushed the supporting poles into the ground. ("Better than a pile driver," Nick observed.) Then the dragons strung up the tarp and secured it at Rhea's and Nick's direction. Evvin was particularly helpful, following directions to the letter.

Once the shelter was finished, they all stood back to examine their work. Rhea noted that it took up less than a quarter of the space, so the dragons still had plenty of room for their usual activities.

"Very nice," Kieran said.

"You humans do good work," Morran said.

"Well, we couldn't have done it without all of you dragons doing the heavy lifting," Nick said.

"Thank you," Thalia said.

Zinnia turned to Thalia. "Morran and I are going to take the humans to see Grandpa and Grandma."

"Greet them for us," Thalia said.

"Can I come too?" Evvin said.

"Stay here this time," Morran said.

Evvin dipped his head, looking disappointed, but said nothing.

Rhea and Nick got into their protective gear, then climbed up and attached their harnesses. The dragons lifted off.

It was not long before Rhea saw tall cliffs ahead. The cliff wall stretched for quite a distance, north and south. She could not see the end in either direction.

Zinnia and Morran headed toward a break in the cliff wall. This was wide enough for the two dragons to fly in easily side by side.

Once through, Rhea saw another cliff wall, maybe half a mile away. In between she saw a flat rocky surface. No plants grew there. Although the sun was fairly high in the sky, the area was completely in shadow. Still, enough light streamed in, near the tops of the cliffs, for clear viewing.

"Looks like dragon statues," Nick said, pointing to the far cliff wall. "Though I remember you said those were hibernating dragons."

"Or dead," Morran said. "I'll show you the one you called Rex."

Morran veered off and Zinnia followed. Rhea began to make out numerous dragon forms. Some were very detailed, others barely distinct, since the arms, legs, and other features had worn away. Probably due to weathering, she guessed.

They landed at the foot of a cliff. Looking up, Rhea could see the form of a dragon, back melded into the cliff wall.

"That's your Rex," Morran said. "From what has been passed down in dragon lore, he hibernated here soon after his human died and never revived."

Rhea looked around at all the dragon forms. "How can you tell which ones are dead and which are just hibernating?"

"It's hard for us to tell sometimes," Zinnia said. "The dragons whose faces have worn away are definitely dead. Ones that look whole could be hibernating or could have died."

A loud cracking sound drew Rhea and Nick's attention. The ground shook slightly. Rhea saw Nick clutching his harness.

"Earthquake?" Nick speculated. "Avalanche?"

"No," Morran said calmly. "Just a dragon coming out of hibernation. We can take you to look."

"Will the dragon mind?" Rhea asked.

"No," Zinnia said. "Besides, whoever it is will be busy awakening."

The dragons took to the air. Rhea could see small rocks falling as the awakening dragon separated itself from the cliff face. It looked like someone pushing off from a wall they were leaning against. The dragon first separated at the neck and head, then the shoulders. The wings came free and spread out. Then the hindquarters and legs followed. The dragon dropped to the ground with a crash.

"Is the dragon all right?" Rhea asked.

"Yes, we can fall a short distance without hurting ourselves," Zinnia said.

As they soared over and past, Rhea saw the dragon flexing arms, legs, neck, and wings. Then the dragon flew away at a low altitude.

"My grandparents are just over there," Zinnia said.

"Kieran's parents or Thalia's?" Nick asked.

"My mother's parents. My father's parents flew away to another community years ago."

"Exploring?" Nick asked.

"Some dragons do," Zinnia said. "We had a dragon fly in and stay for a while a few years ago. He said he was circling the globe. Not many dragons do that, but he did. But my other grandparents, they had friends who grew up on Earth on farms in Ukraine and wanted to live with them. They visit us at home from time to time." Zinnia landed. "Here we are."

After climbing down and looking up from the ground, Rhea could see two dragons who had apparently fastened themselves to the cliff face. Next to her, Morran landed with Nick.

Nick got off and looked up too. "Do they know we're here?"

"Zinnia and I haven't hibernated," Morran said. "Kieran and Thalia haven't, either. But we've heard from those who have that it's like hearing someone in a dream."

Zinnia stretched herself to full height and looked toward the two dragons. "Hi, Grandma and Grandpa. Mother and Father send their greetings. We have humans here with us. Nice humans. We miss you. We hope you'll come see us again."

The dragons on the cliff remained motionless.

Zinnia turned to Morran. "We can go home now."

On their way back, Rhea said to Zinnia, "You spoke to your grandparents in English instead of the dragon language."

"We use both. There are human words that don't exist in dragon language."

"Do your other grandparents speak Ukrainian?" Nick asked.

"Probably," Zinnia said. "We can learn human language if we listen to it long enough. I didn't know many human words until after I came to live with Rhea. I wasn't old enough. I learned most of my human words when I lived with Rhea. But I couldn't speak them yet. I wasn't old enough to say human words until after I returned here."

"Can I ask a question about hibernating?" Nick asked.

"Yes, we want to answer your questions," Zinnia said.

"Why do dragons hibernate?"

"Besides nearing the end of life," Morran said, "dragons hibernate to rest."

"It's like taking a vacation," Zinnia said. "Dragons can rest and think."

"But you can do that without hibernating, can't you?" Nick asked.

"We can," Morran said. "But sometimes a dragon feels overwhelmed. Or wants to do nothing for a time. You don't have to hunt when you hibernate. You can just be."

"Grandma and Grandpa said they wanted to hibernate for a long time. They had raised many dragons, offspring and offspring of offspring, but wanted to wait until after I had come home and found someone to mate with before going away. They'll come back when they're rested."

As they drew closer to Zinnia's family home, they saw dragons circling above it.

"What's going on?" Nick asked.

"I don't know," Morran said. "We'll see when we get there."

There were more dragons on the ground, but they cleared a space when Zinnia and Morran landed.

Rhea and Nick climbed down. Rhea saw Thalia lying underneath the shelter, her stomach and neck on the ground, looking relaxed. Kieran sat outside the shelter, conversing with other male dragons near him in the dragon language. Evvin paced back and forth in front of a rapt audience who listened to him talk about how they constructed the shelter.

Rhea and Nick stood near Thalia. She said, "Dragons have been coming to see our shelter. They heard the sounds when we were putting it together and saw the tarp rise above the boulders and came to see what was going on. Evvin has been entertaining groups of dragons who listen to his story and then fly away so others can hear. Evvin hasn't tired of telling it again and again."

"The other dragons seem impressed," Nick said.

"They are." Thalia moved her head in Kieran's direction. "Some of them have wondered if it is possible for them to have a shelter of their own. Kieran has told them that right now, we should not burden the humans with too many projects at once."

"We don't have enough tarp or tentpoles left to make another, anyway," Nick said.

"We may be able to make some from local materials," Rhea said. When Nick turned to her with a skeptical expression, she added, "We don't know enough about what we have here yet to work with. Arthur built things from what he found here. We may be able to do the same."

"They are saying good things about you and Nick," Thalia said. "Especially your willingness to help us with something we didn't even ask for."

"That's what we do," Nick said.

"We're happy to help in whatever way we can," Rhea said.

"Zinnia said that you would be. She was right," Thalia said. "We're glad you're here."

"So are we," Rhea said.

# CHAPTER 6

As the last of the visiting dragons left, Rhea turned to Zinnia and Morran. "Is this a good time for us to ask you questions about what we read in the books?"

"Yes," Zinnia said. "We can go back to your house and talk."

The four of them returned to the house. They settled down in front of the front door. Rhea briefly went inside and retrieved the books.

"To start," Rhea said, "there are some things we read in the books that you hadn't told us about this world."

"We couldn't tell you everything at once," Zinnia said.

"Of course," Nick said. "And we didn't expect it. But we did want to talk about them."

"We'll be happy to tell you anything you want to know," Zinnia said.

Rhea opened the book. "We wondered about the clinging vines."

"You mean the tangling vines?" Morran asked.

"Arthur wrote that some of the trees had vines that could capture and hold you," Nick said. "And you couldn't get out."

"That's right," Zinnia said. "Dragons could get out, but we're too big to get entangled anyway. Smaller creatures can't get untangled. Eventually they die of starvation or thirst. Then the tree digests the remains."

"If you were entangled," Morran said, "we'd find you and pull you out before that."

"Can you point one of those trees out so we know to avoid them?" Rhea asked.

"Of course, if we see them in our travels," Zinnia said. "But there aren't any close by."

"Another thing about the tangling vines," Nick said. "Arthur wrote that Rex showed him a tree with three sets of human bones there."

"Humans have come here," Zinnia said. "Several have come when they grasped dragons who were returning when their wings grew."

"We quickly take them back," Morran added.

"In the distant past," Zinnia said, "dragons who have gone into the human world to see what it's like have come back with humans."

"Most grab onto a tail," Morran said. "Some were taken back. Others scattered and got lost in our world. Without dragons to help them, they haven't lasted long."

"Some try to climb on a dragon's back," Zinnia said. "They slide off in flight and die in the fall."

"Arthur thought the remains he saw were of pirates who came here to hide treasure," Rhea said. "Arthur found a chest with jewels and gold and traded those for money when he went back to our world to buy things."

Zinnia exchanged a look with Morran. "We don't know anything about that."

Rhea closed the book. "That's all right. You've been very helpful. We mostly wanted to know about the vines and the humans."

"But we also wanted to ask for a favor," Nick said.

"We will help where we can," Morran said.

"We'd like to go back to our world, briefly, to buy more supplies," Rhea said. "Can you do that for us?"

"Yes," Zinnia said. "We thought you might need to go back from time to time."

"Nick and I thought what we'd to is grab the two empty carts. We would go to the large hardware store near campus," Rhea said. "To avoid drawing a crowd, you'd take us there and go back here and wait for a couple of hours."

"We'd give you a timer," Nick said.

"Then you'd come and bring us back here."

"I can do that," Zinnia said.

"What's a timer?" Morran asked.

"It's a device that measures seconds, minutes, and hours," Nick said. "We'd set it and give it to you. An alarm goes off when the time is up."

"All you would have to do is stay here and then come and get us when the alarm sounds," Rhea said.

"Can we see it?" Morran asked.

Nick rushed into the house and came back with it. He showed it to the dragons. "Look. I'll set it for about 10 seconds and you can see how it works."

The dragons watched.

"The lights move," Morran said as the timer counted down.

"Yes, the numbers show how much time is left," Rhea said.

"We can't read numbers," Morran said.

"You don't have to," Nick said, as the alarm beeped. "Just listen for that noise."

"How long is a couple of hours?" Morran asked.

"About the time it took to fly to Arthur and Rex's place," Rhea said.

"You can do anything you want during that time," Nick said. "Just stay close enough to hear the alarm."

Zinnia turned to Morran. "We can get Evvin to watch it. Morran and I can make your ring of stones while he's doing that."

"Yes," Morran said. "That sounds like something Evvin would like to do."

"We also wanted to ask you about the double house you mentioned when it rained," Rhea said.

"If you don't need it as a rain shelter, we thought it would probably work for Dan when he comes," Nick ventured.

"It's a little farther away," Zinnia said. "We can show you."

"Please do," Rhea said.

The dragons led the way. They went in a different direction from the one that Rhea and Nick took earlier when exploring. It was maybe half a mile, but they finally saw two structures like their house, close together.

Rhea and Nick went in and out of each house as the dragons looked on.

"Yes," Rhea said after they had examined the houses. "Dan can use one as his house, and one as his veterinary office."

"We can clean them up for you, as we did with your house," Zinnia said.

"Thanks," Rhea said. "That's very kind of you and we really appreciate it."

"It takes little effort, and we're glad to do it," Zinnia said.

* * *

The next day, after the dragons' hunt, Rhea and Nick stood outside their house with the two empty carts. Rhea had a messenger bag with Arthur's books over her shoulder. Nick had the timer.

Nick set the box down close to Evvin and activated it.

"Oooo, the lights change," Evvin said.

"Yes," Nick said. "Just wait until you hear a sound, and then tell Zinnia and Morran."

"I will, I will." Evvin settled down with his neck and stomach on the ground and watched the timer box. He looked totally absorbed in the task.

Zinnia took them back to the quadrangle and immediately departed. Because it was summer break, the area was unoccupied.

Nick took a breath. "Wow. The air's a lot fresher in dragon country. I hadn't realized it until now."

"Traffic noise here seems louder than it used to be. The environment is much quieter where we just came from."

"Yeah," Nick said, "and I can feel the difference in gravity in my legs."

"I can, too." Rhea took out her smartphone and texted Dan.

Within minutes, they saw him running toward them. "Everything okay?"

"Yes," Nick said. "We're just on a supply run to the hardware store."

Rhea took the messenger bag from her shoulder. "The books that the human who lived on the dragon world are in here. You should find them useful."

"Wow, a first-person account. Thanks!" Dan accepted the bag from Rhea and shouldered it. "Did you read them?"

"We did," Nick said.

"What did you think?" Dan asked.

"It's amazing," Rhea said. "Arthur, the human, recorded what he saw, what he did...there's even a book with drawings and descriptions of plants and animals."

Dan smiled. "Can't wait to read it."

"Just be careful with the pages," Nick said. "It's an old book." He turned back to Rhea. "Let's get going."

"I'll drive you to the hardware store," Dan said. "Do those carts fold up?"

"Yes, they do," Rhea said.

Before the two hours were up, they had shopped and returned to campus with two full carts. Nick also purchased another supply cart to take with them.

"It's going to take a while to outfit the houses we told you about," Rhea said. "Maybe a couple more days."

"That should be just enough time for me to read the books and for the mass spectrometer to come," Dan said. "I have everything else I want stacked up in my office."

"Mass spectrometer?" Nick asked.

"Believe me, we'll need it," Dan said. "Thanks to you, I was able to order the best one money can buy."

"You're the doctor," Rhea said.

Dan smiled. "I wanted to make two other requests, if I could."

"Sure," Rhea said.

"First, it would help to be paired with a dragon, like you and Zinnia. Like you said Arthur and Rex were. Someone who could stay with me most of the time to answer my questions."

"We'll make inquiries," Rhea said.

"Second, my husband, Carlos, would like to join us when his land reclamation project ends. It would be a few weeks more, which gives us time to discuss. I'm sure his knowledge of agriculture could help us out."

Rhea exchanged a glance with Nick. "I don't see why not. I'll bring it up."

Zinnia appeared at that moment. Dan waved a farewell and sprinted away.

Again, dragon, humans, and carts came through perfectly. Morran and Evvin stood waiting for them.

"The box made a noise, and I told Zinnia," Evvin said proudly. "The lights stopped, though."

"They're supposed to do that, Evvin," Rhea said. "Thanks for watching it for us."

"We made the ring of stones by your house and cleaned the other two houses while you were gone," Morran said. "Do you need us to help you with the carts?"

"Right now," Nick said, "Rhea and I need to put away the supplies we bought for ourselves. Then we need to take the original extra cart and the one I just purchased over to the double house."

"After we put our things away," Rhea said, "Nick and I will probably want to rest, so we don't expect to start modifying the double house until tomorrow."

Morran turned to Zinnia. "Zinnia and I can go and play then."

"Yes, we still have those things in our ears," Zinnia said. "You can call if you need us."

"Have fun!" Rhea said. She and Nick waved as Zinnia and Morran flew off.

"I can stay if you want," Evvin said.

"That's nice of you, Evvin," Rhea said, "but most of what we brought back are small items we can handle ourselves."

Evvin dipped his head. He seemed disappointed.

"There is something you can do for us," Nick said. "Remember when you put the posts in the ground for the rain shelter?"

"Oh, yes."

"We have a post with a camera on it that we want to put at Arthur and Rex's place, so that we can see if The Terror appears in the distance. If you don't mind flying that far, you can put it there for us."

"I can do that!"

"It's not too far for you to fly?" Rhea asked.

"Oh, no, I've flown farther than that."

Nick went inside and brought out a long metallic pole. One end was pointed. The other end had a solar collector, a camera, and a transmitter. He showed it to Evvin.

"You'll need to carry it in the middle. When you get there, find a clearing at the top of the hill and stick the pointed end in the ground up to where the red circle is. The flat shiny part should point to the sky and the box with the round glass thing should point to the horizon. That's all that needs to be done."

Evvin grasped it firmly. "I'll do it right."

"I'm sure you will," Nick said. "That's why I gave it to you."

Evvin took off.

When the dragon was a distance away, Rhea turned to Nick. "It occurs to me we're lucky that dragons aren't color blind."

\* \* \*

Rhea and Nick had their purchases put away within a couple of hours. Evvin had not yet returned, so they checked out the ring of stones.

Nick lifted his eyebrows. "Good work. Very neat, almost like a professional mason would do."

"They do have that large ring of stones around their own house, and I don't think that was naturally made," Rhea said. "That indicates they have some experience with construction."

"Well, I'm impressed," Nick said.

"I think we have time to talk to Zinnia and her family about a dragon to help Dan," Rhea said.

Nick nodded.

"I noticed that Morran didn't invite Evvin to come and play," Rhea said as they walked along the path to Zinnia's family home. "And Evvin didn't fly away by himself to play. I wonder if he has any dragon friends."

"Yeah, I felt sorry for the poor guy," Nick said. "Then it occurred to me that we could provide something for him to do."

"It was a good idea. I didn't feel comfortable asking Zinnia or Morran to go back there so soon."

"I suppose we could have asked Thalia or Kieran, but somehow that feels kind of...awkward."

"I know what you mean."

When they reached Zinnia's home, neither Zinnia nor Morran were there. They saw Kieran and Thalia settled on an open space. Kieran was rubbing his neck against Thalia's neck affectionately.

"Oh, sorry," Rhea said, "we didn't mean to intrude."

"You're not intruding," Thalia said.

Kieran pulled back. "You're welcome here anytime."

"We wanted to talk to Zinnia and Morran about something," Morran said.

"You can talk to us, too," Kieran said. "Perhaps we can help."

"You remember that we wanted to bring Dan, the veterinarian, here," Rhea said.

"Yes," Thalia said.

"He asked us if he could be paired with a dragon, like I'm paired with Zinnia and Nick is paired with Morran."

Thalia and Kieran turned to each other.

"Should we wait for Zinnia and Morran to return?" Nick asked.

Kieran turned to them. "There's no need. We would like to help you in any way we can, but I don't think that can be done."

"Is there something that we need to do to make it happen?" Rhea said.

"No, that's not the problem," Thalia said.

"You see," Kieran said. "It all started with Zinnia. She called a meeting of the dragons. Thalia and I had been talking with her about her coming of mating age and wanting to lay her egg in this world."

"Kieran and I wanted that, too," Thalia said.

"Zinnia said that we should get humans to help us," Kieran said. "She had lived with humans and saw them solve problems."

"We had all lived near humans...most of us, anyway," Thalia said. "But not in a human household, as Zinnia had."

"Dragons were in favor of asking for help," Kieran said, "but the problem was that the only human that stayed here a long time and lived had a dragon companion. No one except Zinnia felt that they knew enough about humans to do this well. Zinnia said that she could. That's why she came for you."

"Morran volunteered to help Zinnia," Thalia said. "So when Nick appeared, there was already someone ready to be a second companion."

"So what you're saying is that there isn't a dragon that feels knowledgeable enough about humans to be a companion," Nick said.

"Yes," Kieran said. "Thalia and I will help, as will other dragons, but even we didn't think we knew enough."

Rhea nodded. "We understand."

They all were silent for a few minutes.

Nick said, "I know that you have warned us that Evvin could harm us accidentally, but he hasn't so far. What if we paired him with Dan? He wants to be around humans."

"You have only known Evvin a few days," Kieran said. "We have observed him for years."

"But that was around other dragons," Rhea said. "He knows he can't harm you. But he's been careful with us. In fact, he told the bachelor dragons to go away when they flew too close to us."

Thalia turned to Kieran. "He roared a warning for us to hear so that you could come and help."

Kieran looked at Thalia. "Do you think Evvin could be paired with a human?"

Thalia remained silent for a few seconds, lowering her head as if pondering the question. Kieran watched her, as if also considering the idea.

"After thinking it over, yes," Thalia said at last. "Rhea and Nick said Dan is a veterinarian. I remember the veterinarians who came to the farm where I grew up. They handled animals that were far larger and stronger than them, even if they were stubborn or angry."

"And the farm animals can't talk and discuss," Nick said. "Evvin can."

"Evvin followed our instructions when we were building your shelter," Rhea said. "We just sent Evvin to take a camera to Arthur and Rex's house so we can watch the area."

"That was a good idea," Kieran said.

"We expect Evvin to install the camera just as we asked," Nick said.

"We'll have to talk to Evvin first," Thalia said. "We need to tell him he needs to do what Dan asks of him."

"He will. I'm sure of it," Nick said.

"And you and Rhea have to explain Evvin to Dan before he comes here so that he knows what to expect," Kieran said.

"We can do that," Rhea said.

"There's one other thing," Nick said. "Dan has a mate. He asked if it would be all right if his mate joined him later."

"He has a mate?" Kieran said.

Thalia turned to Kieran. "That is good." She turned to Rhea and Nick. "Dan is older than you?"

"Yes, he's older," Rhea said.

"And more experienced," Nick said.

"Yes, the mate can come," Kieran said. "That would mean there would be two humans to instruct Evvin."

Rhea saw motion in the sky and looked up. "Zinnia and Morran are returning."

"You and Nick should go to your house and wait for Evvin," Thalia said. "It's best if we talk to Zinnia and Morran about this."

Rhea and Nick walked back to the house.

"Evvin has probably planted the camera by now," Nick said. "Let's see." Once inside, Nick pulled out his tablet and sat at one of the desks. Rhea pulled up a chair and joined him.

"The transmitter is working," Nick said. "Let's see if we can get a picture."

Rhea leaned over to watch as Nick brought the image into focus.

"There it is," Nick said. "Just as we saw when we were there."

"Can the camera turn?" Rhea said.

Nick touched the buttons on the app. "There it goes."

"Recording?"

Nick touched the app again. "It is now." He turned to Rhea. "Now we're going to have a 360 view that we can check on fast forward from now on."

"Good." Rhea said.

A sound of distress pierced the air.

"I guess that means that Thalia and Kieran told Morran," Nick said.

Not long after, they heard a rush of wings and looked out to see Evvin landing.

"I put the camera in the ground, just as you said," Evvin reported. "The shiny thing pointed up and the round glassy thing pointed out."

"You did it perfectly." Nick showed Evvin the tablet. "The camera is working."

Evvin leaned over to view the screen. "It's just as if we were there."

"That's how we can keep watch at a distance," Rhea said.

Nick patted Evvin's neck. "Good work."

Evvin lowered his jaw and pulled back his lips in what appeared to be a proud grin.

Rhea heard the thump of dragon feet and turned to see Zinnia and Morran approaching.

Zinnia faced Evvin. "Mother and Father have some good news for you, Evvin."

"What is it?" Evvin asked.

"It's a surprise," Morran said drolly. "Go and see."

Evvin took off quickly on all fours.

When Evvin had gone, Morran said, "I understand that you two thought this was a good idea?"

"Yes," Nick said.

"Dan wants to be paired with a dragon and Evvin wants to be paired with a human," Rhea said. "Besides, Dan has years of experience with working with young dragons."

"I will give him this. He's mated. That shows maturity and smarts, at least," Morran said.

"The veterinarians who came to the farm I was at before I went to Rhea's were very smart," Zinnia said.

"The ones I saw when I was a hatchling living on a human farm were, too," Morran said.

"Besides, Evvin is cooperative," Nick said. "He planted a camera at Arthur and Rex's place while you were gone."

While Rhea and Nick were showing Zinnia and Morran the camera views, they heard Evvin's exclamation of excitement coming from Zinnia's home.

The next day, Rhea and Nick concentrated on outfitting Dan's house and clinic, with the help of the dragons. As they worked, they heard trilling sounds. To Rhea, it sounded like pure joy.

The dragons all raised their heads.

"What is it?" Nick asked.

"A dragon has returned from growing up with humans," Zinnia said.

"All dragons in the community go to greet them," Thalia said, and took off. The other dragons followed.

Rhea turned to Nick. "I always knew that when dragons grew wings, they flew back to the dragon world. I guess I hadn't thought of what happens on this side."

"I'm sure they'll tell us," Nick said.

"If they don't, I'll remember to ask," Rhea said.

In about an hour, Zinnia and Morran returned.

"The dragon is with her parents now," Zinnia said.

"It's important for us to greet a dragon who returns," Morran said. "Some get lost and aren't sure how to find their parents. A few have humans tagging along that we return to the human world."

"This dragon came alone. Most do," Zinnia added.

"We want the dragon to know that they are welcome and we are happy to see them," Morran said.

"I remember when I first came back," Zinnia said. "It seemed as if my parents would never stop nuzzling me. And I felt as if I never wanted them to stop."

"My parents hardly left my side when I first came back," Morran said. "They taught me how and where to hunt. How to fly well, too, since I was awkward when my wings first grew out."

"Everyone's awkward with new wings," Zinnia agreed.

Kieran and Thalia landed.

"Where's Evvin?" Nick asked.

Kieran extended his neck and looked up. "Flittering around somewhere...there he is."

They all returned to modifying the houses. It was nearly sundown when Nick and Rhea evaluated their progress and concluded they had done all they could.

"We can go get Dan tomorrow, if that works for you," Rhea said. "After your hunt?"

"Yes," Zinnia said.

"He'll bring his own equipment for his clinic," Nick said. "We'll all have to be very careful with it and follow his instructions."

"We'll be ready," Morran said.

Rhea and Nick looked around for Evvin. He had settled on the ground nearby with his stomach and neck on the ground. He seemed sad.

Rhea and Nick walked over.

"Aren't you excited?" Rhea asked. "Dan will be here tomorrow."

"What if he doesn't like me?" Evvin said.

"He'll be just as happy about meeting you as you are about meeting him," Nick said. "He wants to be with dragons, and you're a dragon. Perfect."

"Remember when we came?" Rhea said. "It will be just like that. You'll see him, we'll tell him who you are and you'll tell him who you are and then you'll help us move his things into his house. After that, you'll get to know each other, just as you got to know Nick and me."

Evvin lifted his head off the ground.

Nick walked over and patted Evvin's neck. "You'll do fine, buddy. You'll do fine."

"Humans know humans," Thalia said. "There's no need to worry."

"That's right," Rhea said, "and we'll all help you and Dan as much as we can."

Evvin looked reassured and sat up.

Rhea glanced toward Morran. He looked skeptical, but fortunately held his peace.

# CHAPTER 7

Back on Earth, Dr. Daniel Yang made sure that the mass spectrometer had been securely packed. This was the last item that needed to go on the carts. He was ready for Rhea and Nick to reappear with Zinnia and take him to the dragon world.

They had said that they would be back in a "couple of days." Dan used the time to prepare for his departure. Thanks to Nick's generosity, Dan had paid his rent a year in advance and stored his car. All that he needed to do once Zinnia reappeared was to put his keys in the secure lock box on campus.

To pass the time, he called Carlos on FaceTime, hoping he would be free at the moment. Carlos answered immediately.

"Still waiting?"

"Yes, though they could come at any time."

"Ready?"

"Yes, everything's on the loading dock at the University's veterinary clinic, ready to go."

"Nervous?"

"A little. Arthur's books were excellent. Sketches and descriptions galore of flora and fauna. This 'terror' of theirs isn't going to be easy to track. From what Rex told him and what Arthur saw at a great distance, I still think this is an animal predator looking for food."

"From what you told me, I'd say something in their usual food supply changed, and they went after dragon eggs instead. When I was growing up in California, coyotes and bears would come into residential areas when their food supplies dried up."

"That's the usual pattern, yes. Except that this predator leaves no traces of its prey. No bones, no eggshells in the case of the dragons, nothing."

"Be careful. I'm counting on seeing you again."

Dan laughed. "That's what I've said when you've gone to remote places with your projects."

Carlos smiled. "Well, yes, we agreed that we both seem to seek out adventurous assignments."

"Risk-takers, that's us." Dan took a breath. "I don't think that Rhea and Nick fully realize what they're up against. A couple of wide-eyed graduates, out to challenge the world."

"Or worlds. But no different from us at their age."

"Yes, I guess we all go through that stage. That's why Peace Corps volunteers and military recruits are generally at the peak risk-taking age."

"We haven't seemed to have grown out of it."

"At least we have experience on our side."

"True."

A large shadow blocked the sunlight coming through the window. "Oh, my gosh! It's them! They're here! Gotta go. I love you."

"I love you too. Take care."


Dan met Rhea, Nick, and Zinnia in the quadrangle. Zinnia settled into the grass. Since the university was still on summer break, only a small number of onlookers came, standing at a respectful distance. The reporter from the campus newspaper, hoping for a story, had been lingering around the veterinary clinic lately, and now had a clear view of the dragon.

Pointing to the clinic's loading dock, Dan said, "Everything's in carts over there. We just have to bring it out."

With the three of them working, the task only took a few minutes. When they were gathered around Zinnia, Rhea said, "One more thing. You're going to be paired with Evvin."

"The one Zinnia said to watch?" Dan asked.

"He's been behaving himself and has been very helpful," Nick said.

"Mother and Father have talked to him," Zinnia said. "They told him to do as you say."

"You can be sure of that," Rhea said. "He follows instructions to the letter. Zinnia's parents will intervene if he doesn't, but I don't doubt he'll be willing to cooperate."

"He's actually very nervous about your arrival," Nick said. "Asking us where to sit, what to say, how to look. He wants to make the best possible impression."

"We told him to simply sit to one side and wait for you to appear with us," Zinnia added.

"I think I can handle that," Dan said.

"We'll arrive at the double house the dragons cleaned up for you," Rhea said. "One house for you to live in, the other for your clinic."

"Sounds perfect," Dan said.

"Hang on to something," Zinnia said.

Dan, Rhea, and Nick took hold of one of Zinnia's back ridges. The campus disappeared. It seemed as if they were moving through fog.

When the scene cleared Dan saw sky and green grass. He let go of Zinnia and looked around.

"Your home," Rhea said, pointing to a large, maroon, egg-shaped structure with square holes here and there.

Dan saw three dragons sitting together, one smaller than the other two, and one Zinnia's size sitting apart.

Rhea put a hand on Dan's shoulder. "This is Dan, the veterinarian." She gestured to the dragons. "This is Morran, Zinnia's future mate. This is Kieran, Zinna's Dad, and Thalia, Zinnia's Mom."

Dan nodded at them. "Pleased to meet you."

"We're happy to have you here," Thalia said.

Rhea turned slightly and pointed to the lone silvery dragon. "And this is Evvin."

Dan sized him up. His experience in animal behavior told him that Evvin was probably nervous, as Nick had said. He smiled and stepped closer, but not too close, to Evvin.

"Pleased to meet you, Evvin. I'm Dan. We're going to be the best of friends. After I put my things in the houses, we can take time to talk and get to know each other."

Evvin relaxed. "Yes. Yes, I want to do that."

Dan turned to Rhea and Nick. "Let's get the carts unloaded."

Rhea pointed to the houses. "Nick and I already set up solar power, wi-fi, toilets, bathing facilities, bed, kitchen, water supply, and some essential furniture. We made the bed a double for you and your husband, when he comes."

"Very kind of you, thank you. Everything looks great." Dan pointed to a cart. "Let's start unloading this one."

The first cart held his personal items, largely essentials that he needed when moving in an apartment. Once that cart was unloaded, they turned to the second one.

"This has all my lab equipment. The third cart has the mass spectrometer."

"Just wondering," Nick said. "A mass spectrometer isn't usually standard equipment for veterinarians, is it?"

Dan smiled. "No. But I went over to one of the science labs to learn how to use one. I want to be able to analyze organic matter, particularly food sources." He nodded to the spectrometer. "In order to move that, we'll have to set up a table for it, and we may as well get the lab set up first."

Nick nodded. "Just tell us where everything goes."

"We can start with the tables. That's for the mass spectrometer, and next to that is the exam table."

They started moving the tables. As they worked, Nick said, "You're going to put a dragon on an exam table?"

Dan chuckled. "No. Though, while we're mentioning it, I'd appreciate you setting up an outside tent I can use as an exam room for the dragons. Until then, I can work outside."

"We can set one up for you in the next couple of days," Nick said.

"What's the table for, then?" Rhea asked.

"I'll have to gather data on the other animals here, too, such as cell structure, respiration, and so forth. To know how The Terror can consume a dragon as well as cattle, I'll need to know what they're made of. Knowing local cellular structure might give me some insight on The Terror as well."

"Do you think The Terror is an animal?" Rhea asked.

"That's my working theory at the moment," Dan said. "Or it could be something entirely unimaginable to us on Earth. Whatever it is, knowing how life here is put together can only help us."

"You've put a lot of work into this already," Nick said.

"Yes," Dan said. "Arthur's books were essential reading. By the way, I brought them back with me. This is their home, and I think we should bring them back to where they originated."

"But until we have The Terror solved," Nick said. "It's probably a good idea to keep them around to refer to."

"I've covered that," Dan said. "I had them digitized. I went to the history department, thinking they probably had experience with handling old books. They were thrilled to get books that old, and the fact that the books included a record of another world sealed the deal. They have the digital record, I have it in my computer, which I brought with me, by the way, and I have an SD card for you two."

"Wow, thanks," Nick said.

"Do you think you'll make much use of a sophisticated desktop computer without internet access?" Rhea asked. "We just brought our laptops and tablets."

"I brought my tablet, too, but I needed a machine with maximum RAM and memory. I downloaded practically an entire veterinary library. I also need to analyze lab data. The computer will get a lot of use."

Once everything was in the clinic house, Dan, Rhea, and Nick stepped outside. Dan carried his tablet with him.

Rhea turned to the dragons. "It's about dinnertime for us." She turned to Dan. "Would you like to have supper with Nick and me?"

"Thanks, but I'll take a rain check. I brought food with me." Dan gestured to Evvin. "I want to get acquainted with Evvin."

Evvin straightened up.

Morran turned to the other dragons and then to Dan. "We can stay here overnight."

Dan faced him. "Thanks, but Evvin and I will be fine."

"I think you'll want to us to stay overnight," Morran said, with a glance toward Evvin.

"That's a very generous offer, but I'm sure you would prefer to sleep at your home," Dan said.

"Tonight, we can stay here," Morran said. "We stayed with Rhea and Nick the first night they were here in case they needed something."

Dan gestured to Evvin. "If I need something, I have Evvin here."

Morran moved to one side and gestured with his head. "Come over here, human."

Dan started walking in that direction. "My name is Dan and you can call me by my name."

"Come over here, Dan," Morran said. When Dan was a few feet away from his head, Morran added, "I have been a dragon longer than you have, and I say that you need us to stay overnight."

Dan smiled. "I've been a human longer than you have, and I say that we'll be fine."

Kieran raised his head. "If you two are done comparing your claws, I'd like to go home and settle down for the evening."

"They'll be fine, Morran." Thalia turned to Evvin. "Remember, Evvin, you need to do what Dan says."

"Yes, I promise," Evvin said.

Zinnia reached out and put a hand on Morran's forearm. "Time to go home, Morran."

With one more backward glance to Dan, Morran followed the other dragons as they walked away with Rhea and Nick.

When they were all out of sight, Dan rubbed his hands together and approached Evvin. "I have waited for years to meet a dragon just like you, Evvin."

"Me?"

"Yes, you. Would you do something for me?"

"Yes, anything."

He opened the patient app on the tablet he was holding and entered Evvin's name. "Thank you. I want to get more information about you. You don't have to answer my questions if you don't want to, and if anything I do makes you uncomfortable, I want you to tell me so that I can stop."

"But Thalia said to do what you asked," Evvin said.

Dan nodded. "That's right. When I say that I want you to tell me if you don't like something that I'm asking or what I'm doing, that's doing what Thalia said."

Evvin paused again, seeming to consider. "All right."

"Good. I wanted to ask if you are able to stand up on your hind legs with your wings spread out."

"I can do that."

"Can you hold that pose for a while? You won't fall over?"

"No."

"Can you do it now?"

"Yes." Evvin leaned back, straightened his hind legs, and stood, unfolding his wings to their full length.

Dan looked up for a few seconds before realizing he was gaping.

Evvin straightened his neck and held his head up high. "Is this right?"

"Yes. Wow. You are magnificent," Dan said.

Evvin opened his mouth and drew his lips back in what appeared to be a smile.

"I'm going to walk around you so that I can see everything," Dan said. "Can you hold that pose for a while?"

"Yes, I can."

Dan walked slowly around Evvin, taking note of limbs, wing attachments, and other anatomical characteristics. When he was in back and to one side of Evvin, he asked. "Can you lift your tail, slowly?"

Evvin did so.

"That's fine. Go ahead and put it down."

Even complied.

When Dan had completed his circuit, he said, "Can you hold the pose for just a bit longer? I need to go in the lab, pick up something, and come right back."

"Yes."

Dan grabbed his medical bag. He ran back, put the bag on the ground, and held up the tablet. "I'm just going to take some pictures of you."

"Pictures?"

"I'll show you soon." Dan walked around Evvin again, taking both wide photos and closeups. When he completed the circle, he lowered the tablet. "You can relax now, Evvin. Just sit."

Evvin folded his wings and sat.

"Lower your head and I'll show you the pictures."

Evvin faced the tablet.

"That's you," Dan said.

"It's like when I look into still water," Evvin said.

"Exactly," Dan said. "Now I can see you whenever I want, even if you're not around. It's something we humans like to do." He consulted the patient record on the tablet again. "I have another question for you. How old are you? How many years have you been alive?"

"I'm 20."

"Mated?"

"No, this will be my first year to mate. Mating season is in the fall. This is still summer."

"I noted that there's a flap on your lower underbelly near your legs. Is that covering your male organ?"

"Yes. I don't need it unless I mate."

"Do all dragons mate in mating season?"

"Some don't. Older dragons such as Zinnia's parents and grandparents don't mate anymore. It's very rare for younger dragons not to mate."

"Are all the matings with males and females, or do some dragons mate with another dragon of their own sex?"

"Sometimes males mate with males and females with females. They don't produce eggs though."

"I would expect not. What do other dragons think of that?"

"They're happy for them. It's good for all dragons when dragons are happy with their mates."

"I agree. Are you planning to mate with a female dragon?"

"I hope so. I haven't found anyone yet. I may have to wait and see who is available in mating season."

"Whoever it is will be lucky to have you as a mate, Evvin."

"You think so?"

"I know so." He went on to another section of the app. "I want to take a head to tail measurement of you."

"What does that mean?"

"We humans assign units to length and width."

"Like if something is 10 fingers long?"

"Something like that. Would you lie on the ground with your head, neck, and tail stretched out in a straight line?"

Evvin did so. The ground vibrated a bit when he settled down.

Dan walked to the end of the tail, put a narrow spike in the ground, attached one end of a tape measure to it, and walked to the tip of Evvin's nose.

"Thirty-eight feet, four inches," Dan said, and recorded it. "Now, without getting up, can you stretch out a wing, or both, whichever is more comfortable for you."

Evvin stretched out one wing.

Dan walked to the stake, rolling up measuring tape as he went along. He pulled up the stake and placed it at the tip of the wing. Then pulled the tape to the point where the wing met Evvin's shoulder. "Twenty-six feet, two inches." He recorded that and turned back to Evvin. "Thank you. You can fold your wing and sit back up now."

Evvin sat. "Was that good?"

Dan smiled. "Evvin, everything about you is impressive."

Evvin smiled again.

"Now I want to get measurements of your legs, arms, fingers and toes."

That proved easier than the other measurements. Evvin bent and twisted so that Dan could get the readings.

After that, Dan swiped to the next part of the app. "Now let me see if it's possible to measure your weight. You see that large square we put by the second house?"

"Yes."

"That's used to find the weight of large animals on Earth. I'm not sure if it will hold your weight, but we'll give it a try. Can you stand on it? You'll have to hold your tail while doing it."

"I can do that."

As Evvin moved, Dan synced the tablet to the weigh station sensors. When Evvin stood on the weigh station, Dan captured the reading. "Five thousand six hundred ninety-three pounds. You can step off now, Evvin, and go back to where you were sitting."

Dan went back to his medical bag and took out a stethoscope. "I want to listen to your heart, Evvin. Can you crouch so that you're lower to the ground?"

Evvin did so. "Are you going to put your ear to my chest? I used to snuggle against Thalia when I was younger and I could hear her heart."

"That's wonderful, Evvin." Dan held up the end of the stethoscope. "But I need help to hear your heart. I'm going to put this on your chest. It'll help me hear. I'll also have to touch your chest. All you have to do is stay still and not talk."

Dan stepped closer to Evvin, keenly aware of how large Evvin was compared to him. He was much larger than the juvenile dragons he was used to examining. Although he had to move the end of the stethoscope around a little, he found the best place to hear Evvin's heart. He moved the stethoscope a little more to listen to his lungs. Then he moved the stethoscope more, hoping to detect other sounds he had heard in juveniles.

Taking a breath, he put the stethoscope down, took a step back, and started entering more data into the tablet. As he worked he said, "You can relax now, Evvin, and talk. You have a great, strong heart and lungs. I heard other sounds, too. They could be digestion, or something else."

"We dragons hear sounds when we snuggle against each other."

"Do you know what they are?"

"Heart, yes. Others are just said to be sounds of life."

Dan nodded. "They are that." He reached for his portable ultrasound device. "I'm going to run this along your side. You'll hear something and you'll feel something. If you don't like it, I want you to tell me so I can stop."

"All right."

Dan got some ultrasound gel from his bag and rubbed some on Evvin's side. Evvin's scales were slightly warm, smooth, solid, and fit together well. Dan started the ultrasound, putting the device on Evvin's side and moving it across while watching the monitor.

"I can feel it," Evvin said.

"Does it bother you?"

"No. I hear a little noise, though."

Dan let it run a while longer but saw essentially the same organs he had seen in dragon juveniles. He turned it off and put it away. Looking up at Evvin, he asked, "Can you lower your head so I could look in your eyes and ears?"

When Evvin's head was low enough, Dan did a quick check of the dragon's eyes and ears. Everything was clear.

"You're doing great, Evvin," Dan said as he entered the data.

Evvin let out a breath. Dan felt a breeze and noted that the breath had no odor.

"Can you open your mouth and hold it open so I can look at your mouth and throat?"

Evvin complied.

Dan took pictures with the tablet, looked down Evvin's throat as much as he could, noting the features. He saw that most of the teeth were pointed, which was average for a carnivore, and consistent with what he had seen in juvenile dragons. There was also an opening at the side of the throat, near the rear molars, which were flatter teeth. He checked the gums and tongue before telling Evvin he could close his mouth.

"Your teeth are incredibly clean. Do you munch on hard things, like bone?"

"I do," Evvin said. "But we don't use that to clean our teeth. After we hunt, we find a meadow and lie down. We put our chins on the ground and open our mouths. Bugs come and eat the meat between our teeth. Then they go away."

"Now that I would like to see sometime," Dan said.

"They're big bugs. I don't know if they would hurt humans."

"Well, maybe I can get Rhea and Nick to fix a camera to a drone and watch."

"I don't know what that means."

"A drone is a mechanical device that flies. If we put a camera on it, we can take pictures like I took pictures of you."

"Oh! I planted a camera for Nick and Rhea a few days ago. They showed me the pictures."

"I'll have to ask them to show me, too." Dan stepped a little closer to Evvin. "Don't do it now, but tell me how you breathe fire."

"That's easy," Evvin said. "I click my back teeth and squeeze with my neck and jaw right here." He indicated the location with his hand.

Dan pointed upward. "Can you send a little fire upward so I can see?"

Evvin stretched his neck, opened his mouth, and let out a column of fire. He closed his mouth and faced Dan again.

Dan smiled. "Excellent! Thank you." He reached down and picked up his medical bag and instruments. "I'll just put these back." He was halfway back to the clinic house when he heard loud cackling and honking sounds.

He paused and turned to Evvin. "What's that noise?"

"Swimmers," Evvin said. "They're coming back from the lake to the land to sleep for the night."

"Yes, I read about those in Arthur's book." He continued to the clinic house and realized from the thumping of dragon feet on the ground behind him that Evvin was following. He turned at the entrance. "Evvin, I have a lot of delicate equipment in here, so I need to ask that you not come in. I'll leave the door open so you can watch me if you want to."

"I'll stay here." Evvin sounded disappointed but remained where he was while Dan put the equipment back in the clinic house.

Once that was done, he walked back to the entrance and closed the door behind him. He thought about the other house, his new residence, and realized that there should be plenty of room there since he had put most of his stuff against the walls. Besides, according to Arthur's journal, Rex joined Arthur in his house all the time.

"I'm going to my house to prepare and eat a meal," Dan told Evvin. "You can come in with me if you want to."

"I don't need to eat now. I hunt and eat in the morning."

"Yes, I read about that in Arthur's journal." Dan put up a hand, then paused. "Would it be all right if I patted your head?"

"Yes, you can pat my head. It won't hurt me."

"But do you like being patted on the head?"

"Yes. Nick did it. It feels nice."

Dan smiled and patted Evvin's head. "You and I are going to get along fine, Evvin."

Evvin smiled again.

After Evvin followed Dan into the residence, the dragon sat in the middle of the room, watching silently as Dan made coffee and heated a container of spaghetti. He grabbed a plate and utensils and placed them on a table. When he sat down with his food, he faced Evvin. As he ate, Evvin moved his head from side to side, as if fascinated with the way humans ate, or with the strange food that they ate, or both.

When Dan finished eating, he washed the plate, utensils, and container. He refilled his mug with coffee and sat again. "Since we're going to be together for some time, we need to talk about some things that humans do."

"Yes, I want to know."

Dan smiled. "Good." He motioned over to the lavatory. "That area is where I shower, to clean myself, and poop. Humans need to be alone when doing that, so I will be closing the curtains behind me."

"Dragons have special places to poop."

"Everyone goes there?"

"Yes, we all go to the same places to poop."

"Is it crowded?"

"No, they're large places, and we take turns."

"I suppose you don't get dirty. You and the other four dragons I've seen so far are very clean."

"If we need to clean ourselves, there's the lake, and the rivers, and the ocean. Sometimes we stay out in the rain, too."

"I'd like to see the ocean sometime."

"The river is closer. The lake is a little farther in a different direction. To get to the ocean is a long walk, but a short flight."

Dan nodded. "I see. I also wanted to talk about sleeping." He pointed to the bed. "That's my bed. I will be sleeping there."

"Can I sleep with you?"

"You can't get into the bed, Evvin. Even though it's a double bed, it won't hold both you and me."

"I mean can I curl around the bed. On the floor."

Dan considered a moment. "That depends. Do dragons roll over in their sleep?"

"No, dragons don't roll over in their sleep. We sometimes move our tails, or our heads. Maybe flex fingers and feet. But we don't roll over."

Dan remembered from Arthur's book that Rex would sleep next to him in their house. Since that arrangement lasted for about 50 years, Dan thought it ought to be safe enough. "Tell you what. I'll sleep in my bed, and you can sleep where you are now."

Evvin lowered his head, looking disappointed.

"Just for the first night. I need to get used to sleeping with a dragon in the room. I haven't done it before. Later we can talk about your moving closer."

Evvin bobbed his head up and down in what appeared to be a nod. "Yes, I'll do as you say."

"We're going to be great friends, Evvin."

Evvin smiled.

When Dan got ready for bed, Evvin watched curiously as he stripped down to his boxers. Dan crawled into bed and pulled up the covers. "Good night, Evvin. We can talk again after we wake up tomorrow morning."

Dan had turned out the lights and shut the door, but there was still some light in the room from the moon. For a while, it was quiet, except for a soft sound that Dan guessed was Evvin breathing.

In the middle of the night, Dan woke when he felt a weight on his leg. The weight was not heavy, so it could not be Evvin rolling over on him. Still, he looked and saw in the dim light what appeared to be the tip of Evvin's tail. For a moment, he wondered if he should say something, but then remembered that Arthur had reported that Rex habitually touched him with his tail during the night.

Dan rolled over and went back to sleep.

# CHAPTER 8

Morran stuck his head through the doorway as Rhea and Nick were eating breakfast. "Are you going to check on your friend to see if he's still alive?"

Rhea put down her fork and picked up her phone. "I'll send him a text." She paused while she entered the text. "There. I sent him a message. It may take a minute or two for him to respond." She continued to eat. Her phone chimed soon afterwards. She picked it up again. "He replied to my 'Good morning' with 'Good morning.' He's still alive."

Nick turned to Morran. "Were you expecting a different result?"

"I say we still need to check on him."

"We will," Rhea said, "when we've finished breakfast. If you'll wait outside, we'll join you shortly."

Morran let out a huff of breath and backed out.

Rhea sent: *We'll come over after breakfast.*

Dan replied: *Just finishing myself. We'll be expecting you.*

Rhea put the phone down and turned to Nick. "So far, so good."

Four dragons were waiting for them when Rhea and Nick walked outside. They strolled over to Dan's houses. Dan was not in sight, but Evvin was outside.

When he spotted them, Evvin rocked back and forth with excitement. "Oh! You brought me the *best* human! He said I was magnificent!"

Morran turned to Zinnia and trilled something in the dragon language. Zinnia looked at him but did not respond.

Dan came out of the house and faced them. "Good morning. Nice to see everyone again."

"How was your evening?" Nick asked.

"Fine, no problems. Evvin and I got along very well." Dan smiled at Evvin.

Evvin raised his head proudly. "Yes, yes, we did." He swung his head toward the other dragons. "I'm going to hunt now."

Dan nodded at him. "Remember to bring me a swimmer for dinner."

"I won't forget." Evvin flew off.

Morran swung his head in Dan's direction. "Did he sleep with you in your house?"

"Yes. He touched me with his tail during the night."

"Probably wanted to make sure you didn't run off," Morran said.

Zinnia turned to Morran. "You touch me with your tail every night. Several times a night."

Morran looked at Zinnia. "I thought you liked it."

"I do. But you can't blame Evvin for doing something you do as well."

"Besides, I'm not running off," Dan said.

Morran swung his head in the direction of Evvin's retreating form. "Magnificent?"

Dan turned to him. "Yes. No missing or broken scales, wings are fully intact and working. He has the full use of all his limbs. Eyes and ears are clear. No missing or broken teeth. Gums in good shape. Heartbeat strong, lungs strong. A dragon in excellent health and in full possession of his faculties."

Morran trilled something to Zinnia again.

"That's the second time you've said that, Morran," Dan said. "Care to translate for us?"

Morran made a grumbling sound in his throat and lowered his head.

Zinnia turned from Morran to Dan. "He said that humans are easily impressed."

"Perhaps that's because dragons are impressive creatures," Dan said.

Kieran raised his head. "Since we've confirmed that Dan and Evvin are getting along well, I say we go and hunt." He flew away. Thalia followed. After a glance back at the humans, Morran flew off, with Zinnia following.

When they were gone, Nick turned to Dan. "You could tell Morran said the same thing twice? I haven't been able to make out anything except general tones."

"Me, neither," Rhea said, "and I lived with Zinnia for years."

"I do bird calls," Dan explained. "I've been able to do bird calls since I was a kid. I can distinguish between bird species and even recognize sounds among the same species. The dragon language seems to have the same tones. I didn't know what he said, but he did say the same thing twice."

Nick turned to Dan. "I say that you are magnificent."

Dan chuckled.

"You asked Evvin to bring you a swimmer for supper?" Rhea asked.

Dan turned to her. "Yes. In the first place, I need to do an autopsy to get data on organs, cells, circulation, nerve clusters, bone structure, and so forth. Next, we need to start eating the foods here. We can't ask the dragons to go back for groceries every week."

"We agree," Nick said. "We just haven't exhausted our food supply yet. But we're getting low."

"At least we have water," Rhea said. "Besides the condensers, we have rain barrels now. We had rain here a couple of days ago. Ours and yours should be full."

"Yes, show me," Dan said.

They led the way around the house to a large barrel. The top, which had a hinge, was closed.

Dan looked from it to the house. "I see. You gather water in the reservoir on the roof and the chute pipes it down to the barrel."

Rhea nodded. "There's a sensor opening the top when it starts to rain and closes the top when the barrel is full."

"There's a spigot right here," Nick said. "You can either fill a cup from this, or," he reached for something that appeared to be a large pitcher, perhaps two feet high and a foot wide, with a shoulder strap on it, "you can fill this up if you need a lot of water at once."

Dan reached out for the pitcher. When Nick gave it to him, he used the spigot to fill it. "This will be a great start. I want to analyze the water." He started walking to the clinic house.

Rhea and Nick followed. "But we know from Arthur's reading that the water's fine."

"Yes, I read that," Dan said, "but I still want to know if anything's in it besides $H_2O$." Once inside the clinic house, he took out a sterile test tube from a rack and poured water into it. He put the pitcher down and set the test tube in the rack. Reaching for a strip of paper, he dipped it in the water and pulled it out. "Not acidic. That's a start." He then poured the water in the test tube in a machine and turned it on. He watched the screen at the top of the machine as it showed results of the analysis. Rhea and Nick moved closer to watch.

"What are you looking for?" Nick asked.

"Primarily naturally occurring poisons, such as arsenic or mercury," Dan said.

"See any?" Rhea asked.

Dan shook his head. "No. We're in the clear."

"What's next?" Nick asked.

Dan swung around in the swivel chair. "I need to wait for Evvin to come back with the swimmer."

"We need to wait for the dragons to return to put up your tent," Rhea said. "They can drive in the tent supports better than anything we have."

"Since it's just the three of us at the moment," Dan said. "How do you think they'd react if I suggested a dragon autopsy?"

"As a scientist, I can understand the need," Rhea said. "But you can't."

"Meaning they'd be strongly against the idea?" Dan asked.

"No, you really can't," Nick said. "Morran and Zinnia showed us a valley between two mountain ridges. Dragons who are dying attach themselves to the rocks, and when they die, they turn to stone. Morran and Zinnia showed us Rex. He's like a statue."

"Partly worn from weathering," Rhea added.

Dan rubbed his chin. "No dragon just drops from the sky from heart failure?"

Nick shrugged. "Not as far as we know."

"The dragons hibernate there, too," Rhea said. "They attach themselves to the rocks, and when rested, they detach and go on."

"Hibernate? Interesting. Now that's something I could study." He stood from the swivel chair. "Since we have to wait for the dragons to come back, I'll go back to my house and put more of my things away."

"Nick and I will go get the tenting supports and tarps," Rhea said.

"I'll get out the grill, too, so we can barbecue swimmer for supper." Dan said. "Care to join me for dinner?"

"You brought a grill?" Nick sounded impressed.

"Sure, we're going to cook, aren't we?" Dan said.

Rhea turned from Nick to Dan. "We'd be happy to join you for dinner."

Rhea and Nick loaded one of the carts and returned to Dan's house. They found a flat gravelly area near the clinic house and unloaded there. Dan came out to assist.

Evvin came into view carrying something that looked like a large, limp bird. He landed and carefully set it on the ground in front of him.

Dan walked over. Rhea and Nick followed.

"I got you a swimmer, just as you asked," Evvin said to Dan. "Is it what you wanted?"

Dan looked over the swimmer. "I can see where you bit it, just where the neck joins the body."

"That's the best place to bite," Evvin said. "The blood goes out fast and they don't wiggle or honk anymore."

Dan nodded. "Thank you. This is just what I wanted."

Evvin smiled.

Nick walked around the swimmer. "That's a three-foot goose? Duck? With a long neck?"

"It's a swimmer," Evvin said.

"Impressive feathered wings." Rhea turned to Evvin. "And they fly?"

"Yes, yes, they do," Evvin said.

Dan turned to Nick. "Help me get it into the clinic?"

"Oh. Yes, of course," Nick said. He grabbed the place where the torso met the legs.

Dan grasped the shoulders. "On three. One. Two. Three."

They hefted the swimmer and brought it inside the clinic.

Nick came out less than a minute later.

Rhea turned to Evvin. "While Dan is working, can you help Nick and I set up a tent for Dan?"

"Yes," Evvin said. "Just tell me what to do."

The other dragons returned shortly after they started the work. With everyone helping, they had a large tent set up quickly.

When they finished, Dan came out of the clinic.

"We're finished," Rhea said to him.

"Yes, I was watching through the window." Dan turned to nod at all of them. "Good work. Thank you."

"What did you find about the swimmer?" Nick asked.

"I'm not done yet, but as a preliminary report, I analyzed the small amount of blood left inside the animal. The blood similar to animals on Earth. Cell structure is similar. Many of the same organs."

"Is that good or bad?" Nick asked.

Dan took a breath. "Well, if there are a lot of similarities, it means that I don't have to learn entirely new anatomical details." He walked to Kieran and stopped in front of him. "I understand that dragons hibernate."

"Yes, we do."

"Would it be possible for you to pass the word among your fellow dragons that if there's a dragon ready to go into hibernation and would allow me to watch and examine them in that state, to let me know?"

"'Pass the word?'"

"Tell other dragons, who can tell other dragons."

"Yes, I can do that." Kieran extended his neck and tilted his head upward. He let out a long trill. When he stopped, they could hear other trills in the distance.

"Thank you," Dan said.

"Ask for whatever you need," Kieran said.

"It would help if I could examine a dragon who had died, so that I could see the internal organs, but I understand that dragons turn to stone after they die."

"Yes, we do," Kieran said.

Morran ambled over. "What about the bogs?"

"Bogs?" Dan asked.

Kieran turned to Dan. "Younger dragons, especially those just returning from the human world and not yet familiar with ours, sometimes become curious and walk into a bog. They can't get out. They drown, and they don't turn into stone."

"I haven't heard of this happening in many years," Thalia said. "Even before I laid Zinnia's egg."

"They're still in there. I've seen them," Morran said.

"Can we get one out?" Dan asked. "I promise I will treat the body with the greatest respect."

"We trust you," Kieran said. "The problem would be in getting one out without endangering ourselves."

Dan turned to Rhea and Nick. "We have engineers. Maybe they can come up with a plan."

Rhea turned to Nick and took a breath. "Give us a day or two to think it over."

"I'd like to take a look at the bog, first," Nick said, "though it wouldn't have to be today."

Dan nodded. "Yes, I'm still getting settled in myself. I'm sure this would be a day-long task anyway."

"Traveling around here brings up something we need to talk about." Rhea turned to Dan and Evvin. "Evvin will have to learn to fly with Dan."

Evvin drew his head back.

Dan smiled and approached Evvin. He reached over and patted Evvin. "Yes. How about it, buddy?"

Evvin lowered his head. "I...I...I don't want Dan to fall off. He could die." Evvin sounded despondent.

"No, I won't, Evvin," Dan said. "I'll be fine. I know you can do it."

Nick stepped over to Morran. "Evvin, take a look here. See all the supports on Morran?"

"Yes, Evvin," Rhea said. "We don't want to fall off, either. It's up to us to hold on, and Dan will."

Nick climbed on Morran's back and strapped himself in. "Look, Evvin. I'm absolutely secure here. Even if I fell asleep, I'd stay in place. I wouldn't fall."

Morran craned his neck and turned his head in Nick's direction. "If you fall asleep on my back, I'm having Zinnia lift you off."

Nick chuckled, removed the straps, and slid down to the ground. "Don't worry, I'm won't."

Rhea put a hand on Zinnia's side. "Zinnia, would you let Dan fly with you a little? Then Evvin can watch and see that it's safe."

"Of course," Zinnia said.

Rhea waved Dan over. She expected to have to instruct Dan on what do so, but Dan climbed on and strapped himself in without her having to say a thing.

Zinnia turned her head slightly in Dan's direction. "Ready?"

"Anytime you are," Dan said.

Zinnia turned to Evvin. "Now, watch, Evvin. You don't have to do anything special. Just lift off as you usually do. See? Dan is well clear of my wings. They won't even touch him."

Rhea stepped back and watched as Zinnia spread her wings and launched herself into the air.

"Whoo!" Dan shouted. "This is great!"

Zinnia flew in a circle over the two houses. Evvin watched carefully as she landed almost in the exact spot where she took off.

Dan released the straps and slid to the ground. "Thank you, Zinnia, that was amazing!"

"See, Evvin," Zinnia said. "Dan was safe. Now you can try it."

Nick walked over to the newly-built tent. "We have the straps we need here. We can put them on you, Evvin, if you like."

"Morran and I will watch," Zinnia said. "Rhea and Nick know how to do it."

Dan strolled over to Evvin. "What do you think, Evvin? Can Rhea and Nick put the riding straps on you?"

"What do I do?" Evvin said.

"Just stay still and let Nick and I put the straps around you," Rhea said.

Evvin did not move as Rhea and Nick set up the harnesses, though Rhea sensed Evvin trembling slightly.

Dan reached over and patted Evvin's neck. "You're doing fine buddy."

When they finished, Rhea gave the straps a test pull. "Everything's in place."

"You can move now, Evvin," Dan said.

Evvin relaxed.

"How do the straps feel, Evvin?" Rhea asked. "If they're too loose or too tight, we can adjust them."

"I hardly feel them at all," Evvin said.

"That's good," Zinnia said. "Now, let Dan climb up. When he's settled, fly in a circle, the same way I did. I'll fly next to you."

"Are you ready for me to climb up?" Dan asked.

"Yes," Evvin said, though not confidently.

Dan pulled himself up and settled in. "I'm ready."

Zinnia looked Evvin and Dan over. "Everything looks good, Evvin. Just take off."

Evvin did not move at first.

"Should I nibble on your tail?" Morran asked.

Evvin turned to Morran. "No! I can do it."

"Morran," Thalia warned.

Evvin took off. Zinnia launched herself into the air at a safe distance.

"You're doing fine, Evvin!" Dan shouted.

Evvin made the circle, Zinnia following, and then landed where he started.

Dan reached over and patted Evvin's neck. "You did it, Evvin."

"That was easy," Evvin said.

Zinnia landed. "See? It's not hard."

Dan unstrapped himself and slid to the ground. "Now you can take me anywhere, Evvin. Thank you."

"We're proud of you, Evvin," Kieran said.

"Yes," Thalia said, "even Morran. Aren't you, Morran?"

"Yes, that was good," Morran said. "Sorry, Evvin."

Dan put a hand on Evvin and faced Morran. "Now we'll be able to help you out one day, Morran."

Morran did not respond.

Kieran faced Dan. "Is there anything else we can do for you?"

"Yes," Dan said. "I'd like Rhea and Nick to fit some dragons with cameras. When you go out to hunt next time, or the time after, or whenever it's convenient, I want to see what you eat."

"Multiple dragons?" Rhea asked.

Dan nodded. "I presume you don't eat the same thing every day, or even if one dragon does, another dragon may eat something else."

"We eat a variety of things," Thalia said.

"And not the same things every day," Kieran added.

"How about this?" Rhea said. "The dragons can come back to our house and Nick and I can see if we can get cameras to fit. Then whenever they're ready, we can put the cameras on them before a hunt and set them to record."

"I'd be willing to do that," Morran said.

"I think we all would," Kieran said.

"Meanwhile," Rhea said, "Dan, here, can go back to his research, since he has a swimmer to examine."

"Works for me," Dan said.

Dan was standing outside his house with his electric barbecue as Rhea and Nick appeared through the trees.

"You're right on time. The bird is done," Dan said, spearing the meat with the long fork and transferring it to the platter.

"Smells good," Nick said.

Rhea grinned. "Did you analyze it?"

Dan smiled. "Of course. Nothing in the carcass that we need to worry about." He turned off the grill, picked up the platter, and led the way inside. The table, already set for three, had a space for him to place the platter. "Have a seat."

"Anywhere?" Nick asked.

"Anywhere you want," Dan said.

Rhea and Nick took adjacent chairs at the small square table, while Dan took the carving knife and served the meat. When everyone had meat on their plate, he sat.

Rhea reached for a pitcher. "Is this coffee?"

"Yes, help yourself," Dan said. "Packets of sugar and powdered cream in the middle."

"You brought coffee?" Nick took the pitcher from Rhea when she was finished and poured it into his mug.

"Enough to last for months," Dan said. "I wasn't about to do without it."

"The baked potatoes and butter are from our Earth, I take it." Rhea reached for those serving dishes.

"Yes," Dan said. "But we'll need to start eating the tubers Arthur described. I want to see if Evvin or one of the other dragons would be willing to bring a cow and calf from the herd so we can have dairy products."

"Can you make butter and cheese?" Nick asked.

Dan nodded. "Comes from being around farmers...and having a sister who's a chef as well as a husband who's an agriculturalist."

"How about flour? Arthur had a hand mill," Nick said.

"I have a food processor. That's even better," Dan said. "I sent Evvin to gather some grain. After I showed him Arthur's sketches, he said he knew where it was."

"Speaking of dragons," Rhea said, "Nick and I were able to fit cameras to each of the dragons, so they'd stay in place but not interfere with their hunting or eating. We're ready to put them on again whenever they're ready."

"I can't wait to see what those recordings show," Nick said.

Dan chewed and swallowed a piece of meat. "No."

"No?" Nick queried.

"Only I am going to see the camera recordings," Dan said.

"Why?" Rhea said.

"Because," Dan said, "once you see your kind, friendly Zinnia and Morran chase down an animal, rip it open, and devour it, you won't be able to unsee it."

Rhea opened her mouth to reply, thought about it a moment, and nodded. "I guess I see your point."

"What about you?" Nick asked.

"We veterinarians cultivate a degree of detachment," Dan said. "I interned all over the place, with wild animals as well as farm animals."

Rhea looked from Nick to Dan. "We can have the camera images sent to your computer."

"We'll do that before we leave," Nick said.

"Thank you," Dan said.

Rhea took another bite of meat. "This is really good."

Nick raised his fork. "Yes. Not like chicken, maybe a little like turkey? But not game-y at all."

"Has what my sister would say 'good mouth feel' despite not having much of a fat content."

"Do you have any barbecue sauce?" Nick asked.

Dan turned to him. "No, just the salt and pepper packets on the table. Did you need it?"

"No, no," Nick said quickly. "It's delicious. I just wondered how it would taste with it."

"I don't think we could make our own," Rhea said. "The main ingredient is tomato, and I don't remember Arthur describing anything that resembled a tomato."

"Though something similar may grow in a place Arthur didn't know about," Dan said.

"Speaking of Arthur," Nick said, "I was wondering whether we could teach the dragons to read?"

Dan turned to him. "First, we need to consider whether their brains are wired for reading. Nearly all the dragons spent their early years on Earth, where they picked up our oral language, but with signs and notices all around, none of them learned to read."

"My younger sister read books to Zinnia," Rhea said, "Zinnia would look at the pictures, but even though she read elementary books, such as 'A is for apple' and so forth, Zinnia can't read."

"Besides, what would they read?" Dan said. "There aren't any signs around here."

"Arthur's book, for a start," Nick said. "We could teach them to write, too."

"Again, their brains may not be wired for it," Dan said. "There aren't even any drawings from them that I or Arthur have ever noticed."

"Zinnia never made any drawings, even with her claws in the sand," Rhea said.

"Second reason," Dan said. "We aren't colonizers. It isn't for us to decide what's best for them and then compelling them to do it."

"I wasn't thinking about compelling, just asking," Nick said.

"Let them ask first," Dan said. "They've had plenty of opportunity to do so, particularly when telling you and Rhea about Arthur's book. As in, 'We can't read Arthur's book, but you can...and by the way, can you teach us to read?' That would have been an opening."

"When you put it that way, that makes sense," Nick said.

"We did build a rain shelter for them," Rhea said.

"Did they ask for one?" Dan said.

"No, we offered to make them one, and they said yes," Nick said. "When the other dragons saw it, they wondered if they could have one."

"Should we have done that?" Rhea said.

Dan shrugged. "Who knows? Just by our being here, we're affecting dragon society. The best we can do is try to leave as small a footprint as we can."

"Sort of our own non-interference directive," Rhea said.

"Though they invited us in," Nick said.

Rhea nodded. "But it's more like they hired us as employees."

"Yes," Dan said. "They're giving us food and shelter and resources in exchange for our services."

"And if they don't like what we're doing," Rhea said, "there's nothing preventing them from grabbing us, taking us back to Earth, and dumping us there."

"I don't disagree with anything you're saying," Nick said, "but I've been thinking of this as helping someone in need."

"That too," Rhea said, "Or doing a favor for a friend."

"In my case, or helping a patient."

"I only hope we can help them," Nick said. "This is going to be a tough one."

"I think of it this way," Dan said. "The dragons had been laying eggs for what? Millennia? Then, a little over 100 years ago, something changed. We may not be able to change it back, but I hope we can help them to make some sort of accommodation so that they can keep their eggs safe. It's just going to take time."

# CHAPTER 9

When they had finished eating, Dan packed up the leftovers and sent half of them home with Rhea and Nick. Soon after they departed, he heard the sound of wings beating the air and walked outside.

Evvin landed and set the sheaves he carried on the ground. When Dan walked over, Evvin said, "I looked a long time to find the best ones. Is this what you wanted?"

Dan picked up a sheaf. The grains seemed ripe. "Yes, this is exactly what I want. Thank you."

Evvin grinned.

Dan gathered a few more sheaves. "Are they hard to find?"

"Good ones, yes. They grow all over, but we eat a lot of them and it takes three or four moons for them to grow back again."

"I take it they're tasty."

"Yes."

"I'll tell you what," Dan said. "These are all I need for now. You can eat the rest of them."

Evvin seemed pleasantly surprised. "That's very nice of you."

From what Rhea, Nick, and Zinnia had told him of Evvin before he arrived, he had gathered that Evvin was awkward and unsure of himself. Since Dan had arrived, could see how they had reached that conclusion, but he felt Evvin had a good heart and the potential to grow to be an amazing individual if nurtured properly. He did his best to be reassuring. "Friends share. Friends help each other." He turned toward the door of the clinic. "I'm going into the clinic house to analyze these. You can stay outside at the doorway and watch, and we can talk while I'm working."

Evvin followed him to the house but remained at the entrance while Dan walked inside and sat at the lab table. The dragon lay flat and rested his chin on the threshold.

As Dan prepared the grains for the mass spectrometer, microscope, and other testing equipment, he glanced over at Evvin. "I wanted to ask you about an animal Arthur described and sketched in his book. Flat, round, four legs, and rows of ridges on the back. Do you know what it is?"

Evvin let out a trill. "I don't know the human name."

"Arthur didn't give it a name, either. He referred to it as a walking manhole cover. Have you seen them? Are they near here?"

"Yes, over by the river. It's a different path from the one to Rhea and Nick's house."

"Can you show me later?"

"Yes. There's a track. Animals go back and forth."

"What can you tell me about them?"

"They're nice for a snack. Crunchy. The little ones are better since the ridges aren't hard, but they're small."

"Do you eat a lot of them?"

"Not many. There are better things to eat. They drink lots of water, but they can't swim. They drown, and they go over the waterfall. Dragons find them at the bottom of the waterfall."

"They aren't hunted?"

"Not very much. The big ones, you have to turn them over and eat from the belly. They don't like being turned over or touched there. They make a lot of noise, and they thrash around a lot. If you approach the little ones, the big ones will crawl up your leg and make loud noises. Then they'll turn around and poop on you."

"Do they bite?"

"Not dragons. They seem to know that we can't be bitten. Scavengers they will bite if the scavengers get close enough."

"Are they meat eaters?"

"No, they only eat plants. They bite to defend themselves or the little ones."

"Do they leave you alone if you don't look like a threat?"

"Yes. Animals here don't attack unless they feel there's a danger or want to eat you."

"Good to know." Dan noted the results of the quick tests and let the longer tests run. He stood from the chair. "I'm done for now. Can you show me the path you talked about?"

When Dan stood outside, Evvin pointed. "That's the way to the river. All the animals we talked about go there in the morning to drink water and eat plants. There have nests all around."

"What do the nests look like?"

"Round. Made of dried reeds mostly. They rest on the ground."

Dan nodded. He pointed in a different direction. "And that's the way to Rhea and Nick's?"

"Yes."

Dan saw seven silvery dragons flying in the distance. "Are those the bachelor dragons Rhea and Nick told me about?"

Evvin looked up. "Yes."

"Do you know them well?"

"A little. They aren't nice to me."

"Do they hurt you?"

"No. Dragons don't attack other dragons. But they make fun of me, or don't pay attention to me."

"You're right. That's not nice." Dan kept watching the dragons. "They seem to be flying in this direction. Were you expecting them?"

"No."

"Well, I think we can handle them. Kieran, I understand, told them to behave themselves."

"All the dragons did."

"Then I know we can handle them. They're probably just curious." Dan turned to Evvin. "I'm going to stay close to you. They're big, and they might step on me accidentally. I'll need you to protect me."

"I will."

"If you see them getting too close to me, just say, 'Stop. Step back.' You don't have to say it loudly. Often, others will pay more attention to a low voice."

"I'll do what you say."

Dan reached up and patted his arm. "You're a good friend, Evvin."

The dragons landed close to the tent as a group. For a few seconds, they just sat there, heads up, turning from side to side.

"I see you," Evvin said to them.

"We want to meet the new human," one of them said.

Dan raised his hand and waved. "My name is Dan, and you can call me by my name. What's your name?"

"Brutus."

Dan smiled. On Earth, the Dragon Appreciation Society cataloged common names farmers gave dragons, and this was one of them. "Pleased to meet you, Brutus. Did you come just to see me?"

Brutus turned to the tent. "The golden dragons made one of these for themselves. We wanted to know how."

"The golden dragons." Dan turned to Evvin and said in a low voice, "The unmated females?"

"Yes," Evvin answered.

Dan considered for a moment. Rhea and Nick had told him that the other dragons had wondered whether they could all have a shelter. Apparently, the unattached female dragons had already figured out how to build one by themselves. Since the word was out now and could not be retracted, there was no reason to hide the knowledge. Sharing it might even make these dragons more cooperative. Dan turned back to Brutus. "I'm not an engineer, like Rhea and Nick. I'm sure they'd be happy to help you if you asked."

The visiting dragons lowered their heads.

Dan lifted his chin. "Oh, I get it. You feel awkward going to them after what you did. Not to mention they're closer to Kieran."

The dragons kept their heads low but said nothing in response.

"Why not ask the golden dragons, then?" Dan said. After another long silence, Dan added, "I see that dragons also have a degree of masculine pride. All right. Have you seen their shelter?"

"Yes," another dragon said. "They used branches from fan trees on top. On the side, spire trunks or piles of rocks."

Dan nodded. He remembered Arthur's descriptions and drawings of the trees that had branches like fans and the trees that looked like pillars. "And what is your name?"

"Skipper."

"Pleased to meet you, Skipper."

Another dragon spoke up. "They sleep under it whether it's raining or not."

"And you are?"

"Gus."

"Pleased to meet you, Gus."

"They sleep snuggled together," said yet another dragon.

"Your name is...?"

"Hunter."

"Pleased to meet you, Hunter. And you're jealous of this?" When they did not answer right away, he guessed, "You're thinking of life after mating? Snuggling as a couple? Might make you more attractive to them if you can show you can make a shelter for them?"

The heads went up.

"Well, I'll see what I can do," Dan said. "First, let me get everyone's name. He pointed to a dragon. You are...?"

"Stan."

He pointed again.

"Mitch."

"Last one," Dan said.

"Logan."

Dan clapped his hands together. "All right. I'm not an engineer, but I did go camping with my youth groups in my younger days, and I know something about putting up a tent." He started walking toward the shelter. He heard Evvin walking behind him, staying close. When he reached the tent, he added, "Evvin helped put up this tent as well as the shelter at Kieran and Thalia's home. He and I are going to explain supports and coverings."

Evvin enthusiastically related how he and Zinnia's family had put up the tent at Rhea and Nick's direction. When he finished, Dan took over, walking to the supports and explaining why they were placed the way they were and how the coverings were attached.

"Stop. Step back."

Dan lifted his head at Evvin's voice. He had not noticed that the other dragons had begun crowding around him. Skipper, in particular, was within arm's length.

All the dragons scuttled backwards a few steps when Evvin spoke. Evvin craned his neck and turned his head so that he looked the other dragons in the eye.

Dan moved closer to the shelter of Evvin's body. "Let's continue. But you're not going to get a good view if you're crowded together, so separate a little more."

The dragons obeyed.

When Dan felt he had given the dragons a basic plan, he said, "Now you can try it yourselves. Don't worry if you don't get it right the first time. Keep trying until it works. If you have questions, you can come back and ask. Evvin and I will be happy to give you advice."

Brutus stepped forward...but not too close. "You can come to us if you need anything, too. We will help."

"Thank you," Dan said.

The dragons gathered together and flew away.

Dan turned to Evvin. "Thank you for watching out for me, Evvin. You saved me from being squeezed, at the very least."

"It worked," Evvin said, sounding a little astonished.

Dan patted Evvin's arm. "I knew you could handle them."

The next morning, Dan's cell phone buzzed as he was finishing cleaning up after breakfast. The text came from Rhea: *The dragons want to use the cameras today. We fitted them before they went to hunt. Nick and I are coming to put a camera on Evvin.*

*We'll be ready*, Dan answered.

He walked out of the house to see Evvin munching on the extra grains he had brought the day before. "Evvin, Rhea and Nick are coming over to put a camera on you so I can see what you eat when you go hunting. Are you ready for that?"

Evvin swallowed. "Yes."

Rhea and Nick arrived soon afterwards. They fitted Evvin with a camera and checked with him to be sure the camera was comfortable and would not interfere with his hunting. Then Evvin flew off.

"You should see the images on the computer when you open the camera app," Nick said.

"Thanks," Dan said.

"By the way," Rhea said. "We saw the bachelor dragons flying in this direction last evening. Did they come here?"

"Yes, they did," Dan said.

"Morran wanted us to check to be sure they weren't causing any trouble," Nick said, "but before we could answer, Kieran told him that Dan could handle it and would call if he needed help."

"We did fine," Dan said.

"What did they want?" Rhea asked.

Dan waved in the direction of the tent. "Apparently, the single golden dragons made their own shelter after seeing the one you made for Zinnia's family home. The bachelors wanted instruction on how to make one themselves."

Rhea and Nick exchanged an astonished look. "The golden dragons made a shelter all by themselves?" Rhea asked.

"That's what the bachelors said," Dan answered.

"I'd like to see that," Nick said.

"I suggest that Rhea ask Zinnia about taking you there, in case the golden dragons prefer to talk to other females," Dan said.

"But the bachelors know about it," Nick said.

"They could have seen it on a flyover," Dan said.

"Well, there's that," Nick said.

"Did you tell them how to do it?" Rhea said.

Dan shrugged. "I saw no reason not to, since the word had already been spread around. I wanted to send them to you, but they seemed embarrassed about doing that. Besides, they now seem more willing to help."

"That's a plus," Rhea said.

"If you'll excuse me, I want to go and monitor the hunt," Dan said.

"Of course," Rhea said.

"See you later," Nick said.

"Yes, come for supper." Rhea pointed. "We're just a short distance that way."

When Dan sat behind his computer screen and opened the app, he saw five windows with live views, labeled with the name of each dragon. He saw Kieran and Thalia chasing long-necked animals that reminded him of llamas? Alpacas? Zinna and Morran's views were similar, showing they were hunting together as well, though they seemed to be at edge of a riverbank, wading into the waters, dipping their heads in, and coming up with large fish. Elsewhere, Evvin had already taken a swimmer.

Through the cameras, Dan was able to observe other dragons nearby. A number of dragons were in the air. He saw that most of them drank water from waterfalls, which fell from cliffs and escarpments along the mountain range.

As the dragons soared, looking for food, Dan saw fields of not-yet-ripened grain. Edible plants also grew on the sides of the mountains. Dragons clustered at a particular site where pods of various sizes had sprouted. They relieved themselves on the mountainsides, and plants grew in abundance around those sites. Dan guessed that after the dragons ate certain plants, they excreted seeds with the manure which washed down the slopes when it rained and then grew in the valleys. He knew from his experience of encountering dragons at farms that their manure was a potent fertilizer.

Eventually, every dragon with a camera settled in a meadow, stretched out, stomach and jaw on the ground. After they opened their mouths slightly, showing their teeth, beetles about the width of the palm of a human's hand emerged from the undergrowth. They fed on the leavings stuck in the dragon teeth and gums, then disappeared again in the short grass. The dragons took to the air again.

Dan picked up his phone and texted Rhea. *The dragons are returning. I received good videos from the cameras. Can I keep Evvin's camera and use it to observe other animals?*

*Yes, of course* was the response.

Dan grabbed the tablet loaded with Arthur's drawings, walked outside, and watched as Evvin approached and landed. He took the camera off Evvin's head and held it in front of him.

"Did you see what I ate?" Evvin asked.

"Yes, thank you. I had a question for you."

Evvin tilted his head.

"All the other dragons I watched stopped at some point and ate the pods." Dan held up the tablet so Evvin could see what he was talking about. "Don't you like them?"

Evvin dipped his head slightly. "I like them, yes. But other dragons like them too. It's hard to get through the crowd."

"Yes, I noticed that the dragons were clustered at those points, even pushing and shoving each other."

"They taste really good."

"So I gather. The dragons were ignoring the smaller pods. I take it those aren't ripe yet?"

"Yes, if you eat those, they taste bad."

Dan nodded. "I see." He heard a noise behind them and turned. Rhea and Nick walked out of the forest path, followed by four dragons.

"Did the cameras help?" Thalia asked.

"Yes, they did, thank you."

"Can we help in some other way today?" Kieran asked.

"As a matter of fact, you can. This is a delicate question among humans, so forgive me for any awkwardness."

"You can ask us anything," Kieran said.

"Now that I know what you eat, it will help if I analyze your poop. Would it embarrass you to drop it nearby next time?"

"That is not a problem with us," Kieran said.

Dan pointed to a flat grassy area not too far from where they stood. "I'll put markers there so you can tell where to go. Zinnia, I'll put up a green marker for you; Morran, I'll put up a red marker; Thalia, I'll put up a blue marker; Kieran, I'll put up a yellow marker; and Evvin, I'll put up a white marker."

"We can do that," Kieran said.

"You only have to do it once," Dan said.

"Anything else?" Kieran asked.

Dan approached Morran. "I have a task especially for you, Morran."

"Me?"

"Yes. Next time you're out hunting, bring me one of these pods." He held up the tablet so Morran could see the picture.

"Uneaten?"

"Uneaten. Can you do that for me?"

"Not easy, but I will."

"Thank you. I appreciate the effort." Dan turned to Kieran. "That's all I can think of for now. You've all been very kind."

"Tell us if you need anything else." He turned and walked back on the path. The other dragons followed. Nick and Rhea exchanged good-bye waves with Dan before leaving themselves.

Dan turned to Evvin. "I'm going to put the camera away and set out the stakes."

"What can I do?" Evvin asked eagerly.

Dan thought for a moment. He had not considered that he might have to keep Evvin busy. But without any apparent dragon friends or a future mate, he may not have anything to do.

He took a breath. "Eventually I'll want to have a pen for animals. You've been to Arthur and Rex's place, you've seen the enclosure Arthur built?"

"Yes."

"I guess you can't nail boards as Arthur did, but can you get some rocks and build a wall?"

"I can build a dragon home."

"How is that built?"

"Dragons make homes by surrounding a flat area with rocks. The place where Kieran and Thalia and Morran and Zinnia and I live is like that. We stack the rocks taller than we are."

"Well, I don't need a wall that high. Maybe this high off the ground?" Dan held a hand out at the height of his shoulder to show the distance.

"Yes, I can do that."

"Let's walk around and find a place."

For the next hour, he and Evvin walked around the two houses until Dan found what he felt was a suitable spot. He indicated where he wanted the walls and the entrance. Evvin seemed to be giving him undivided attention.

Once they had established boundaries, Dan said, "Of course I don't expect this to be completed in a day, or even several days. Take your time and do what you can whenever I need to do something alone."

"Yes, it takes time to build something good," Evvin said. "I can start now, though."

Dan patted Evvin's arm. "Thanks, Evvin."

Evvin flew off.

That left Dan to put out the markers, which he did quickly. His objective, however, was to find the animals that Arthur had described. Already, he privately called them tanklets.

Taking the camera and strapping it on like a bodycam, he started along the path that Evvin had pointed out. The route consisted of compacted brown dirt about three feet wide. Looking from side to side, he saw what Arthur and the dragons called fan trees: trees with branches that spread out like fans. He stopped to examine a branch and found that the twigs and leaves were tightly woven. He could see that the golden dragons could use them effectively as a roof.

Walking on, he came to a clearing with a large round nest on the ground. In the nest huddled small round creatures, who squeaked. As he watched, one of the kits—somehow his brain automatically supplied a name for the little ones—climbed over the side of the nest and slid to the ground outside.

As a veterinarian, he knew that picking up the kit and putting it back into the nest was a bad idea. But he edged up to the kit to take a closer look after surveying the area to be sure that a parent was not in sight.

Basically, the kit looked like a hedgehog. The back showed the beginnings of the rows of spikes it would have as an adult, but those were not stiff or solid. The head definitely resembled a hedgehog, as did the feet. Each of the four legs had one knee joint. There was a tiny pointed tail.

Dan also examined the nest, as well as he could at a distance. There was an open-weave pattern, so that air could circulate at the sides as well as the top. The nest was amply large for the seven kits he counted, with room for them to fit even when they grew to twice the size. Craning his neck, he also saw the remains of crushed shells at the bottom of the nest, which seemed to reinforce the foundation. The nest appeared free of excrement and relatively clean overall. A branch from a nearby fan tree hovered above the nest, which presumably would keep the nest dry when it rained.

A loud chattering drew his attention. Directly ahead of him was an adult, presumably one of the parents. It marched toward him with determination, complaining all the way. Dan quickly backed up, trying to keep the parent in sight as he did so, but he tripped on a tree root and landed on his back. Before he could pick himself up, the tanklet walked over his legs, over his abdomen, and stood on his chest. Fortunately the animal was lightweight enough not to crush him.

Dan had been scolded by animals before, when he came too close to a nest of birds or squirrels. The sound he heard did not resemble a bark or a chirp, but he definitely was being reprimanded.

In veterinarian school, he was told that his first duty was to avoid being harmed by the animal, or else he could not help the animal at all. He could raise his hands, grab the creature on either side at the diameter of the circular body, only about eighteen inches wide, and lift the tanklet off. But he was so delighted and excited at being this close to an animal seen only once before by a human, that he could not help but remain still and observe as the tanklet cussed him out.

The breath was not unpleasant. The teeth were flat, typical of herbivores. While the top, what he could see of it before the creature climbed on him, was stiff and ragged, the underside looked soft and furry. He was tempted to pet it there but remembered what Evvin had said about the tanklets getting upset if touched on the stomach. There was a seam by the tail that reminded him of the flap on Evvin concealing his male organ, so this was almost undoubtedly a male. Like the dragons, the feet had retractable claws, which fortunately were retracted at the moment.

The tanklet stopped chattering. He let out a huff, turned in the other direction, tromping on Dan's chest and ribs as he did so, and walked over Dan's legs to the ground. Remembering what Evvin had said about the creature defecating, Dan quickly scrambled to his feet and fled to shelter behind a tree. Looking around the trunk, he saw the tanklet raise its tail and poop noisily in his direction. Without looking back, the tanklet trotted back toward the nest, head held high in what appeared to be a triumphant gesture.

Still holding on to the trunk of the tree, Dan took deep breaths to calm himself. His heart was racing. In the—what was it, two days?—he had been there, he had focused on getting his houses set up, getting to know the dragons as well as getting better acquainted with Rhea and Nick, and getting to work to show that he was earning his keep. Only now had he allowed himself to feel the excitement of being here – with dragons! Dragons he saw every day. As time went on, he learned more and more about them, the fulfillment of his fondest wish. And now, he had met, face-to-face, within inches, one of the other intriguing creatures that Arthur had written about. This was an experience that surpassed his greatest expectations.

This made Dan even more determined to identify and defeat The Terror. He promised himself that he would not rest until he found a way to keep the dragons and other animals safe from it.

# CHAPTER 10

Dan remained holding on to the trunk of the tree for a few moments more. Looking up, he decided that this was a spire tree: narrow trunk, rising straight up, no branches at his height or below, but dozens and dozens of short thin branches and leaves going up to the top. According to Arthur, when these trees died, the trunk solidified, or petrified, and the branches simply fell off, leaving a straight pole soaring to the sky.

He let go of the tree and touched the camera on his shoulder. The recording light glowed, showing that it had been sending images to his computer at home all along. He pulled the camera off and held it in his hand as he crept toward the nest again.

When he heard squeaking, he stopped. He could not see the nest right away, but looking through branches of low trees, he finally was able to get a direct view of the clearing. The kit had been placed back into the nest. Another larger tanklet had joined the one he had met earlier. This one's behind was shaped differently. Dan concluded that this was the mother, and the shape of the hindquarters allowed the eggs to pass more freely.

Taking the camera straps, Dan secured the camera to the tree at his eye level. He checked the view finder to be sure that it was recording the nesting area before turning and walking home.

As he approached clinic house, he heard the sound of rocks clashing. Walking around the structure, he saw a pile of rocks, ranging from the size of bowling balls to the size of a standard oven. Evvin reached into the pile and placed rocks on the ground, beginning the base of the enclosure. The dragon reached under his armpits and smeared something on the rocks before placing other rocks on top.

"This looks good so far, Evvin," Dan said. "But what are you putting the rocks?"

Evvin held out a hand. Dan saw a transparent gel there.

"This gets the rocks to stick together," Evvin said.

"And the substance comes from the armpits?"

"The back of the arms at the shoulder," Evvin said. "I squeeze the muscles there and it comes out. If I wanted to hibernate, it would come out all over. That would let me stick to the rocks."

"Evvin, can I have a little of that to analyze?"

In answer, Evvin moved his hand in Dan's direction.

Dan held up a finger. "Give me a moment. I want to get a slide."

He rushed back into the clinic house and grabbed a petri dish and a slide. He also put on gloves. When he came back to Evvin, the dragon smeared the gel on both.

"Thanks, Evvin. I'm going inside to run tests. You can continue to build the wall. You're doing fine." Dan pivoted and took a step toward the lab, then pivoted back. "Evvin, have you ever hibernated?"

"Not yet," Evvin said. "I might later, if I want a long sleep."

"Do all dragons hibernate at some time in their lives?"

"No, there are dragons that never feel like hibernating."

"Thanks, Evvin, that's what I wanted to know."

After Zinnia, Morran, Thalia, and Kieran returned from their morning hunt, Rhea and Nick removed the cameras.

"Did Dan see what we ate?" Thalia asked.

"Yes, he texted us to tell us the cameras worked," Nick said.

Rhea approached Zinnia. "The bachelor dragons told Dan last night that the golden dragons had made a shelter for themselves. I wonder if it would be possible to take Nick and I to see it?"

"They made their own?" Thalia turned to the others. "Clever dragons."

Zinnia turned to Rhea. "Yes, Morran and I can take you and Nick."

"They won't mind me coming there?" Nick asked.

"The unmated singles tend to stay in their own groups until they mate," Morran said, "but they don't keep others out."

"Can we go now?" Rhea asked.

"Yes," Zinnia said. "Just climb aboard."

The flight to the home of the golden dragons was brief. From the air, Rhea could see that their home was similar to Zinnia's: a flat, smooth, rocky area surrounded by tall boulders. At one end of the enclosure stood a structure topped by fan tree branches.

Zinnia and Morran landed in an empty area of the enclosure. The golden dragons had been lingering under the shelter but moved out when they saw visitors.

Rhea and Nick climbed down.

Zinnia approached the group. "These are Rhea and Nick, the humans we brought here." She turned and added, "These are Henrietta, Flo, Luna, Astra, Ora, DeeDee, and Cleo."

"Pleased to meet you," Rhea and Nick said.

Henrietta, who was nearest to them, said, "We're glad Zinnia brought you here to help with The Terror. We all want to lay our eggs in the hatchery during birthing season."

"What's the hatchery?" Rhea said.

Zinnia stretched herself to her full height and indicated the mountain area. "There's a place at the foot of the mountains by the main river. It gets the sun most of the day and is very warm. There are lots of reeds there for nesting. It's an excellent place to lay eggs. Dragons laid eggs there for a very long time until The Terror came."

"You don't stay with the eggs until they hatch?" Nick asked.

"We have to go and hunt, still," DeeDee said.

"Our weight could crack the egg prematurely," Flo added.

"Evvin's parents tried to keep his egg at their home," Henrietta said, "and still had to go to the hatchery because the shell wasn't hardening properly. They stayed with the egg there and The Terror killed them both."

"We mourn their loss as well," Rhea said. "We'll do everything we can do see that you can lay your eggs there safely."

"If we can help in any way, tell us," Henrietta said.

Nick indicated the shelter with a wave of his hand. "We wanted to see the shelter you built. Can we get closer?"

"Of course," Henrietta said.

The dragons separated so that Rhea and Nick could approach. Rhea saw that the supports consisted of either spire trees, pulled out by the roots, and jammed upside-down into the ground, or by stacked rocks. She walked inside the shelter and looked up. Turning back to the golden dragons and pointing up, she said, "It looks like there's a net supporting the fan tree branches."

"There are flowering plants on the mountainsides that look like nets," Zinnia said. "The stems are very strong."

Rhea turned to Zinnia. "I wanted to ask you about that. Back on Earth, you loved to eat flowers, but I haven't seen that many here. I've looked down as we've flown and all I see is an occasional blossom."

"There are lots of flowers in the birthing season," Henrietta said. "But we eat nearly all of them and they don't bloom again until the next birthing season."

"The flowers you see from the air are just wildflowers that sprout here and there," Morran said. "Not enough for even a mouthful."

Nick pointed to the shelter's ceiling. "I can see that the roots from the upside-down trees provide some support for the top, but doesn't it slip?"

Henrietta reached behind her and brought out a hand. Rhea and Nick saw a transparent gel. "This is sticky. If we hibernate, this is how we attach to the rocks."

"It's how we attached the netting and branches to the trees and rocks," Ora said.

"And we use it when we stack the rocks so they stay in place," Luna added.

Rhea looked at Zinnia. "I don't recall seeing that when you were living with me on Earth."

"We can only produce it after we're old enough for wings," Zinnia explained. "We flex the muscles behind our arms and it comes out."

"It's impressive work," Nick said. "And you built it just by seeing the shelter we built and listening to Evvin explain how we put it up?"

"Yes," Ora said. "We talked together and agreed we could make one too."

"Then we discussed the best way to do it," Cleo said.

Nick and Rhea left the shelter.

"Thank you for showing it to us." Rhea walked over to Zinnia. "Can we pay the bachelors a visit?"

"Yes," Zinnia said.

They saw the bachelor dragons working at building a shelter when they arrived. Materials—rocks, spire tree trunks, fan tree branches, net flower vines—had been arranged neatly nearby.

"How are you doing?" Nick asked upon landing.

All the dragons stopped and dipped their heads.

Morran let out a huff and turned to the bachelors. "The humans are just here to see what you are doing, not to scold you." He turned to Nick and Rhea and made introductions.

The bachelors relaxed.

Nick and Rhea walked around the site. The dragons had already constructed supports, mostly spire trees that had been rammed into the ground upside-down.

Rhea grabbed one of the planted spire trees with both hands and pulled on it. "Looks good so far. The supports are solidly planted."

Nick turned to them. "What were you planning next?"

Brutus pointed upward. "Fly up with the net vines and attach them to the top. Then spread the fan branches over them."

"That's what the golden dragons seem to have done," Hunter said.

"Yes, that will work," Rhea said.

"More netting and branches on the side, and the rocks can hold them steady," Gus said.

"Looks like you're doing it right," Nick said. "Just keep on doing it. We'll be happy to help if you have questions."

Rhea and Nick had the swimmer leftovers warmed up by the time Dan arrived for supper, followed by Evvin, who remained outside. Dan suggested that Evvin visit Kieran and Thalia before joining Rhea and Nick at the dinner table.

Dan set a basket on a counter and lifted a cloth. "I made some bread from the grains I put through the food professor. Arthur's recipe. Tastes pretty good if I say so myself." He brought it to the table and set it among the other serving dishes. "I've already sliced it." He sat in one of the chairs.

Rhea and Nick also sat.

Nick reached for the bread. "Can't wait to taste it."

"Just help yourself," Rhea said to Dan. "I see that you changed clothes."

"I took a shower and checked for ticks, since I was deep into the undergrowth earlier. Either there aren't any ticks here or they don't like humans."

"That's a relief." Nick had buttered the bread and took a bite. When he had chewed and swallowed, he added. "This is good."

"What were you up to in the undergrowth?" Rhea asked.

Dan smiled. "I found one of those animals that Arthur sketched. The 'walking manhole cover.' I call them tanklets."

"Uh-oh," Nick said with a grin. "You name them, and they become family."

"They're all our family here," Dan said. "And yes, I named the adults Win and Nona. The little ones I didn't name individually— yet—but I've been calling them kits."

"I'd love to see them," Rhea said.

"I wouldn't do that yet," Dan said. "They're not happy about intruders. I got walked on and scolded by Win after I tripped and fell. Win's treading on my chest left a few shallow bruises, nothing serious, but I'd wait until I've observed them at greater length. I put the camera you gave me at a discreet distance to watch them."

Rhea nodded. "I can wait. We have enough to do as it is."

"What were you two up to?"

"We went to see the shelter the golden dragons put up," Nick said. "They didn't mind my being there. Looked pretty good."

"We went to the bachelor pad too," Rhea said. "They're just starting but are making good progress."

"We found out that for adhesives, they can use some sort of biological glue they get from around their armpits," Nick said.

Dan nodded. "Yes, I found out the same from Evvin. He gave me a sample. I was careful analyzing it, wore gloves so my fingers wouldn't stick together if I got some on me. It's potent stuff, binds better than our best household glues once it dries. When it's wet, it's flexible and you can smear it."

"What's it made of?" Nick said.

"I was able to compare some of the molecules with compounds from glues I looked up in my database, but other substances in it were unidentifiable...I presume unique to this world."

"We were bound to find those," Nick said.

"The golden dragons also told us that the dragons used to lay their eggs in an area they call 'the hatchery,'" Rhea said. "The shells seem to need lots of sun and fresh air to harden."

"And nesting," Nick said. "They talked about nesting."

Dan nodded. "That's consistent with what I saw on the farms. The mother dragons laid their eggs in sunny places where there were piles of hay or weeds or other plants to cushion the egg. I'll have to ask Evvin some time to take me to that hatchery area."

"Since we're talking about going places," Nick said. "Kieran suggested we visit the bog tomorrow and see if we can extract a dragon there."

"After the hunt?"

"Yes," Nick said. "Does that fit into your schedule?"

"Fits just fine," Dan said.

Dan and Evvin returned to their home just after sunset. The moon was out, so there was sufficient light to see by. "I want to watch the camera I set up in the forest earlier," Dan said. "You can wait at the doorway if you want or go back to building the enclosure."

"I'll build," Evvin said. "It's fun."

Dan smiled. "Good." He sat in front of the computer screen and turned on the camera app. It had night vision capability, though the image was just black and white. Win had settled into the nest, perfectly covering it like a lid with his body. The kits presumably were underneath, getting air from the sides of the nest. Nona seemed to have her own shelter at the foot of the fan tree, made of fan branches. She disappeared into it.

Win had his eyes closed. Nothing happened at first, and Dan almost leaned over to switch off the app—the camera would still record—when an animal shaped like a lizard approached the nest, nosing around. It got within inches of the side of the nest when Win quickly stretched his neck, turned his head, and bit the lizard just behind the shoulder. There was no sound, but Dan could imagine the bones breaking. Win shook the lizard fiercely and tossed the body aside.

Almost immediately, three animals rushed out from the underbrush. These had to be the scavengers Arthur had sketched, which vaguely resembled weasels. They feasted on the remains. Then, as quickly as they came, they vanished into the underbrush, leaving nothing, not even bones, behind.

The next day, after Evvin went out to hunt, Dan again sat at the computer watching the tanklets. The adults helped the kits scramble out of the nest, then Win led them away. Nona brought up the rear and kept the kits from straying from the path. Every once in a while, a kit would stop, poop, and waddle on.

When they were out of sight of the camera, Dan grabbed a couple of sample cases. He had a large cylindrical carrier to put larger animals in, but he left that behind in favor of smaller cases. He lined an empty one with a sanitary liner and put some stoppered test tubes and tweezers of various sizes in another. That should be enough to collect anything he saw of interest.

He hurried down the path until Nona, at the end of the line, was barely in sight. Keeping a discreet distance, he followed until they emerged into a clearing and padded down a hillside, temporarily out of sight.

When he reached the clearing, he saw a river rushing at the bottom of the hill. Turning to his right, he saw and heard the top of a waterfall. To his left, the tanklets had spread out and grazed on the grasses.

As quietly as he could, he made his way to a hill by the waterfall, hoping he was far enough away for the tanklets to ignore him. They did. He got out his binoculars for a better view.

Up the river he saw two other tanklet families. At a considerable distance away, an adult and two kits sampled the grasses. At a closer distance, he spotted two tanklet adults and five kits. None intruded on the others' territory.

Hearing scolding sounds from Win, he turned his binoculars in that direction. A salamander-like animal had approached the kits. Win marched toward it. It turned and retreated back to the riverbank, disappearing into the waters. Win returned to his family and his grazing.

Toward the top of the hill he saw another rise topped by a spire tree. It was the tallest landmark in the area. A short distance away, downhill from there, Nona was digging. She came up with a tuber, purple, maybe six inches long and four inches wide and shaped like a thick turnip. It had a green stem at the top. Nona clamped down on that with her teeth to carry it to her family. The kits squeaked excitedly and surrounded the tuber. The parents joined them in the feasting.

This had to be one of the vegetables that Arthur had written about. It fit the description well. When the family finished eating and waddled to the riverside to drink, Dan stealthily went to that area. He rummaged for the digging tool in one of the sample cases, located a stem, and managed to unearth a tuber for himself. He placed it in a sample case and scurried back to his observational spot.

Once the tanklets had their fill of water, they ambled back up the path, presumably toward home. Dan took the opportunity to go around the rise and look down the waterfall and out to the continuation of the river, which stretched as far as he could see. He took out a test tube from a sample case and dipped it in the water, thinking to analyze it later. After stoppering the tube and placing it back in the case, he turned his attention to the base of the waterfall. A tanklet kit lay on a rock. At first, he thought it might be sunning itself, but when he took the binoculars for a closer look, he realized that the kit had probably drowned and been washed down the river and over the falls. He had counted the tanklets in the families he had seen, and none were missing, so he guessed it must be from a family of tanklets farther upstream.

As he looked down from the rise, wondering if he could find a safe path down to retrieve the kit, a large silver dragon, about Kieran's size, flew toward the edge of the falling stream. He hovered there and took a long drink. When finished, he looked over to Dan, flew toward him, and settled nearby.

"You're the new human I heard about?"

"Yes, I'm Dan."

"I'm Icarus. It's nice to have humans nearby again. I'm happy here, but I miss the humans near me when I was younger. Humans had so many things we don't have here. They build things."

"There are a lot of interesting things, here, too."

"You looked like you needed some help."

Dan pointed downward. "I'd like to have the little animal there to examine, but I don't see how I can go down there."

"Yes, the rock's in the middle the stream, and the scavengers can't reach it. I'll get it for you." He flew down, picked up the kit, and settled next to Dan again.

Dan opened the sample box. "Just put it here." When Icarus did so, Dan closed the box and said, "Thank you."

"Ask if you need something else." Icarus flew away.

Dan walked back to his lab, sorted and put everything away, and placed the kit carefully on the necropsy table. Just to be sure the animal was dead, he got out his stethoscope and listened for any sign of life. He heard no heartbeat, no lung action.

Reaching for gloves and a mask, he said to the kit, "I'm sorry, little one. You ought to be out playing with your family, not lying on a cold necropsy table."

# CHAPTER 11

When Zinnia, Morran, Thalia, and Kieran returned from the morning hunt, Rhea and Nick were ready for them. They all walked to Evvin and Dan's place.

"Ready to go out to the bog?" Rhea asked.

Dan motioned to the tent. The side flaps had been rolled open and secured. "The space is ready over there if we can bring the remains of a dragon back."

Nick handed Dan a helmet. "This is a riding helmet to use when you fly with Evvin. There's a microphone inside."

Dan put it on. "Thanks."

Rhea approached Evvin. "I have a Bluetooth to put on your ear, Evvin, like the ones Zinnia and Morran have."

Evvin remained still while Rhea clipped it on and showed Evvin how to turn it on and off.

"Now I have one, too!" Evvin said excitedly.

They all flew to the bog, Morran and Nick leading the way. They flew over the bog, which resembled a large swamp with golden specks on the top of the water and tall grasses at the edge. Because of areas of clearer water, Rhea could make out dragons underneath the surface. She felt sad for them, trapped for years, if not centuries, in the water.

The dragons landed a distance from the shoreline. When Rhea, Nick, and Dan slid off, Zinnia said, "We can't come any closer. The ground gets soft nearer the water."

Nick rubbed his chin. "I got an aerial view, and I see the problem. If we had some heavy equipment, we could dredge the bog."

"I don't think we can bring heavy machinery here, even if we could find someone to loan us some," Rhea said.

"We have a smart hook," Nick said, "but looping it around a dragon body would be tricky."

"Damn near impossible," Rhea said.

Nick turned around and surveyed the woods behind them. "There are trees. Maybe some spire trees lashed together? The dragons could sit on them and lift one out?"

"I don't think we could get enough and they wouldn't extend that far," Rhea said.

"I'm not trusting my weight to plants," Morran said.

"How about rocks?" Zinnia said. "We can take rocks, drop them into the water until they make a pile, stand on them, and then lift a dragon out."

"It would depend how deep the bog is as to whether it would be practical or not," Rhea said.

"I don't know a lot about bogs," Dan said, "but my impression is that they're fairly shallow."

"Let's try it," Thalia said.

As if in agreement, the dragons flew off.

For the next half hour, the dragons came back with rocks and dumped them into the water, being careful not to drop one on a submerged dragon. The rocks stacked quickly, and the dragons arranged them around a particular submerged dragon so that there was a stack on either side and another stack at the shore.

Eventually, Morran said, "That ought to do it. Now we need to lift the dragon out."

"I can help!" Evvin offered.

Morran turned to Evvin, as if evaluating him.

"He's been very helpful to me," Dan offered.

Thalia nodded at Morran.

Morran blew out a breath before speaking. "Here is what we do. Evvin, you stand on the ones by the shore. You'll lift and pull backwards while Kieran and I stand on either side and lift the head and tail."

When they were in position, all three dragons leaned forward and got their forelegs underneath the submerged dragon.

Morran looked from side to side. "Ready? Evvin, lift and fly backwards."

Evvin did so while Kieran and Morran pulled up. They quickly got the submerged dragon on solid ground.

Rhea moved close to the dragon. Water ran off the dragon's side. Dan pulled gloves out of his pocket, put them on, and pressed on the dragon's side. The body seemed to be soft.

"Thanks, everyone." Dan walked to the dragon's head. "Anyone you know?"

The dragons gathered around and lowered their heads. One after the other, they said, "No."

Morran moved his head toward Dan. "What next?"

"Now we need to fly this dragon back and place the dragon under the tent you saw."

Morran turned to the other dragons. "Thalia, Kieran, you fly this dragon back while the rest of us fly with the humans."

Kieran and Thalia arranged themselves side-to-side. Thalia put her forelegs under the neck and shoulders, Kieran under the hindquarters.

"Ready?" Thalia said. "Lift!"

They all flew back to the tent without incident. Kieran and Thalia put the dragon underneath the tent.

"Thank you," Dan said. "We need to roll the sides down. Then I'll examine the dragon. When I'm done, I'll come out."

Rhea saw Dan go into the clinic. He emerged dressed in a smock and hair covering, wearing goggles as well as gloves. A cart held a lot of equipment, including a powered bone saw. He wheeled the cart to the tent and disappeared behind the flap. All they could hear was the sound of whirring.

"How long will this take?" Thalia asked.

"I don't know," Rhea said. "But dragons are large. It may take until our dinnertime."

"We'll be back, then." Thalia turned to Evvin. "Evvin, come with us."

The dragons took off.

"Where are they going?" Nick asked.

"No idea," Rhea said.

"Should we hang around?"

"I guess so, in case Dan needs something. Let's get some chairs and stay within earshot."

Dan did call for them to bring him things from the clinic every so often. They passed the objects to them through a flap in the tent.

A while later, while Rhea and Nick sat outside the tent, they heard dragon trilling. After more time had passed, their friends returned with two other dragons, a silver one and a golden one, both the size of Kieran and Thalia. They sat silently, respectfully, watching the tent.

At last, Dan pulled a flap aside and walked out. He took off the goggles and gloves.

"Did you find what you wanted to know?" Thalia asked.

"Yes, though I had to work quickly because the dragon was hardening even as I worked. The incisions are closed now and we can lift the tent flaps."

Rhea and Nick set to work while Kieran approached Dan. He indicated the two dragons next to them. "This is Roc and Duchess."

The golden dragon, Duchess, took a step toward Dan. "We wondered if this could be our Barney. He disappeared into the bog soon after returning from the human world. We go there from time to time to mourn him."

Dan nodded. "I, too, mourn him, and thank you for letting me learn more about dragons because of him."

Roc moved toward the corpse, examining the head. "Yes, this is our Barney."

"You're free to take him back," Dan said.

Rhea took a good look at Barney. He was silver when they took him out of the water, but now he was gray, and solid as stone. He looked like the statue of a sleeping dragon.

Duchess and Roc and Thalia gathered around Barney and pulled him from the tent. Then they took off. Morran, Zinnia, and Evvin flew away behind them.

"Shall we come, too?" Dan asked Kieran.

"No, you can stay here," Kieran said. "We're taking Barney to the cliffs." He lifted off and followed the others.

Rhea turned to Dan. "What did you find?"

"A lot of things," Dan said. "Here, let me get a chair and join you." He disappeared into the clinic with the cart of equipment and came out with a chair. Sitting facing Rhea and Nick, he said, "The most interesting thing I found was the interior tubing supporting the fire breathing. It seems that there is sort of a biological tube coming from the stomach and intestines which siphons off the digestive gasses to the mouth. The back teeth there are harder and as Evvin explained to me, they squeeze with their jaw muscles to release the gas, click the back teeth making a spark, and that's how they breathe fire."

"So it's essentially their burps and farts," Nick said.

Dan smiled. "Crudely put, but correct."

They heard a keening sound coming from the mountain area.

"Sounds like a dirge," Rhea said.

"Dragon funeral would be my guess," Dan said.

For several minutes, they sat quietly, respectfully listening to the sounds of mourning. Eventually, the sounds faded away.

"I wish we could have joined them," Rhea said.

"So do I," Nick said, "but we have to respect their wishes."

"It's possible they thought we wouldn't understand," Dan said.

Rhea nodded at Dan. "I hope what we're doing is going to help them."

"We're definitely making progress," Dan said.

"Find anything else interesting with the dragon?" Nick asked.

"My theory that that they expel wastewater with their excrement is correct. I suspected it when I examined dragon manure on Earth. They have only one hole for elimination for solid and liquid waste."

"What about their other organs?" Rhea said.

"Largely the same as I saw in the swimmer: heart, lungs, stomach, liver, kidneys, that sort of thing. There is an organ I couldn't identify. I would have liked to have removed and kept it, but as I said, the dragon solidified too quickly."

"Any guesses as to what that is?" Nick asked.

Dan shook his head. "Not yet. But when I put my stethoscope to a dragon, both on Earth and here, I hear a motoring sound, like a well-oiled engine, in addition to the heart and lung sounds. At first I thought it was the sound of digestion, and maybe it is. Or it could be something unique to this world."

"A power core?" Nick guessed.

"Perhaps an internal energy source. That's another of my guesses."

"Maybe we could get another dragon from the bog to analyze?" Rhea said.

Dan shook his head. "No, I think we've done enough for now. I have so much other research to do."

"What next?" Rhea said.

Dan gestured to the field. "Analyze the manure. All five dragons stopped in the middle of the hunt to drop their excrement and flew away again. Oh, and I dug up one of those tubers that Arthur wrote about."

"The one like the purple potato?" Nick asked.

"Yes. I plan to plant a garden if my analysis confirms it's good to eat." He got out of his chair. "Speaking of digging in the ground, I examined a tanklet this morning. Poor little thing drowned. I didn't want to leave the body out to be eaten, so I wrapped it in burlap and I'm going to bury it."

"Can we see it?" Rhea asked.

"Yes, I closed the incisions." Dan stood and walked toward the clinic.

"Where's the shovel we left with you?" Nick asked.

"Just inside the clinic," Dan called.

Nick retrieved the shovel and Dan came out with a bundle of burlap. He opened the burlap to show Nick and Rhea.

"It's still small, so it doesn't have that hard round back that the adults have," Dan explained.

"It's adorable," Rhea said.

"I can see the beginnings of the ridges," Nick said.

Dan walked to a spot in the nearby field. Nick started digging. When he had a sizeable hole, Dan rewrapped the tanklet and gently laid it there. Nick filled the hole and stomped on the dirt to flatten it. He sniffed the air and indicated the piles of manure in the field. "Pungent smell."

Dan shrugged. "I've worked on farms. I'm used to the odor of manure."

Rhea looked up. "The dragons are coming back."

This time only Evvin, Zinnia, and Morran landed. Morran seemed to be carrying something.

"Everything go well?" Rhea asked Zinnia.

"Yes," Zinnia said. "Duchess and Roc were sad, but comforted to have their nestling back."

"Having dragons around them helped," Morran said.

"It's the same with humans," Dan said.

Morran extended his arms. "I got two pods for you during the morning hunt. It wasn't easy, but when I said that the veterinarian needed them, the other dragons gave way."

Dan took the pods. Each was golden brown, about the size of a melon, but shaped like a large bean. "Thank you."

"What are you going to do with those?" Nick asked.

"I'm going to analyze them and see if humans can eat them, too," Dan said. "The dragons seem to love them."

"We do," Zinnia said.

Rhea moved toward Dan to get a closer look. "I don't think Arthur mentioned these."

"He didn't," Dan said. "All the more reason to analyze them."

"We'll leave you to your analysis, then," Rhea said. "Join us for supper?"

"I'll take a rain check today," Dan said.

"See you later, then," Nick said.

Rhea and Nick walked back to their home with Zinnia and Morran.

While Evvin became busy with the retaining wall again, Dan sat in the clinic. First, he organized the data that he gathered from the dragon examination and put it in the same folder as the results of the tanklet necropsy. Both animals had the mysterious extra organ, as had the swimmer. Those organs he had saved and preserved. Next, he sliced up the purple tuber for analysis. While the machines were doing their scans, he got a large knife and opened up the pods. They insides were less like melons and more like jackfruit...or dragonfruit, which was a real Earth staple.

While slicing up the pod contents for analysis, he looked at the live camera of the tanklet nest. There was a stand of grain there, not enough to attract a dragon, but apparently enough for the tanklets. Win and Nona nibbled on the middle grains of a stalk while the kits nibbled on the lower grains. Dan watched for a while to see whether Win and Nona would attempt to bend them to get at the topmost parts, or perhaps push rocks or plant parts to stand on to get at the upper grains, but they showed no inclination to make any sort of tool. They did, however, climb a little rise to get at the grains ripening there. When they climbed down, Dan realized that the rise was surrounded by enough grains and grasses for him to hide there and watch the tanklets more closely.

When the pod parts had been distributed to the analyzers, he walked outside and offered Evvin the second pod, since he had more than sufficient fruit to use from the first one. Evvin ate it eagerly.

"I'm going to take some pictures of the tanklets," Dan said. "I think you would scare them, so just keep working on the wall."

"Yes, it's better that they not see me," Evvin agreed.

Dan grabbed his camera and camouflage covering. The greens and browns of the covering would blend in well in the wooded area, whereas his denim pants and shirt would not. The covering had an opening where he could look out and point his camera. He walked to the nesting area, crouched on the rise, wrapped the covering around him, and waited, camera at the ready.

Not long after he heard squeaking behind him. He shifted his weight, waiting for the kits to come around him and into view. They did not appear right away, but the covering somehow started to slip off. He turned. The covering came all the way off, pulled by the kits, who held on by their teeth.

"Hey," Dan said softly. "That's not a plaything and it isn't good to eat." He pulled off the tops of nearby stalks of grain and threw them on the ground. As he hoped, the kits let go in favor of nibbling on the grain. Now that he was no longer hidden, he draped the fabric over an arm. Looking straight down, he saw Nona looking up at him, chattering. He broke off the top of another stalk and tossed it next to her. Nona eagerly devoured one of the grains, looked up, chattered again, and returned to grazing.

"You're welcome," Dan said, and walked away.

When he returned to the house, he put down the camera and fabric. He sat watching the nest video on the computer. Win had joined Nona in feasting on the grains.

Suddenly, he had an idea. He walked to the house and found the large platter with the raised middle. The platter had shallow indentations around the edge for condiments. He went outside and filled the water pitcher from the rain barrel. Slinging the strap over a shoulder, he made his way back to the nesting area. He walked around the tanklets to a place not sheltered by the fan tree, set the platter on the ground, and poured in water.

Almost immediately, the tanklet family surrounded the platter and started drinking.

"There," Dan said. "The rains will refill it and you'll have a local source of water."

The tanklets ignored his remark and continued drinking.

He smiled at them and walked back to the house, returning the water pitcher before going back to the clinic.

By that time, some of the machines had done their work and had data to share. While he was checking the results, he heard the sound of wings. Out the window, he saw Evvin still working on the wall, so it had to be another dragon.

He walked out to see Kieran landing. Another silver dragon, about Kieran's size, landed next to him.

"This is Titan," Kieran explained. "He's about to hibernate and remembered that you wanted to see a dragon hibernate."

"Yes!" Dan turned to Titan. "I want to listen to your heart and lungs as you settle in, take your temperature at your ear, and come back later after you've settled in and listen again. Would that be all right with you?"

"Yes, that would be all right," Titan said.

"Just let me get my equipment." Dan hurried into the clinic, put a tablet, stethoscope, and ear temperature gauge into a carry pack, and walked out again.

Facing Titan, Dan said, "By the way, is there a particular reason for going into hibernation?"

"To rest," Titan said. "To have a time where I don't have to get up every morning and hunt. I can just relax and dream."

"I understand," Dan said. "What do dragons dream about?"

"Other dragons," Titan said. "Dragons I know now, dragons I've known in the past. Places I've been. Flying."

"When do you know when you're finished hibernating?"

"When I feel rested. Or when I hear something I want to investigate."

"Do you hear well when hibernating?"

"Sounds get through, though they seem faint. Mostly I ignore them."

"Thank you," Dan said. "I appreciate the information." He turned to see Evvin standing next to him, apparently realizing that he needed a ride.

They flew to the eastern mountains. Dan saw an opening in the rock wall, and then a valley between the cliffs. Figures that seemed to be dragon statues had adhered to the walls. Dan realized those were either dead or hibernating dragons.

Titan looked over the far cliffs, apparently seeking a comfortable spot, then backed into a cliff, folding his wings behind him. Evvin maneuvered closer as Titan closed his eyes. Dan could see the biological glue seeping from Titan's pores, attaching the dragon to the rock. The tail, forelegs, and back legs relaxed.

Evvin found a ledge next to Titan and settled there. Dan attached a lifeline to Evvin's harness and edged his way toward Titan. He placed the temperature gauge gently into Titan's ear and leaned over to get the sounds of the heart and lungs. Gradually, the heartbeat slowed and the respiration rate decreased. Dan stood listening for several minutes until both heart and lungs reached what seemed to be a stable minimum rate. Then he stood back, recorded the numbers in his tablet, removed the temperature gauge and recorded its output, and took a photo of the place where Titan had fused into the cliff wall.

Kieran had hovered nearby all this time. "Is that what you wanted to see?"

"Yes, thank you." Dan climbed back onto Evvin. As he watched Kieran fly away, he said to Evvin, "Can you show me where Barney is?"

"Yes," Evvin said. He flew to a spot at the foot of a cliff where the fossilized body of Barney had been set.

Dan slid off, walked close to Barney, folded his hands in front of him, and stood for a minute in respectful silence. Evvin also remained still while Dan stood there.

Dan climbed onto Evvin's back. "We can go home now."

On the return flight, Dan looked down and spotted, as he did on the way to the cliffs, dragon residences: roughly circular flat areas surrounded by boulders, some currently occupied, some not.

One place looked different. Instead of a stony floor, he saw what seemed to be a pile of debris.

Dan leaned forward. "Evvin, can you land in the spot just below us?"

"Yes."

When they landed, Dan climbed off Evvin's back and found himself standing at the edge of a hoard made up of gold and silver plates and coins, as well as steel chains and cables. Scattered among the collection he saw pieces of jewelry: rings, necklaces, bracelets, medallions. On top of the pile lay, stretched out, a great golden dragon. The scene reminded him of the legendary dragons who slept on hills of riches.

The dragon lifted her head. "Welcome. You must be Dan, the veterinarian. I'm Minerva, keeper of dragon treasures."

Dan motioned to the dragon's bed. "That's an impressive pile."

"Gathered through countless generations of dragons who visited your home, or humans who left things here."

Dan nodded. "Is it comfortable to sit on?"

"Yes." Minerva shifted her weight, which caused some of the pile to slide over the sides, making a clinking sound. "Are you looking for something to wear? There's lots here to choose from."

Dan raised an eyebrow. Apparently, the part of the legend where the dragon held on to every bit of accumulated goods did not apply here.

"No, I don't need anything," Evvin said.

"I don't, either, but what do other dragons take?" Dan asked.

Minerva moved her head closer to Evvin. "Lately they want something to put around them, like Evvin and Morran and Zinnia have." She moved her head back.

Dan glanced back at Evvin. *So, the cables that allow me and Rhea and Nick to ride have become a fashion statement.* He turned to Minerva again. "You said that this collection has been here for generations of dragons. How did you come to call this place home? Did your parents live here before you?"

"No, the keeper here selects a successor from someone who knows the lore of dragons well."

A thought occurred to Dan. "Before The Terror?"

"Long before, yes."

Dan took a breath. "Did anything happen here just before or just after The Terror first appear, such as an earthquake?"

"Yes. The dragons used to live nearer the ocean. But we had to move here because there was a large flow of hot, fiery rock that covered the area and destroyed the plants and the places we made our homes."

"A volcanic eruption?"

"Eruption?"

"Lava, the hot rock, spewing upwards. A tremendous sound. Ash falling from the sky. The sun not visible for a length of time. The air becoming colder than normal."

Minerva raised her head. "No, nothing like that, just the lava. Not just here. Dragons traveling from community to community said that it was the same where they lived. Dragons moving from near the ocean to farther from the ocean because the lava covered everything."

"Did dragons usually live near the ocean?"

"Almost all of us. The ocean is still nearby, just not as close as it used to be."

"How about the hatchery? Did that have to be moved, too?"

"No, that stayed the same. The hot springs there are good for hardening the eggs. But dragons couldn't lay eggs there anymore. The Terror came and ate them."

Dan nodded. "Thank you. You've been very helpful. If I have other questions for you, could I come back?"

"Of course. It is my task to share knowledge and stories with other dragons."

Dan smiled at the thought that Minerva considered him an honorary dragon. He climbed onto Evvin again.

Evvin and Minerva exchanged brief trills before Evvin took off and flew home.

Since the test results confirmed Arthur's observation that the purple tuber was safe to eat, Dan prepared it for supper, cooking as if it were a potato. The tuber had a top like a carrot. Dan had been able to pull that out and found seeds at the end of the carrot top. He set those aside to plant later.

The analyzers showed that the pod fruit was also safe and equally as nutritious as the tuber, but Dan wanted to hold off on trying that. Arthur had never eaten it, and while it might be safe, it also might cause stomach or intestinal distress. Dan was not currently in the mood to weather a case of diarrhea or stomach cramps.

After dinner, Dan started analyzing the dragon manure. He expected to find bone fragments and rocks, since he had found those among the dragon manure he had analyzed on Earth. When the results started coming out, they were basically the same as the results he found on Earth. Except for Evvin. Evvin's lacked some elements the other four dragons had. The only difference in Evvin's diet seemed to be that Evvin was not eating the fruit.

Dan remembered that when he was younger, he was a fussy eater. He felt all right, but when his mother brought him to the doctor for a routine checkup, the doctor suggested that he start taking vitamin supplements. After that, Dan felt even better, more alert, more energetic. Could something similar be happening with Evvin?

He went outdoors where Evvin continued his building. The enclosure was taking shape. "Evvin, can I talk to you for a moment?"

Evvin stopped building and walked over.

Dan had brought his tablet that had photos he had taken of the purple tubers before analyzing them. He held it up. "Do you know what this is, Evvin?"

"Yes. The little animals eat them."

"Do dragons ever eat them?"

"Sometimes, if the little animals leave them out."

"Have you ever tried one?"

"Yes."

"Do they taste good?"

"Oh, yes."

"Do dragons ever dig them out to eat?"

"No, dragons don't dig. We can dig, but we mostly don't. We don't need to dig for food like the little animals."

Dan lowered the tablet to talk to Evvin directly. "I think that since you can't get to the pod fruit, this would be good for you to eat. It can make you feel even stronger if you eat things that taste good to you."

"But where would I find them?"

"Good question. Let's walk around and see if we can find some close by. If the little animals can find them, so can we. Let me get a digging tool and a pouch and we can look together."

They walked around the flat, grassy areas. Dan told Evvin they were looking for green leafy tops. It took a while, but they finally found one. Dan dug it up and put it in a pouch.

"Look, there's more," Evvin said.

Dan walked over to Evvin. Evvin was right, between them and a little brook, Dan saw a number of the leafy tops.

After watching Dan dig another one, Evvin extended his claws and dug one up to. Soon, Dan's pouch was filled.

"That's all we need for now, Evvin. We can get more whenever we want."

"Can I eat one?"

"Absolutely." Dan held one out.

Evvin rinsed his claws and the tuber in the brook, then ate it eagerly. "Evvin, every day before or after you go out for your hunt, I want you to eat one of these tubers."

"I will. They're good."

"I've watched many animals under my care become stronger and happier when I've changed what they eat. I think this will work for you, too."

"Yes. I am happier when I can eat food that tastes good."

Dan patted Evvin's shoulder. "That works for humans, too."

# CHAPTER 12

In the morning, Dan rose early. After dressing, shaving, and combing his hair, he walked past an unusually quiet Evvin to the kitchen area.

Generally in the morning, Evvin was on his feet, moving around, sitting up, talking, and watching Dan. Today, Evvin was lying on the floor where he was the night before, eyes open, tail tip swishing from side to side, but otherwise still.

Dan decided to give him some space and ate breakfast. After he cleaned up, Evvin still had not moved from his spot, so he took a chair and sat at a comfortable distance from Evvin's head.

"Is everything all right?"

Evvin raised his head slightly. "I've been thinking."

"About?"

"Thinking."

"Can you tell me more about that?"

"I'm thinking better," Evvin said. "It's like I've been seeing through a cloud, and now it's clear."

Dan nodded. "We humans call it 'brain fog.' The fruit and vegetable you ate yesterday had high levels of choline in it, among other vitamins and minerals. It helps with thinking."

"It's like a part of me has been hidden all these years, but now it's not."

Dan sighed and nodded. "I know how that feels."

Evvin moved a bit more. "Things that happened before, that I didn't understand, I understand them now."

"Such as?"

"Thalia wanting me to do everything you said. She was afraid that I might do something bad without meaning to."

"You did very well, I think."

"But I didn't know. Now I do."

"You're starting to put things together."

He raised his head slightly. "I'm not a hatchling anymore."

"At age 20, and ready to mate this year, you are definitely not a hatchling anymore."

"Evvin is a hatchling name. It's a good name, but I'm going to call myself something else. My father's name." He raised his head and trilled.

Dan imitated the sound the best he could.

"Almost." He trilled again.

Dan matched the notes.

"Yes. It means 'strong.' Can you think of a good human name for me. Something strong?"

Dan thought a moment. "Strong. Let's see. There's a human legend about someone named Atlas. He could lift the world on his shoulders."

"An entire world?"

"It's just a story, but yes, it means strong."

"Atlas." He paused. "I like it. Yes. Atlas."

Dan pushed back the chair and stood. "Let's go tell Thalia and the others."

They walked side-by-side to Rhea and Nick's house. Rhea and Nick stood outside with Thalia, Kieran, Zinnia, and Morran. Dan knew from previous conversations with Rhea and Nick that the dragons checked in with them every morning before going off to hunt.

"Morning," Dan said.

"Morning," Rhea and Nick answered.

"Something on your mind?" Rhea said. "We didn't get a text."

"Wanted to show you and Nick something," Dan said, "but first, we had something to discuss with all of you."

"Do you need our help with anything today?" Kieran asked Dan.

"Yes, I was thinking of going out and gathering medicinal plants."

"Which are?" Morran asked.

"The plants that induce sleep. Others that can heal wounds or soothe pain."

"We can find the ones that induce sleep," Morran said. "But be careful. We know where they are because we sometimes when we look for missing dragons, we find them in a field, sleeping. We have to drag them out by the tail before they can wake up."

"I plan to wear protective clothing," Dan said.

Atlas stepped into the center of the assembly and raised his head. "I have something to say."

The other dragons also raised their heads.

"What is it?" Thalia asked.

"Evvin is a nice name for a hatchling, but I'm not a hatchling anymore. I want to be known by my father's name." He trilled.

"That is a good name," Kieran said. "Your father would be proud."

Atlas turned to Dan, then back to the dragons. "I asked Dan for a human name. Atlas."

"Atlas is a good name," Nick said.

"I am going to keep helping Dan like Zinna and Morran help Rhea and Nick. You do not need to watch me closely anymore. I can work with Dan on my own, as Zinnia and Morran do."

Morran turned to Dan. "Are you sure?"

Atlas strode up to Morran. "Dan is my friend, but not my guardian. If you have a question to ask about me, you can ask me."

Without a word Morran drew himself to his optimum dragon height. He stood on his hind legs, spreading his wings.

Atlas faced Morran squarely. He rose to his own maximum height and spread his wings to match Morran's. Although Atlas was the smaller of the two, he had stretched his neck, limbs, and wings to full length to give the appearance of a larger size. He looked Morran straight in the eye.

After a full minute of steady staring, Morran folded in the contest, lowering himself slowly to the ground. Atlas followed.

"Now that we're done comparing claws," Kieran said, "let's hunt."

Kieran had just finished speaking when Atlas boldly launched himself into the air. He rapidly flew away, not looking back.

Morran turned to Dan. "He grew up fast. What did you do?"

"First, I respected him as an individual," Dan said pointedly. "Second, I found he was undernourished. It turns out those pods that you love so much have important nutrients, and he was missing them."

"I don't understand everything you're saying," Thalia said, "but I do understand you're telling us eating pods is important. I would have done something if I had known."

Dan turned to Thalia. "Of course you would have. I don't doubt it. Now we know. It turns out that the food that the little animals dig up can supply the same sort of nourishment. We found a source, so Atlas doesn't need to compete for the pods."

Nick said in a low voice, "Looks as if he could compete for them successfully now."

Zinnia turned to the other dragons. "This is why I said we need humans. They know things."

"In turn," Rhea said, "this is why we humans need dragons. As you have observed, humans don't do well here without dragon help."

"I think humans call that teamwork." Kieran turned to the other dragons. "Time to hunt." He took off. The other dragons followed.

Nick turned to Dan. "Atlas sure changed suddenly."

Dan took a breath. "Probably not as fast as it seems. Atlas is a keen observer. He's been watching us and has probably been pondering how things could be different. In a sense, he was primed for a change. He just needed a little boost in the right direction."

"Can a change in diet work that quickly?" Rhea said.

"It can," Dan said. "I've seen it in animals many times. Give them the right medication or the right nutrition, and you can get overnight results. Besides, these are not Terran animals. There are a lot of similarities, yes, but that mysterious organ tells us that there are important differences that we don't yet understand."

Rhea nodded.

"So you're going to seek out those medicinal plants that Arthur wrote about?" Nick asked.

"Carefully, yes," Dan said. "I'll wear protective clothing and put on a respirator."

"Do you need our help?" Rhea said.

"Probably best that you don't go," Dan said. "I only have one protective suit."

"We can go at a distance," Nick said.

"You could, but I have something to keep you busy." Dan reached into his pocket and took out a handkerchief. Holding it in his hand, he unfolded it to display a flat black rectangular object about the size and shape of a stick of gum.

Rhea and Nick came over and scrutinized it. "What is it?"

"I found it in the dragon manure," Dan said. When Nick and Rhea stepped back, he quickly added, "It's fine. I cleaned it."

Rhea and Nick stepped forward again.

"I didn't see this when I analyzed dragon manure back on Earth," Dan said. "But it was in every manure pile here."

"Something they're eating?" Nick said.

Dan nodded. "It got into their digestive system somehow. And get this: it's not metal, and it's not stone. I've examined it under the strongest microscope I have with me. It's cellular."

"It's alive?" Nick asked.

"Not now," Dan said. "But it once was."

"An animal they ate?" Rhea guessed.

"If so, it wasn't digested. Why would they eat an animal they couldn't digest? And why bother eating an animal that isn't any larger than a stick of gum?"

"What does Atlas think?" Nick said.

"I haven't shown it to him yet. I wanted to get your opinion first."

"I guess we could analyze it." Nick turned to Rhea.

"We would see if it's magnetic, or radioactive," Rhea said.

"You brought a Geiger counter?" Dan smiled. "Nice."

"We wanted to be prepared for anything," Nick said.

Dan pointed to it. "Careful how you handle it. The sides are smooth and rigid, but the flat part is like Velcro. Hard to see, but there are little spiny things sticking up from both sides. When I had more than one to look at, I found they can stick together." He folded the handkerchief again and held it out.

Nick took it. "Can we smash it?"

Dan considered. "At this point, I wouldn't recommend it. Not until we know more about it. We might find ourselves releasing spores or something else that we don't want to deal with."

"We'll be careful," Rhea promised.

"Very careful," Nick added solemnly.

"We're not in Kansas anymore," Dan emphasized.

When Dan returned to the clinic, he checked the monitor focused on the nest. The tanklets had left to graze. Perfect. He grabbed the portable weigh station he had used successfully in the wild on Earth, thinking it would be the best way to get the weight and dimensions of the tanklet adults. The scale base had been etched with measured grid lines and a camera had been attached to the end of a gooseneck at the side of the base. Sensors would record weight. He looked forward to adding data for Win and Nona to his notes.

He carried the weigh station to the nest area, placing it about a meter away. Then he gathered some grain tops and placed them just beyond one edge of the station. He hoped that Nona or Win would walk across the base of the station, stop at the edge, and eat.

The site where the video camera monitored the nest seemed to be the best place to hide. He stepped behind the tree there and found a place to watch through the leaves.

About ten minutes later, he heard squeaking. The kits came into view. They headed straight for the weigh station, Win and Nona following. The kits gleefully scuttled across the base and began to nibble the grains. Win followed, but instead of eating the grain, he chattered at the kits, shooing them away. Nona herded them toward the nest. Win stepped off the base, turned, and began to scold the weigh station.

Knowing that scolding preceded pooping, Dan lunged from his hiding place and reached the weigh station in a few quick strides.

"No, no, no, you aren't pooping on my weigh station." He picked up the contraption by the gooseneck and lifted it up. Win craned his neck to look up at Dan, though this time his chattering did not indicate scolding, but conversation.

Dan looked down. "All right, I get the message. I'm taking it home. You won't see it again." He started back to the clinic, still holding the weigh station above the ground.

Win ambled beside him, chattering all the way.

"Yes, yes, I get it, you want to be sure it's gone," Dan said.

When he reached the clinic, Dan shoved the weigh station inside and quickly shut the door.

Win turned from the door to Dan.

Dan looked down, touched his fingers together, and spread his arms. "It's gone. It'll never bother your kits again."

Win chattered conversationally, turned, and trotted back in the direction of the nest.

Dan returned to the clinic and opened the door. His next task was to gather the protective suit and sample cases. Taking the cart, he loaded everything he needed on it before rolling it outside, ready for Atlas to come back from the hunt.

When he did, he saw Win coming toward him, carrying a tuber in his mouth. He walked up to Dan, dropped it at his feet, looked up, and chattered. Then he lowered his head, turned, and trotted back toward his nest.

Dan bent and picked up the tuber. "I guess this means I'm an honorary member of the nest and I'm going to be provided for."

Rhea and Nick returned before the dragons came back from the hunt.

Nick handed the handkerchief and the tile back to Dan. "It's not radioactive. It conducts electricity well, and there's a low magnetic field."

Dan pocketed the handkerchief. "Anything else?"

"High tensile strength," Rhea said. "We didn't try to break it, but we pulled at it little by little, making sure we weren't cracking it open."

"Doesn't deform," Nick added. "Not bendable or flexible."

"You're right about the clinginess," Rhea said. "Adheres to cloth, rock, metal—hard to remove, but not impossible."

Dan nodded. "By the way, do you think that Zinnia would be willing to make one more trip back to Earth? I need some rakes and other tools for the garden. I think if I just spread the dragon manure over the ground, the seeds within the manure will start sprouting."

"Rhea and I wanted to make a quick trip, too," Nick said. "I want to bring the solar powered all-terrain vehicle that she and I constructed as our senior project."

"That way we don't need the dragons to fly us over short or medium distances," Rhea said.

"Sounds good," Dan said. "We won't need much in the way of groceries from now on. I cooked a tuber last night and it was delicious. Atlas and I collected even more. The pods are safe and nutritious, but since Arthur never tried one, I thought I'd hold off eating a piece in case it gives me indigestion."

"I'll try it," Nick said.

Dan gestured. "Let me put the tile in the clinic. Then I'll go over to the house and cut off a slice for you." He accomplished this quickly and handed Nick a slice of pod fruit on a napkin.

Nick took it and popped it in his mouth. "Mmmm." He chewed and swallowed. "This is good. Real good. Sure you two don't want to try some?"

"I can wait," Dan said.

"Me, too," Rhea said.

Atlas came into view and landed. He walked toward the humans.

Dan gestured at the protective suit in the cart. "This is for going out and collecting samples of plants."

"I can help," Atlas said.

"I want Zinnia and Morran to go with us, in case there's a problem," Dan said.

"Rhea and Nick will come too?" Atlas asked.

"No, we're staying here," Rhea said. "Dan needs to do this without us."

Atlas turned to Dan. "I want to make my own shelter."

"Like the shelter you helped build where Kieran and Thalia live?" Dan asked.

"Yes. But mine should be close to your home so I can stay with you."

Dan gestured around. "Build anywhere you like."

Nick pointed to the area beside the clinic. "How about the tent?"

"That's for Dan to use," Atlas said.

"Fair enough," Dan said.

"Do you need a tarp and some supports?" Nick asked. "We probably have enough for one more small shelter. We can bring them if you wish."

"Yes, that would be nice," Atlas said.

Zinnia and Morran landed.

Dan took out the tablet and held it up. "Here are the plants we're looking for."

The dragons huddled together and looked at the screen as Dan scrolled through the images.

"We can find those," Zinnia said.

"Good," Dan said.

"It will be a long flight," Morran said.

Dan zipped up the suit, strapped the respirator over his face, put on the goggles, got the helmet on, pulled on gloves, and gathered his sample cases. "I'm ready."

The dragons took off. Dan looked around, enjoying the view. From the sky, he could see his double home, plus Rhea and Nick's home. Farther away, he saw the river and the lake. Turning in the other direction, he saw that the forest consisted of areas of trees interrupted by clearings and watered by brooks. Grassland bordered the forest in all directions.

Morran, Zinnia, and Atlas landed in grassland.

When Dan slid off, Morran pointed. "See that patch of shiny green leaves? That's what you want."

"Thanks." Dan took the sample case and garden shears. He waded into the area. Being careful to avoid touching the leaves, he held a stem and clipped it near the base. After putting three stems full of leaves in the sample case, he walked back to the dragons.

Dan lifted his head, hearing a sound he did not recognize.

"Whee-whoo! Whee-whoo!"

Dan turned in a circle. "What's that?"

"Ground birds," all three dragons said at once.

"Calling to each other," Atlas added.

"I haven't heard them near the houses," Dan said.

"They travel from place to place," Morran said. "You'll see them near your house soon when they come to the streams to nest."

"I can't see them here, though," Dan said. "Are they far away?"

"They are difficult to see in the tall grasses," Zinnia said.

"Do they fly?" Dan asked.

"A little," Morran said. "They can't fly higher than a dragon's height. They mostly run."

"They're fast," Atlas said.

"Can you fly over some on the way to our next destination?" Dan said.

"Yes," Atlas said.

When they were in the air again, Atlas circled over a grassy area. In places where the grasses were thinner, Dan saw birds that resembled quail, though they were larger than the quail he was familiar with. They had brown and gray feathers, and they did run quickly.

Their next stop was a stand of trees. Plants with long, narrow leaves surrounded the trunks. Arthur identified these leaves as good for healing wounds. Dan gathered his samples and walked back to Atlas.

Next, the dragons landed on a rise at the edge of a forest overlooking flat grasslands. When Dan slid to the ground, he saw the netting plants Rhea and Nick had described, growing between some of the trees, anchoring on the branches and trunks.

A few steps away he saw the last of the plants he was looking for. This plant was one that Arthur had described as having the property of numbing pain. He collected numerous samples and returned to the dragons, who were surveying the grasslands. Turning in that direction, he saw a herd of the cattle that Arthur described, resting in the warm sun.

Morran turned to Zinnia. "Shall we have a treat before going back?"

"They don't run from you?" Dan said.

Morran swung his head in Dan's direction. "If they see us, yes, but they're napping now. They're slow to wake, and they won't know we're there until we're upon them."

Dan put a hand on Atlas's shoulder. "Would it be possible to bring an adult female and calf back with us? The enclosure you built for me is nearly done."

Zinnia moved closer to Dan. "It would be better if Morran and I each took one and Atlas flew you home." She faced Morran. "We'll have to do without eating them this time."

Morran let out what sounded like a sigh. "Yes, there's always another time."

Zinnia turned her head toward the forest. "Each of us can take a net plant, wrap it around one of them, and hold them close. The plants will make them feel comfortable and mask our smell."

Dan raised an eyebrow. He had never detected any more than a faint metallic odor around the dragons, which was not unpleasant. On the other hand, the cattle might have more sensitive olfactory cells. "Can you tell which are the females?"

"Yes," Zinnia said. "The heads are shaped differently, and the males don't usually nap with the calves."

Zinnia and Morran worked quickly, gathering net plants and flying to the herd. While Dan and Atlas hovered over the plain, Zinnia and Morran approached a cow and calf napping together at the edge of the herd. They spread the net plants over them, lifted them up, and held them close to their chests as they spread their wings and ascended.

On their flight back, Dan heard faint lowing sounds. Presumably the cow and calf had awakened. They sounded amazingly similar to cattle of Earth. Glancing over to the other two dragons, he saw no signs of struggle.

At last, they made it back. Zinnia and Morran set the cow and calf gently into the enclosure, pulling off the net plants as they did so. Dan gathered his sample cases and slid down Atlas's side. He set the cases on the ground and hurried to the opening.

"Thank you," he said to the dragons. "One last thing: can you bring a couple of spire tress to put across this opening until I can build a gate?"

The dragons obliged, taking off and returning quickly with the trees, which they stacked in front of the opening.

"Thank you," Dan said.

"Is there anything else?" Zinnia asked.

"Yes," Dan said. "Rhea and Nick and I need to return to Earth for a while. We won't ask you to do it today, but soon?"

"Tomorrow?" Zinnia asked.

"I'll go whenever you and Rhea and Nick are ready. I'd recommend discussing it with them."

"We will." Zinnia and Morran flew off.

Dan watched the cow and calf for a while. The calf ambled close to its mother. The cow nuzzled the calf before turning to graze on the grasses within the enclosure.

Turing to Atlas, Dan said. "After your hunt every day, can you gather some grasses for them to eat? Just dump them inside the enclosure."

"Yes," Atlas said.

Dan realized they would also need water. Fortunately, there had been enough rain during recent nights to keep the rain barrels filled. He took a bucket, filled it, and placed it within the enclosure. A trough would be better. He would need to buy one on Earth along with a gate for the enclosure.

After dinner that evening, Dan received a text from Rhea:

*Zinnia and Morran flew off to play. Nick and I bringing materials for Atlas to make a shelter.*

Dan texted *be expecting you* and turned to Atlas, who had been watching him put the dishes away. "Rhea and Nick are coming with what you need to build your own shelter. Let's go out and meet them."

Rhea and Nick arrived soon after, pulling carts with tarps and poles.

"We brought the materials for Atlas," Rhea said.

Atlas walked over and inspected the contents of the cart.

"If it's all right with you," Rhea said to Atlas, "Nick and I have been thinking about what the best place for your shelter to be."

"Yes, I want to build a good one," Atlas said.

Nick motioned to a patch of ground. "Right here is opposite the entrances to Dan's house and clinic, so you can be near Dan and see when he comes out. The ground is firm and flat but rises slightly above the surrounding grassland. It would provide good drainage when it rains. Do you think that would be a place that's comfortable for you?"

"Yes," Atlas said enthusiastically.

"Do you need our direction," Rhea asked, "or did you want to set it up by yourself?"

"By myself," Atlas said.

Nick motioned to the carts. "Have at it, then. We'll stay and talk with Dan in case you have questions."

Atlas pulled the poles out of the cart.

Rhea turned to Dan. "We heard that you have a cow and calf. Can we see them?"

"Sure." Dan led them to the enclosure. The cow grazed while the calf wandered around near her.

"They're smaller than Earth cows," Nick said.

Dan nodded. "About three-fourths of the size of Jersey cows, I'd estimate."

"About the same shape," Rhea said, "with brown and white coloring."

Nick tilted his head. "I see an udder. Think you can milk it?"

"I've milked cows before," Dan said. "Remember, I've spent a lot of time on farms."

"But will she let you?" Rhea said.

"Arthur wrote that his cow, at least, was friendly. I can do what he said he did. Approach, pat, start milking. Arthur said that the cow he had even got used to Rex being around."

"Good luck, then," Nick said.

They went back to Dan's house, got chairs, sat, and watched Atlas build his shelter.

At one point, Rhea leaned toward Dan and said softly, "He's doing pretty good."

When Atlas was finished, they all stood and walked toward the new shelter.

"Would it be all right if we took a look at it?"

"Yes," Atlas said proudly.

Dan watched as Rhea and Nick examined the shelter, pulling the tarp at various points to determine whether the attachments were firm, testing the supports to see whether they had been solidly placed.

At last, Nick turned to Atlas. "Great work, Atlas."

Atlas smiled and turned to Dan. "I can sleep here. You can find me if you need me."

"Of course," Dan said. "Just like Zinnia and Morran sleep separately from Rhea and Nick."

Rhea touched Dan's arm. "By the way, we're not quite ready to go back to Earth yet. We're still putting together our shopping list. We told Zinnia maybe another couple of days."

"That's fine," Dan said. "I need to go to the ocean tomorrow, in that case. Minerva, the dragon Atlas and I talked to earlier, said that a lava flow near the ocean took place just before The Terror appeared, and that the dragons had to move because of it. I want to see the area. It may help solve the mystery."

"We'll come with you," Rhea said.

# CHAPTER 13

When Dan rolled over in bed and opened his eyes the next morning, he was startled to find Atlas missing. After a moment, he remembered that the dragon now had a place of his own. Dan realized that he missed Atlas being there in the morning, and the touch of his tail during the night.

After breakfast, and after the dragons flew away to hunt, Dan sat in the clinic house. He began carefully analyzing the plants he had gathered the day before. He started with the pain-reducing plant, thinking that might be the easiest to test on his own skin.

Later, taking a break, he watched the monitor for the nest, and found that the tanklets had returned from their morning grazing, but he did not see Win. He put down his instruments and walked out of the clinic to check whether Win was coming his way with another tuber.

He did see Win, but Win was limping, favoring his right front foot. Instead of Win's usual chatter, Dan heard low murmurs.

Dan approached cautiously and crouched. "What's wrong, buddy?"

Win stopped and lifted his paw a little.

Dan craned his neck. Something had stuck there, maybe a thorn? He reached out to pick up Win, putting his forearm across the furry stomach and turning him sideways a little. Win did not protest or try to wriggle free.

Once inside the clinic, Dan carefully placed the tanklet on the fresh sanitary covering of the examination table. Arranging cushions under sterile drapes, he cautiously laid Win on his side.

Win's eyes closed.

Dan quickly leaned closer to Win to check his breathing. Win seemed to be inhaling and exhaling regularly, strongly. He got out a stethoscope to listen to the tanklet's heart and lungs. Although he had been warned not to rub or pat the tummy, he knew that Win routinely slept over his kits, who undoubtedly bumped him in the stomach all evening. Dan guessed that a stethoscope would not disturb him.

Having confirmed that the heartbeat was strong and the lungs clear, Dan reached for a packet of sterile instruments and set them near the injured foot. He opened the pack, then put on a gown, gloves, mask, and hat, keeping an eye on Win as he did so.

Win slept on.

With the vitals established, Dan took one of his instruments and carefully probed the item stuck to the foot. It appeared to be one of the black tile things that he had gathered from the dragons' manure piles. The Velcro-like sticky things had attached to the skin. His previous examination of a tanklet kit told him that the skin at the bottom of the tanklet foot was thick and leathery, and Win's looked even more so. Careful examination showed that the tiny burrs had not pierced the tough epidermis, not drawn blood, but had firmly stuck to the bottom of the foot.

Carefully, Dan removed the tile and placed it in an empty petri dish. He cleaned the foot with sterile water before taking a magnifying glass to be sure there were no cuts in the skin. There were none. He wondered briefly if he should try the medicinal leaves he had gathered, but he was unsure of the dosage. Since the foot had not been pierced, he decided to leave it as is, at least unless Win appeared to need medication.

Dan raised the side rails on the exam table so that Win would not fall. Removing his gown, gloves, mask, and hat, he reflected that the tanklets were learning quickly: Win had twice visited Dan's home, indicating he knew where they were, and he had come to Dan for help, indicating that he considered Dan as someone friendly who would give aid in a crisis.

Dan walked outdoors and filled the water pitcher. The tuber Win had brought earlier lay in a box. Dan placed it in a bag and returned to the clinic house.

Soon afterwards, Win opened his eyes and stirred.

Dan approached him and said softly, "How are you doing, buddy? Ready to go home?"

Win rocked to one side and stood on his feet on the table. Dan noted that the tanklet did not wince or cry out in pain, so the foot probably was not causing any great distress. Nonetheless, Dan slung the strap for the pitcher and the strap for the bag over a shoulder and picked Win up.

"Here, buddy, I'll give you a ride home."

Win did not protest but chattered softly all the way back to the nest.

When Dan came into view, the kits swarmed at his feet and looked up, squeaking.

"Daddy's home," Dan said. "Let me put Daddy in the nest, and then you can give Daddy all the hugs you want."

Dan lowered Win carefully, feet first, into the nest. Win sighed deeply and closed his eyes. Still squeaking excitedly, the kits climbed into the nest, burrowing under their parent and disappearing. One poked his head up at Win's side, squeaked at Dan, and disappeared again.

"You're welcome," Dan said.

Nona came up to Dan's feet as Dan unslung the water pitcher and the bag. "I brought you food and water so you could stay with Daddy and not have to leave him to forage for the rest of the day." While Nona watched, Dan filled the ceramic dish and set the tuber next to it.

Nona looked up at Dan, chattered, and turned to drink from the dish.

Dan shouldered the pitcher and bag again and walked to the riverbank. Looking through the clear water to the riverbed, he saw another black tile had settled there. Before he could reach for it, the current dislodged it from its location and carried it away.

Looking toward the falls, Dan understood how the tile got into the manure: the dragons drank from the river, particularly from the waterfall, and the tiles went over the waterfall. Undoubtedly the dragons swallowed the tiles as they drank.

He turned to look upstream. That was where the tiles must have come from. He knew that waterfalls cascaded from the cliffs overlooking the ocean. Dan guessed that the river must wind its way from the base of a waterfall, and then to where he currently stood. He made a note to himself to watch for this when the dragons returned to take him to the oceanside.

After Dan returned to the clinic house, he resumed his plant analysis. Eventually, Rhea and Dan showed up at the clinic door.

"The dragons should be back soon," Rhea said. "We told Zinnia and Morran to meet us here. Ready to go?"

Dan stood. "Yes, but I want you to see something first. Remember the black tile?"

"Of course."

"Sure."

Dan pointed. "Take a look at this."

Rhea and Nick walked over to peer into the petri dish.

"It just looks like the tile again," Nick said.

"If you look closely, you'll see it's two tiles, stacked," Dan said.

"Two?" Rhea said.

Dan nodded. "See the empty petri dish next to it? Win limped over this morning with a tile stuck to his foot. I removed it and put it in the dish."

"It isn't there now," Nick said.

"That's right. It was there when I took Win home, but when I came back, the tile had moved to the other petri dish and they had stuck together."

Nick raised his eyebrows. "I thought you said they were dead."

"They are. I checked. I double checked. It isn't living tissue, at least not now. It was once, but not now."

"Then how...?" Rhea asked.

"I don't know," Dan said. "I have to study this further. But we definitely are not in Kansas anymore."

"Wow," Nick said.

"Oh, before I forget," Dan said. "Any stomach or digestive problems, Nick?"

Nick shook his head.

"Good," Dan said. "That means that we can add the pod fruit to our menus."

Dan had gathered his sample cases, and parceled a couple out to Rhea and Nick, by the time the dragons returned. Once in the air, the dragons flew north. At the horizon ahead, Dan saw a field of blue water to the left, and land to the right. As they drew closer, Dan saw that the water formed a cove, hills rising from the shore on the western side, and a large sandy beach on the other side. Overlooking the beach was a circular ridge…a volcanic caldera perhaps?

The beach rose to a flat, its width stretching from the circular ridge to grassland beyond. The flat's length extended to the ocean. East of the flat he saw a plateau rising from the flat that extended to the ridge of mountains in the distance. He could see waterfalls cascading from the cliffs. One of the waterfalls fed a river, which meandered from the base of the cliffs over the plateau. Instead of draining into the ocean, however, the river made a turn near the place where the rising beach met the flat and flowed southward toward dragon country.

The dragons landed on the wide flat overlooking the beach. Dan noted the ground was cracked, and grasses grew in those cracks. Dan, Nick, and Rhea slid to the ground and looked over the area. The ocean waves surged and receded over the sandy beach, the same as they did on Earth. Dan recognized the salt water scent.

Nick pointed. "What's that? Looks like a beached whale."

"Is it in distress?" Dan asked. "Do we need to shove it back in the water?"

"No, it's just sleeping," Morran said. "The seaskimmers come out of the water to take naps."

"How do you know if it's sleeping or dead?" Rhea asked.

"If they're dead," Morran said, "their mouths are open and their tongues hang out."

"We don't see dead ones very often," Zinnia said. "The dead ones usually sink to the bottom where the sea scavengers eat them."

"What about the dead ones on the beach?" Dan said. "Do you eat them?"

"No," all three dragons said at once.

"They taste awful," Morran added. "There are plenty of beach scavengers who eat them, though."

"The fish in the ocean are good to eat," Atlas said. "You have to hold your breath and dive deep to get the best ones."

"Can we go down there and look?" Dan asked. "Will the seaskimmer hurt us if it wakes up and we're too close?"

"It won't attack," Zinnia said. "They follow us sometimes when we walk on the beach."

"Let's go, then." Dan turned to Rhea and Nick. "Don't touch anything unless we can determine it's safe."

Dan, Rhea, and Nick made their way down a gentle slope to the beach. The dragons followed, walking on all fours. A quick survey told Dan that this appeared to be a typical ocean beach. He saw seaweed, shells of unusual shape, and small animals moving around. Some resembled sea urchins. Others resembled starfish, except the legs were longer, narrower, and more numerous.

Dan stopped a pace away from the seaskimmer's head. On closer examination, it looked more like a manatee than a whale. "It's alive all right. It's snoring softly."

Rhea crouched down near the water line. "Can I pick up the shells?" she asked Zinnia.

"There's nothing in them," Zinnia said. "They wash up when the animals inside die."

Dan hurried over. "Let me pick it up with tongs and put it in a sample case, just to be safe. There might be an irritant on the surface that doesn't affect dragons but could affect us. I'll give it back once I've analyzed it." He pulled out the tongs and put a shell in the sample case.

Rhea stood again.

Nick ambled along the beach, looking down. "The fish look pretty much the same."

Dan looked over to where Nick stood and saw a few dead fish, washed up on the sand.

"Those we can eat." Morran picked one up and put it in his mouth. They heard the crunch of bones breaking as Morran chewed.

A quick motion caught Dan's attention. He looked to see what appeared to be a black crab, scuttling along the sand. Except instead of legs, it seemed to be walking on its claws. "What are those?" Dan asked.

"Beach scavengers," Morran said. "We call those sandgliders."

"Are they good to eat?" Nick asked.

"We don't know," Morran said. "We can't catch them. They move too fast."

"If you try to follow one, you'll see," Atlas said.

The sandglider had stopped. Dan approached cautiously, noting that Rhea and Nick followed behind him. Taking the tongs, Dan bent to grab the sandglider, but it raced away. After a distance, it stopped again. Dan crept closer. Again, the sandglider scrambled away. Just to see what it would do, Dan kept following. The sandglider kept darting away up the sandy beach, toward the flat, close to the river bend on the high plateau. When they reached the border between the beach and the flat, the creature quickly burrowed into the sand and disappeared.

"That's what they do," Atlas said.

"Their homes are underground," Morran added.

"Ever try to dig and see if you can find their homes?" Dan asked.

"Oh, yes," Morran said. "Lots of dragons have tried. You end up with a large hole and no sandglider."

Nick turned to Dan. "Their homes must be pretty deep in the ground."

Dan nodded. "Probably the case." He lifted his head toward the plateau and gestured toward the river bend.

"Is this the river that goes through the dragon settlement?" Dan asked.

"One of them. This is the one with the waterfall we drink from," Atlas said.

"If there's a heavy rain, there's a big flood," Morran added.

"How often does that happen?" Rhea asked.

"Just whenever there's a lot of rain," Zinnia said.

"You can hear the flood coming," Atlas said.

Dan turned to him. "Sounds like a flash flood. If you hear it coming, can you tell me?"

"Yes," Atlas said.

"It won't reach to where you are," Zinnia said. "It just doubles the width of the river for a little while."

"It passes quickly," Morran said. "The river goes back to its usual flow before most even notice."

Nick put his hands on his hips and drew a long breath. "Anything else we need to see here?"

Dan looked around. "Say, there's another sandglider over there. By the riverbank. It's not moving at all. Is it dead?"

The dragons looked in that direction.

"No, it's not dead," Morran said. "I've never seen a dead sandglider. Every once in a while, they grow a new shell and the old shell comes off. That is an old shell."

Dan walked over to it and crouched next to it. "Rhea, Nick, you need to see this."

They walked over to Dan. Nick bent over. "What are we looking at?"

"Do you see the structure?" Dan said.

Rhea and Nick moved closer.

"Tiles," Dan said. "It's made up of tiles."

"The same tiles you showed us before?" Rhea said.

"I'm pretty sure of it." Dan took the tongs and clamped on the shell. It immediately broke apart into rectangular sections. Some slid into the river. Dan still managed to snag some of the rectangles and place them in his sample case.

Dan stood. "I'll bet when I take a look at these with the microscope, it'll be the same."

"Well, that tells us where the tiles came from, at least," Rhea said.

Dan pointed. "I want to see where the flat area meets the ocean. I have a feeling this flat is the lava flow Minerva mentioned. If I can see a cross-section, a weathered segment, that might confirm it."

"Careful," Zinnia said. "The ocean wears away the side and there are frequent landslides. Better let us guide you."

The dragons, again walking on all fours, led the way around the flat, through the sandy area, to the ocean shore. They gathered there and turned to the rock face.

Dan saw a drop-off from the top of the flat to the ocean. The dragons were right: the rocks were crumbling from the edge into the ocean. Apparently the ocean waves ate away the rock at the bottom, and then the rocks above fell into the sea.

Pointing, Dan turned to Rhea and Nick. "I didn't get beyond common core geology, but there's a definite layer cake effect there."

"Thin layers," Rhea said.

"The top layer is what we were walking on," Dan said, "and right underneath it, a compressed layer. But it doesn't seem to be rock, but compacted vegetation."

"Yes, I see," Nick said.

"The giveaway is the grasses growing through the cracks in the top layer. Even more, see the sprouts growing on the exposed face of the layer? It looks like tiny versions of the pods the dragons eat."

"Not large enough to eat," Morran said.

"But trying to grow, at least," Dan said. "That's consistent with Minerva saying that the lava flow covered the plants that grew by the ocean. You probably saw on the other side of the flat, there's a vast area of grassland. That seems to indicate fertile soil where the lava didn't flow."

"Yes, the dragons had to move when the lava came," Zinnia said. "But that was a long time ago."

Dan turned to the dragons. "I think that when the lava flow occurred, it covered the food that The Terror was used to eating, and my guess is that food was the pods. On Earth, volcanic soil can be fertile under the right conditions, but apparently that's not the case here, at least in this area. So when The Terror couldn't get its usual food, it started eating dragon eggs."

"But dragon eggs are animal matter," Nick said. "If what you say is right, it was vegetation that was covered."

"Many species are omnivores," Dan said. "Humans eat both plants and animals. Dragons eat both plants and animals. The Terror could, too."

"If so, why didn't The Terror just move to a different food supply?" Rhea asked. "There are pods elsewhere, though a long distance away from here. They could have gone there."

"Maybe they can't," Dan said. "Humans can migrate. Dragons can migrate. Maybe The Terror can't move beyond a certain distance from its home. It goes to the hatchery. It eats cattle herds that graze close to the ocean. But never gets as far as where Arthur and Rex lived. They only observed The Terror from a far distance."

"How does that help with The Terror?" Zinnia asked.

Dan swept the area with an arm. "If we can grow an abundance of food right here that The Terror wants to eat, they might leave dragon eggs alone. After all, they did leave them alone for centuries, if not millennia, before the lava came."

"How would we do that?" Zinnia asked.

"My mate is an agriculturalist. That means he knows how to take care of plants and animals that humans want to eat."

"Like a farmer?" Zinnia said.

"Yes. He helps farmers. I'm sure he can help us get plants to grow here. When we go back to Earth again, I'll ask him."

"That would be good," Zinnia said.

"Are you sure it would work?" Morran said.

"Not completely," Dan said. "I can't guarantee anything. But it's something to try, and even if it doesn't work, we can learn from our attempt and then try something else."

Zinnia turned to Morran and Atlas. "That is why I said we need humans."

Dan opened one of his sample cases. "Let me get some of that rock crumble, the crumble that came from the surface of the flat. I want to analyze it."

After Dan got the sample and closed his case, they heard a noise: *Bloop! Bloop!*

"What's that?" Nick said, looking up and around.

"Mud holes," Zinnia said.

"Can we see those?" Dan asked.

"Of course," Zinnia said. "Short flight, long walk."

The humans climbed on the dragons, who flew them to where the river curved. From the air, Dan saw what reminded him of the surface of tomato paste in a pot, boiling on the stove.

Atlas landed about a pace away to let Dan get off. Zinnia and Morran landed behind him. The humans walked up to where the mud was bubbling up and spilling over.

Rhea bent down. "Is it hot?"

"Not too hot," Atlas said. "It cools fast and then gets hard."

Dan waved at Nick. "Your sample case has a scoop. Let me get some of this."

Dan took the scoop from Nick, crouched, and managed to get about a cup of mud. He could feel the heat: warm, but not searing. He poured the mud in the sample case, replaced the scoop, and handed both back to Nick to carry home with him.

Rhea walked over to the river. "I think I can see what causes the floods. The mud flows down to the river and hardens. Water pools behind it. In a heavy rain, the water pressure would cause the mud dam to break and release the water in the pool."

Nick gestured. "The river still can flow over and around the blockage in the meantime, which is why we still see it over by the dragon community."

Dan kept watching the mud hole. "The mud seems to have stopped coming up."

"It doesn't do that all day," Atlas said. "Just some of the day."

Dan looked around and faced the circular ridge. From this vantage point, he could see a red lake of steaming lava inside the circle. "My guess is that's the caldera of the volcano that overflowed and resulted in the flat." He turned to Atlas. "Does the lava flow very often?"

"Not for many lifetimes of dragons," Atlas said. "Not since the flow Minerva told you about."

"The lava just sits there," Morran said. "Nice for getting close to for a heat bath, but it never goes anywhere."

Dan chuckled. "You dragons must be extremely heat resistant. A human would be killed getting that close."

Zinnia turned to Morran and Atlas. "We need to remember that."

"Unless Rhea and Nick want to continue exploring, I have what I need," Dan said. "We can go home now."

Rhea turned to Nick. "We're fine. Thanks for bringing us here."

"If you need to come back, just ask," Zinnia said.

The humans climbed on to the dragons, who flew them home.

# CHAPTER 14

Rain pounded the roof all night. The storm clouds had moved on by the time Dan climbed out of bed to prepare breakfast.

He was just finishing washing the breakfast dishes when Atlas poked his head in the door. "The flood is coming."

Dan's first thought was of the tanklets. "I have to check my camera in the clinic." He rushed over. The tanklets had already gone. "Damn." Quickly, he snatched thick gloves, shoved them onto his hands, grabbed the cylindrical animal carrier, and raced out the door.

He stopped in front of Atlas briefly. "I'm going to get the little animals before the flood gets here. If they see you, they'll run away or right into the flood, so you need to stay back."

"Yes. I know they'll run if they see me."

Dan raced to the river. Glancing up the riverbank, he saw that the other tanklet families had already gone. Win, Nona, and the kits, however, were drinking at the riverbank. He ran up to the kits, grabbed them from behind, and started to stuff them into the carrier. He could not hear or see any sign of the flood—yet—but he had the feeling that if he could hear the sound, it would be too late.

As he feared, the thundering sound of the flood approaching reached his ears just as he was about to grab the last kit. Win and Nona raised their heads. The kit sprinted away, squealing in panic, out of Dan's reach. Knowing he had only seconds, and that he could lose all the others if he went after the one kit, he seized Win with one arm and Nona with the other and sprinted to the rise at the top of the hill next to the spire tree.

When he felt he had secure footing, he turned to see a surge of water coming down the river course. The sound was even louder now. Win and Nona tucked their heads under his armpits. The surge rushed by, spraying water at him, but not reaching the top of the rise. Although Dan felt relieved that the tanklets he had were safe, he could not help but feel that somehow he should have been able to grab the last kit, too. He reminded himself that if he had, they all might have been washed away. Still, he could not help but feel grieved at the loss.

Although it seemed he stood there forever, only minutes passed before the surge went by. The sound diminished and the water receded.

He looked across the river to see Zinnia and Morran hovering in the air, Rhea and Nick on their backs.

"Are you all right?" Nick called.

Slowly, Dan walked down the hill. "Yes. I lost one of the kits, though," he said sadly. He put Win and Nona on the ground. Taking off the carrier, he set it next to them and opened the end of the cylinder. The kits scrambled out. All appeared to be uninjured.

Win herded them toward the path to their nest.

"I have the hatchling," Atlas said.

Dan turned to see Atlas landing nearby. Atlas's hands were closed. He opened them to show the kit.

Dan let out a breath. "Thank you, oh, thank you, Atlas." He took the kit, and put it in the ground next to Nona, who waited at his feet. Nona then nudged the kit to follow Win and the other kits.

Feeling spent, Dan leaned against Atlas. Atlas put one of his arms around Dan and nuzzled him.

Zinnia and Morran landed nearby. Rhea and Nick slid off and hurried over.

"You sure you're all right, man?" Nick asked.

Dan straightened up, took a deep breath, and exhaled slowly. Atlas released him. "Yes, I'm fine." He turned to Rhea and Nick. "I don't ever want to go through that again." He pointed upstream. "You're engineers, do something!"

Rhea followed Dan's gaze upstream. "Um, yes, I mean, we've done some flood control projects."

"Then it's about time you put those skills to use, don't you think, instead of just sitting there?"

"Hey, hey, hey," Nick said. "You've had a shock, Dan."

"Damn right I had a shock! I almost lost my little family! That's what we came here, for, isn't it?" He gestured at the dragons. "We're supposed to help them, and everyone else, here, too."

"We are doing that, Dan," Rhea said.

"Then it's time to get moving, isn't it?"

Nick put a hand on Dan's arm. "Come on. Rhea and I will go back to your house with you. The dragons have to go hunt. We were going to go to Earth when they came back today, but maybe we'll just take the day off."

"We're not taking the day off," Dan said firmly.

"All right, whatever you want," Nick said.

"We can go back to Earth today," Dan said. "In fact, I insist on it."

Rhea turned to Nick. "We can look up some flood control measures and see if we can get some materials while we're there."

"Good idea," Dan said.

"Go ahead and take off," Nick said to the dragons. "We'll be at Dan's place."

Morran walked up to Atlas and trilled something. Atlas did not respond but flew away. Zinnia and Morran launched into the air behind him.

Dan walked back to his house. Rhea and Nick walked with him. None of them said anything until they were through the door.

"Dan, why don't you just lie down for a few minutes," Nick said. "Rhea and I will get you coffee."

Feeling genuinely weary, Dan stripped off his gloves and lowered the cylindrical carrier to the ground. After removing his shoes, he stretched out on the bed cover.

He had not realized he had napped until he heard Rhea's voice.

"Dan? Coffee's ready."

He opened his eyes to see Rhea standing at the bedside. After slipping his shoes back on, he walked to the table and sat with both of them.

Nick slid a mug in his direction. "Feeling better?"

"Yes, thank you." He took a sip of coffee.

Rhea slid a plate of sliced pod fruit in Dan's direction. "We raided your food storage unit. Hope you don't mind."

Dan reached over for a piece. "Not at all."

Nick munched a slice and swallowed. "It is very good."

After eating the slice, which was delicious, he turned to Nick and Rhea. "Sorry for losing it back there. I didn't intend to snap at you two. And goodness knows what the dragons will think of that."

"No problem," Rhea said. "I think I would have lost it, too. As for the dragons, I think they'll understand."

"We have done flood control projects before," Nick said. "It might be worth a look to see whether we can do anything. If nothing else, we ought to be able to set up an early warning system so that we don't have to wait for the dragons to tell us if there's a flood coming."

When the coffee and fruit had been consumed, Nick volunteered to wash up.

"Anything we can do for you?" Rhea asked.

"I was thinking of checking on the cows," Dan said. "Their water bucket, at least, though it was probably filled by last night's rain."

"When we go back to Earth," Nick called from the sink, "we can bring some extra tarps and poles so that we can construct a shelter in their pen."

"Thanks," Dan said. "That would be useful."

After Rhea walked out, Dan grabbed the gloves and the carrier and put them back in the clinic. He walked out and saw Nick coming toward him.

"All cleaned up," Nick said. "We just have to wait for the dragons to return from the hunt."

"I'll talk to them," Dan said.

Nick gave Dan a hug. "It'll be fine."

Just then, they heard chattering. They turned to see Win marching toward them. Dan saw a tuber on the ground behind him. Win must have brought it and dropped it.

Win stopped when he reached Nick's feet, looked up, and started scolding him.

"He must think you were attacking me," Dan said.

Nick put out a hand and bent down. "It's all right, buddy...."

"Nick, they don't want to be petted," Dan said quickly.

Win bared his teeth and snarled at Nick.

"Oh, a snarl!" Dan said. "I haven't heard that before."

Nick put his hands up. "What do I do?"

"Back slowly to the clinic and shut the door."

Nick did so. Dan did his best to interpose himself between Win and Nick, though Win kept trying to go around Dan, scolding all the way.

When Nick slid the door shut, Win turned and pooped. He waddled over to Dan, lifted his head, chattered conversationally, and then padded away.

"Is it safe to come out now?" Nick said through the door.

"Yes, but watch your step. Win pooped at the entryway."

Nick slid the door open, saw the droppings, and carefully stepped past them.

They heard a giggle. Rhea had appeared from around the clinic house.

"Did you see that?" Nick asked.

Rhea, grinning, closed the distance. "Oh, I saw the whole thing."

"I have the supplies to clean that up," Dan said. "It'll give me more samples to analyze anyway."

Atlas arrived from the hunt first.

Dan walked over to him. "Atlas, Morran said something to you by the river. Would you mind telling me what it was?"

"He said I need to get my human under control."

Dan considered that for a moment. "Sounds like Morran. What did you think when he said that?"

"Morran thinks he understands everything, but he doesn't. He's said things about me, too."

Dan nodded. "I'm glad you saved the kit. Thank you."

"I thought I should follow in case you needed help. I flew up and behind the hatchling. It didn't see me."

Dan reached over and patted Atlas's shoulder. "You did very well. I'm proud of you."

"I always want to help," Atlas said. "I'm happy when I'm around you."

"I'm happy around you, too, Atlas." Dan rubbed Atlas's shoulder again.

At that moment, Zinnia and Morran landed nearby.

Zinnia walked up to Dan. Before Dan could say anything, she said, "You care about us. All of us."

Since that was not what Dan expected to hear, it took a moment for him to answer. "Yes, of course. We all care. That's why we came."

"That's why I wanted you to come," Zinnia said. "We can take you to Earth to get what you need now."

Rhea walked up to Zinnia. "I was thinking...you can see us on Earth, can't you?"

"Yes."

"Instead of a timer, let's arrange a signal you can see when we're ready to come back. We don't know how long it will take this time."

"What sort of signal?"

Rhea raised both of her arms above her head, brought them down to her side, and then above her head again. "Can you see that."

"Yes."

"We may be bringing a lot of things back this time," Dan said. "Maybe Morran could come with you to help?"

Before Morran could say anything, Atlas said, "I can come. I can watch."

Morran drew his head up and back. He threw Atlas a skeptical look.

"How about this," Nick said. "Zinnia brings us to Earth. When Rhea and I are ready, we signal to Zinnia, and when Dan is ready, he signals to Atlas."

Zinnia said, "Yes. We can do that."

"Atlas hasn't been to Earth before," Morran said. "Are you sure he can do this?"

"Any dragon can do it, whether they've been to Earth before or not," Zinnia said.

"But does Atlas know where to land?" Morran said.

"I can go with him. I can show him," Zinnia said.

Morran raised his head again and let out a breath but said nothing.

Dan, watching the exchange, guessed that Morran probably felt satisfied that Zinnia could competently guide Atlas, even if Morran felt he could do better.

Nick turned to Rhea and Dan. "We'll try to coordinate so we'll be ready at the same time."

After Zinnia dropped them off at the quadrangle, still largely deserted over the summer term, Nick and Rhea left to go to a hardware store. Dan drew out his phone and called Carlos.

"Dan!" Carlos said. "I'm here! In our apartment!"

"Weren't you supposed to be gone another month or so?"

"I came back early. I wanted to join you as soon as I could."

"Glad to have you. Need your expertise. And I missed you."

"I missed you, too."

"I'll be there in a few minutes," Dan said.

Coordinating with Rhea and Nick by phone, Dan and Carlos went shopping by themselves. When finished, they met at the quadrangle with carts full of supplies.

"What happens now?" Carlos asked.

"Rhea is going to signal the dragons," Dan said. "When they get here, we make sure that we and our supplies are touching them, and they take us back to the dragon world."

Rhea waved her arms. Within a minute, Zinnia and Atlas appeared over the quadrangle. When they settled down, Rhea and Nick went to work placing the carts next to Zinnia. Dan pushed his part of the supplies next to Atlas.

Carlos stood staring at the dragons.

Rhea and Nick went over to help Dan before returning to Zinnia.

Dan put a hand on Carlos's arm. "You okay?"

"Um, yes. Just a little overwhelmed."

Dan smiled. "I know what you mean." He guided Carlos gently to Atlas's side. "Just put your hand here." He turned to Atlas. "Atlas, this is my mate, Carlos Morales. Carlos, this is Atlas."

Carlos nodded at Atlas.

"Ready?" Zinnia said.

Dan stood next to Carlos and put a hand on Atlas's side. "Ready."

When they appeared on the dragon world, Morran, Thalia, and Kieran stood waiting for them. Atlas and Zinnia stepped back and joined the other dragons.

Carlos remained standing next to Dan.

Morran approached and walked around them.

Dan folded his arms in front of him. "Morran, you do not need to inspect my mate."

Carlos had his hands out in front of him, as if expecting to ward off a tackle. "Oh, is that what he's doing?"

Morran rejoined the other dragons. "He's big for a human."

"Yes, he's six-two, which is taller than most humans, and more muscular, stronger," Dan said.

Nick gestured to the dragons. "If you can help Rhea and I move everything to our house, that will leave Carlos and Dan to do what they need to do."

Atlas turned to Dan. "Do you need my help?"

"No, but thanks for the offer," Dan said. "Go help Rhea and Nick."

Once Rhea, Nick, and the dragons were gone, Carlos sighed and leaned against Dan, putting an arm around him. "Wow. Now this is what I call an adventurous assignment."

"Risk-takers," Dan said. "That's us, all right."

"I've never seen animals so enormous," Carlos said, "especially those big ones sitting in the back."

"That's Kieran and Thalia, Zinnia's parents. Parent dragons tend to be significantly larger."

"I wasn't expecting them to be so...." Carlos let Dan go and waved his hands.

Dan smiled slightly. "You've seen dragons before, Carlos."

"Yes. Smaller ones, at farms."

"Even they are still the size of calves."

Carlos gestured in the direction of the path to Rhea and Nick's place. "All the smaller dragons want to do is play. These guys look serious."

"They are," Dan said. "But they're friendly and playful, too. Atlas, in particular, is friendly and eager to please."

Carlos shook his head slightly. "Takes getting used to, I guess."

"They want us here, Carlos." Dan gestured at the house and clinic. "They made sure we had places to live and food to eat."

As if on cue, the cow mooed.

"Is that the cow you told me about?" Carlos said.

"Yes. Let me show you." He led the way to the enclosure.

Carlos leaned over the wall. The cow walked over. He stroked her head. She seemed to appreciate it. "What's her name?"

"Haven't named her yet. Or the calf."

"Bessie." He reached down the stroked the calf's head. "Let's call this one Tessie. Is this a female?"

"From what the dragons told me, yes, since the shape of her head is the same as her mother." Dan waved at the purchases they brought with them. "We need to take the trough over here so they aren't drinking from a bucket. We also need to milk Bessie. Arthur had some advice on how to approach her for that." Dan turned and pointed toward the field. "There are seeds in those piles of dragon manure over there. We need to use the rakes to spread those out so we can start growing edibles. There are already sprouts in the mounds."

Carlos turned to him. "Looks like I have my work cut out for me."

# CHAPTER 15

After they had moved supplies into the clinic and the house, Dan and Carlos sat down for a cup of coffee. Dan noticed that Carlos seemed to become more and more at ease as time passed.

When they finished the coffee, Dan said, "Shall I text Rhea and Nick that we're coming over for dinner?"

"You can text here?"

"Rhea and Nick set up wi-fi."

"I approve."

"The dragons will all be at Rhea and Nick's. Think you can handle it?"

He nodded. "I can now, I think."

"Good."

The four of them had purchased "heat and eat" dinners on Earth. After texting, Dan transferred them from food storage to the microwave. Then they took the food and walked over to Rhea and Nick's.

The dragons had clustered outside.

Realizing he had not done introductions, Dan said, "This is Carlos, my mate. Carlos, this is Atlas, Zinnia, Morran, Thalia, and Kieran."

"We're glad you're here," Zinnia said.

"I'm glad to be here," Carlos said.

"We're eating dinner with Rhea and Nick," Dan said.

Nick called from inside the house. "We're ready. Come on in."

They had already talked while on Earth, shopping, but dinner gave Dan, Rhea, and Nick an even better chance to tell Carlos what they had done so far.

When Dan and Carlos said their goodbyes, Nick came over to Carlos with a helmet. "Take this. You'll need it for riding a dragon."

Carlos took the helmet. "I think I'll hold off on that for a while, if you don't mind."

"Whenever you're ready," Rhea said. "No rush."

Atlas followed Dan and Carlos back to the house. When they reached the door, Dan pointed. "That's where Atlas sleeps at night." He turned to Atlas. "Atlas, Carlos and I need to be alone at night. We'll close the door when we're ready for bed, and open it in the morning when we're ready. If we need you during the night, we'll come and find you."

"I'll be here," Atlas said.

"Good night, then." Dan and Carlos walked inside the house and slid the door closed.

The next morning, Rhea found a text from Dan on her phone. The text said that he and Carlos were going to work around their house that day.

She turned to Nick and relayed the message. "I guess we can head toward the ocean and see if there's anything we can do about the flooding."

"Yes, I think a drainage channel or rock berm might be enough," Nick said. "Those would be fairly easy to construct. I think most of the problem is that the mud wall can give way too easily."

"We have to be sure we aren't affecting the terrain too drastically," Rhea said. "I think either of those won't disturb the plants or animals near there."

When Zinnia and Morran returned from the hunt, Nick rolled out the ground penetrating radar device he had purchased. "This will help me see what's underneath the lava flat."

"Underneath?" Morran said.

"Before we build anything, or do any digging," Rhea said, "it's important for us to see whether the ground is soft or hard, rocky or crumbly."

Nick looked Morran over. "Can we strap this around a back ridge?"

Morran picked it up. "I can carry it."

Nick grinned. "Thanks." He climbed up on Morran's back. "We want to go near where the river bends."

Once Rhea was firmly seated on Zinnia's back, they left for the ocean. As Zinnia circled for a landing, Rhea saw a seaskimmer on the beach. This time, the seaskimmer's mouth was open and the tongue was hanging out. *Poor thing*, Rhea thought.

Morran landed and set the radar device on the ground. Nick slid off.

Rhea slid off Zinnia and joined him. "I want to look around first."

"Good idea," Nick said.

The mud had started to build again and a pool had started to form behind it.

Rhea waved. "If we can build a sturdy enough barrier here, it could hold back the water. The dried mud is too easy for the water to break through."

Nick nodded. "Let me see what the radar device shows."

As the dragons watched, Nick activated the radar device and guided it over the lava flat. Rhea followed, watching the screen with Nick.

"Looks like there's a lava tube underneath us," Rhea said.

"Not too far underneath, either. Let's see how far it goes."

They followed the lava tube until they neared the drop-off near the ocean.

"Careful," Zinnia warned.

"Yes, the ground is definitely getting more gravelly," Rhea said.

Nick turned around. "Morran, can you circle around and see if you can see a cave opening anywhere along the drop-off?"

Morran obliged. They saw him fly over the width of the drop-off. When he came back and landed, he said, "Yes, there's a cave opening over there." He pointed.

Nick turned to Rhea. "The lava tube opening."

Rhea nodded. "Let's go back to the river bend." Once there, she added, "If we can dig here and reach the lava tube, then when the water rises, it'll flow into the lava tube and then into the ocean."

"The only problem then," Nick said, "is that there's solid rock between where we're standing and the lava tube underneath. We can't just use a shovel."

"Yeah," Rhea said, "we'd need a jackhammer."

Nick looked around the area, turning slowly. He snapped his fingers. "I have an idea. The surface below us is solid rock, yes, but it's only thick enough to support us and the dragons comfortably. Say Morran and Zinnia each took a large rock and dropped it from a height. That might break through the flat to the lava tube."

"Accuracy could be a problem," Rhea said.

"The tube's fairly wide," Nick said. "Besides, what's the harm in trying? It might work."

Rhea turned to the dragons. "Zinnia, Morran, what do you think? Would you be willing to each take a large rock and see if you can drop it right..." She stepped to one side and pointed down. "...here."

"Dragons play games with rocks all the time," Morran said. "We see how close we can hit a spot at a distance."

"Morran and I are good at it," Zinnia said.

"Let's try it then," Nick said.

"First, move the radar device a safe distance off the lava flat so it won't be crushed when the rocks fall," Rhea said.

"Good idea." Nick rolled the radar device off the flat and about 50 feet over the grassland. When he returned, he climbed on Morran's back. "Let's go."

Rhea climbed on Zinnia's back. "We'll tell you how high to fly to drop the rocks from." She took out her smartphone and did some quick calculations.

The land around the ocean had rocks of various sizes in abundance. Rhea was impressed that both Zinnia and Morran each pulled up a boulder of tremendous size.

Morran positioned himself over the spot first. Nick called Rhea through his helmet microphone. "High enough?"

"Yes, go ahead."

Morran dropped the rock. It hit the lava flat with a tremendous crash. A hole opened up. The sides of the hole fell in. Rhea could see the boulder lying at the bottom of the hole.

"Excellent, Morran!" Nick said.

"Let's widen the hole," Rhea said. "Zinnia, can you aim for the edge of the hole nearest the river?"

Zinnia dropped her rock. Again, they heard a resounding crash. The boulder rolled to one side.

"Go ahead and land so we can see," Nick said.

"Not land," Zinnia said. "The ground is still falling in. We'll hover."

"Yes, hover close," Nick said.

The dragons descended and hovered around the hole.

"Looks great," Nick said. "Good work, Morran and Zinnia."

"Yes, I think that will prevent flooding from now on, though we won't know for sure until after the next heavy rain. We can put a monitor here, and—what's that buzzing sound?" Rhea looked up and around. She saw a black cloud moving over the sand toward the seaskimmer. The cloud moved through the seaskimmer as if it were air, leaving nothing behind.

"It's The Terror!" Rhea said.

"Let's get out of here!" Nick said.

"Fly!" Morran and Zinnia said at once.

The dragons changed from hovering to racing away from the ocean in an instant. Morran trilled something. Zinnia trilled back.

Rhea looked behind. The cloud was chasing them!

The dragons, still making incredible speed in relation to the ground, began to climb. The air became cooler. The Terror followed them. The dragons performed a deep dive, pulling up just before they hit the ground. Rhea rocked with the G-forces and hoped The Terror would crash. Instead, it continued to pursue.

The dragons trilled at each other again and separated. The cloud separated, following each dragon. Zinnia and Morran flew together again, and the cloud merged.

Rhea could see that they were heading toward the dragon hibernation area, avoiding the dragon habitations.

"Evasive maneuvers aren't working," Nick said to Rhea.

Rhea took out her phone. "I'm calling Dan."

"I don't think he can do anything," Nick said.

"He needs to know. In case something happens to us."

"You're right." Nick pulled out his phone and pointed it behind him. "I'm taking my phone out to record this, in case they can find our phones."

Dan answered right away. "Hi, Rhea, what's up?"

"Dan, we're being chased by The Terror."

"What?"

"The Terror. It's chasing us."

"Where are you?"

"The dragons are heading to the hibernation area. They're flying very fast and are breathing heavily. I don't think they can even trill right now. I don't know how much longer they can hold out. I think they're hoping to find a hiding place among the rocks."

Rhea could hear Atlas through the phone. "We need to go!"

"No, don't come after us!" Rhea said.

"They couldn't get here in time," Nick added.

"What do you want us to do?" Dan said.

"Nick is recording all this on his phone," Rhea said. "If we don't survive, see if you can find it. Find a way to defeat this thing." She saw the cliff opening ahead. "I have to end the call now, so we can be quiet if we find a place to hide." She switched off the phone before Dan could say anything more.

The dragons swerved into the cliff opening. Rhea could not see the cloud anymore and hoped it would not follow.

Zinnia and Morran slowed. When they reached the spot where Zinnia's grandparents were hibernating, Morran turned to the cliff opposite. At the base, Rhea saw a recess with an overhang. The dragons landed and walked into it sideways, huddling together, breathless, panting.

Rhea and Nick slid off, staying between the dragons for shelter. They looked out.

"Do you think it followed us?" Nick whispered.

"I don't know." Rhea heard a rumbling. "Oh, great, a landslide, just what we need."

Nick nudged Rhea. "There's The Terror. It followed us." He hugged Rhea. "I love you, Rhea."

"I love you, Nick."

Nick held up his phone to continue to record The Terror.

Before it could reach them, an enormous silver dragon flew in front of it, hovering. Opening his mouth, he let out a roar that would have deafened Rhea and Nick without the protection of their helmets.

The sonic boom caused the cloud to stop. It deformed due to the shock wave, and for an instant Rhea hoped it was defeated. But it surged forward again. This time, the silver dragon let out a flame so hot that Rhea and Nick crouched between Zinnia and Morran to avoid being singed.

When the temperature cooled enough to raise their heads again, Rhea saw the cloud surge forward and go completely through the dragon as they did the seaskimmer. Nothing was left of the dragon except silver flakes raining to the ground.

A golden dragon, just as large as the silver one, roared at the cloud. The cloud paused. She roared again. The cloud drew back before moving forward again. The dragon let out a horizontal column of fire, which did nothing to slow the cloud. It consumed this dragon, too. Only golden flakes remained.

Rhea clung to Nick, expecting the cloud to target them next. Instead, it turned and flew away.

Dragons and humans remained still for a time. Rhea did not know how long she stood there, just staring, when she heard soft sobs. Turning, she realized that Zinnia was crying.

"Grandpa. Grandma," Zinnia said softly.

Rhea looked up and across the divide and saw that Zinnia's grandparents had come out of hibernation to defend them.

Rhea put a hand on Zinnia's shoulder to try to comfort her.

Morran stirred. "I need to help Zinnia," he said in a gentle voice.

Rhea and Nick moved aside to let Morran snuggle up to Zinnia and nuzzle her, making low soothing crooning noises.

Rhea leaned on Nick and started to weep. Nick put an arm around her. Looking up at him, she saw tears in his eyes as well.

After texting Rhea saying he and Carlos would stay home that day, Dan resumed his research at the clinic. He had offered to help Carlos with the planting and with the cows, but Carlos said, only partially joking, that Dan would just get in the way. Atlas, meanwhile, took the tarp and poles that Rhea and Dan had provided and was constructing a shelter within the enclosure for the cows. They had already set up the gate and put in the water trough.

Dan turned his attention first to the sandglider shell sample that he had gathered at the ocean. He confirmed that the tiles in the shell matched the tiles he had found in the dragon manure and on Win's foot. After a time, he heard a distant boom. He walked out of the clinic and looked at the sky. No lightning, no approaching thunderstorm. Clear sky lightning, perhaps? Or maybe the volcano had rumbled? Perhaps later he would ask Atlas to take him to the ocean briefly. Another boom reached his ears as he turned to enter the clinic again. Then he remembered that Rhea and Nick had gone to the ocean to see if they could construct something to prevent another flood. Maybe that was it. He returned to the lab and sat down.

Some minutes later, Atlas settled outside the clinic door. "I made the shelter while the cows were napping."

Dan stood and looked out the window. "Good work, Atlas." His phone buzzed. The ID said it was Rhea. "Hi, Rhea, what's up?"

"Dan, we're being chased by The Terror."

"What?"

"The Terror. It's chasing us."

"Where are you?"

Rhea explained.

Atlas said, "We need to go!"

Despite Rhea and Nick's urging that they not follow, once Rhea ended the call, Dan grabbed his helmet, shouldered the emergency pack with the first aid kit and sample case, and rushed out the door, where Atlas had positioned himself to take off. He climbed on Atlas's back.

Carlos called from the garden. "Where are you going?"

"Emergency!" Dan shouted as Atlas took off. He glanced back at Carlos, who threw up his hands, before turning his attention in the direction Atlas flew.

Atlas made straight for the cliffs. Dan thought he saw movement at the entrance to the cliff face as they flew over and past the dragon settlement.

Suddenly, Dan heard a sonic boom, coming from the cliffs. "What's that?"

"That's Zinnia's grandfather, roaring."

"You can tell?"

"Dragons have different voices."

This was followed by a red flash. "He must have come out of hibernation," Dan said.

"Yes."

Another sonic boom. A short pause, and another boom.

"That's Zinnia's grandmother," Atlas said.

Dan saw another red flash. "Must be quite a fight."

They had moved close enough to the cliff entrance when Dan saw a black cloud emerge from the opening and head toward the ocean.

Dan pulled out his phone and dialed Rhea. The connection had been made, but all he heard at first were sounds of weeping.

"Rhea, are you all right?"

"Dan...The Terror...it destroyed Zinnia's grandparents," Rhea managed to say between sobs.

"What?"

"Just...disintegrated."

"What about Nick and Zinnia and Morran?"

"They're here. The Terror didn't attack us."

"Stay there. I'll come for you. Right now, we're following The Terror."

Atlas had already moved to pursue.

"Are you out of your frickin' mind?" Nick yelled.

"If we're going to get rid of this thing, we need to know where it lives and what it does. Atlas and I are going to find out." Seeing movement at the dragon settlement out of the corner of his eye, he turned to see a multitude of dragons in the air, flying toward the cliffs. "Help is on the way. Dragons are coming. Just stay put." He closed the connection and said to Atlas. "Keep the cloud in sight but stay as far back as you can."

"Yes," Atlas agreed.

The black cloud did not waver. It moved over the hatchery, over the river, over the lava flat, but once over the sand, it stopped. Dan saw the cloud expand and separate. Instead of one black cloud, dozens upon dozens of small buzzing black objects hovered there. Each black unit coalesced in the shape of a crab. Then, as Dan and Atlas watched from a height, each crab zoomed with great speed into the sand and disappeared.

"Atlas, go and hover over the sand."

"Yes."

When they got there, they saw nothing but multiple indentations, as if giant thumbs had pressed the surface of the sand.

"Land on the lava flat overlooking the beach."

Atlas did so. Dan slid off.

Both of them looked over the area.

"They're sandgliders. The Terror is a cluster of sandgliders."

"Yes."

Dan sat on the lava flat to take this in, fingers on his temples. "A hive animal."

"What's that?"

"On Earth, like bees and wasps. If you disturb the hive, they can form a swarm and come after you." He stood and walked around. Seeing the hole near the bend of the river, he looked down and saw a boulder there. "The vibration of these boulders falling must have disturbed the nest." He heard the sound of a dirge coming from the direction of the cliffs.

Dan turned to Atlas. "Mourning Zinnia's grandparents."

"Yes. They were nice to me. I'm sad, too."

Dan placed a hand on Atlas's shoulder. "So am I." He turned in that direction. "Would it be all right if we went there?"

"Yes."

The dirge faded away as Dan and Atlas approached the opening in the cliffs. A couple of dragons flew past them. Many dragons remained a brief distance away. They cleared a space for Atlas to land as they approached.

When Dan slid off Atlas's back, he walked cover to Rhea and Nick. They sat on a rock, leaning on each other, arms around each other.

"I'm glad that you're alive," Nick said.

"I'm glad you're alive, too," Dan said. "Are you injured?" When they shook their heads, he added, "How about Zinnia and Morran?"

They all looked over to Zinnia's family. Morran remained close to Zinnia, nuzzling her. Atlas had walked over to Thalia and Kieran, nuzzling them and being nuzzled in return.

"Traumatized and exhausted, but not physically hurt," Rhea said.

Nick turned to Dan. "I think the same could be said of Rhea and me."

"I don't doubt it," Dan said.

Rhea pointed. "It consumed them. That's all that's left—those gold and silver flakes on the ground."

Dan turned. He noticed that the dragons were avoiding that area. Walking up to Kieran and Thalia, he said, "Do you want me to gather the remains for you?"

"I don't think you can," Kieran said.

"I have a sweeper with me, and a sample case, if you don't mind a little dust. I don't think I can gather the gold and silver scales separately, though."

"Yes, we would be happy if you could gather them for us," Thalia said.

Dan put down his emergency pack, got out the sample case, and took out the sweeper, extending the handle to its full height.

As he began work, Brutus took a step in his direction. "Is The Terror coming back? Are we safe?"

Dan glanced at him as he carefully swept up the scales. "No, I don't think The Terror is coming back, at least not until its usual time to appear. Yes, I think it's safe."

"What did you find?" Nick asked.

"They're like hive animals on Earth," Dan said. "The cloud is made up of a dense group of smaller animals, like a swarm of bees or wasps."

"What set them off?" Rhea asked.

Dan continued to sweep. "Rhea and Nick, what happened just before you saw The Terror?"

"We were trying to create a relief channel," Nick said. "I used the radar device and found that there was a lava tube under the flat, with a relatively thin layer of rock over it. We dropped a couple of boulders on it and the rock layer collapsed, exposing the tube."

"I could hear the boom, rather, two booms, at my clinic," Dan said.

"Yes, it was loud," Nick said.

"And, it probably shook the ground in that vicinity, maybe a hundred feet around and perhaps that much depth," Dan said.

"Probably," Nick said.

"What are you getting at?" Rhea asked.

Dan took a deep breath. "The Terror cloud is made up of sandgliders." He paused. Nick and Rhea gasped. The dragons let out exclamations of surprise.

"You shook their home," Dan said. "They came out and attacked, like a swarm of angry bees."

"But Dan," Rhea said. "We saw them. The cloud didn't look anything like a bunch of sandgliders."

Dan finished sweeping the remains into a pile, then put his open sample case on the ground and swept the pile into it. He presented it to Kieran. "Will this do?"

"Yes." Kieran took it and flew to a ledge at the spot where the grandparents had been hibernating. He gently placed it there and flew back.

Dan put away the sweeper and straightened up. "Atlas and I saw it. The cloud reached the sandy area on the beach, and then came apart." He made a gesture as if pulling taffy. "Once the cloud separated into individuals, the individuals shaped themselves into sandgliders. Then they all dove straight into the sand and disappeared."

"Yes, that's what happened," Atlas affirmed.

Dan turned slowly as he talked to the dragons. "Rhea and Nick and I have analyzed the building blocks of the sandglider shells. Even the dead cells have the ability to find each other and stick together. They can rearrange these building blocks into the forms that suit them."

"But we go to the ocean all the time," Gus said. "The Terror has never bothered us there."

"You never disturbed their nest," Dan said. "That's why it's safe to go back to the ocean. As long as you don't shake the ground, the sandgliders won't attack."

"But what about the eggs?" Thalia said.

"The Terror comes out in birthing season, yes?" Dan said.

"Yes," Thalia said.

"It's probably their birthing season, too. Outside of birthing season, they're fine scavenging whatever washes up on the beach. But for reproduction, they need more energy, more food. So they get together and go out seeking as much food as they can consume."

"But why eat Zinnia's grandparents?" Rhea said.

"Reforming themselves probably takes a tremendous amount of energy," Dan said. "They wanted to drive away presumed attackers, yes, but they also needed fuel to get back home. Apparently, they need to eat at the end of their pursuit."

Rhea sighed and turned to Thalia and Kieran. "I'm so sorry. We didn't realize we would awake The Terror."

"There is no blame," Kieran said. "You did not mean to do harm. Only The Terror did harm."

"Any of us could have awakened The Terror without knowing it," Brutus said.

"What do we do now?" Thalia asked.

"Do we kill them?" Brutus said.

"From what we found about their cells, they're damned near indestructible," Nick said.

Dan turned to Brutus. "Nick's right. I doubt it could be done. You know from your own experience that you can't catch them, can't dig far enough to get them. Their nest is probably buried so deep into the rock it would be nearly impossible to reach them, and we would never know if we found all the nests. Besides, it's not a good idea to kill an entire species. They have a place in your ecosystem, in nature. They were harmless to you until the world lava flow. If we restore the conditions before that happened, they should be harmless again."

"How do we do that?" Kieran asked.

"Give them a food supply," Dan said. "The lava flow buried their food. My mate, Carlos, knows how to cultivate food. That's what we're working on now. By the time the next birthing season comes, we hope to have enough grown so that The Terror doesn't attack you again." Dan turned to Kieran and Thalia. "Is there anything else I can do for you right now?"

"Yes," Kieran said. "We'll escort Zinnia and Morran home. Can you humans go with Atlas?"

Brutus stepped up. "I can take a human. I'm wearing those straps you use for riding." He turned to one side to show them better.

"So am I," said a golden dragon.

Rhea turned to Nick. "What do you think? I go with Henrietta, and you go with Brutus?"

Nick shrugged. "Why not?"

As Rhea and Nick walked up to the respective dragons and pulled on the braces, testing whether they were secure, Dan turned to Thalia and Kieran once more. "We are sad about your loss, too. We'll do everything we can so it doesn't happen again."

"We know you care," Thalia said. "We are grateful."

Dan's phone beeped. He picked it up, seeing it was Carlos. Rhea and Dan had connected it to the wi-fi earlier.

"Uh, I know you don't want to be bothered in an emergency, but something's strange is going on. Loud booms. Dragons flying everywhere. Then this trilling that sounded like a dirge. Then everything went very quiet. Are you all right?"

Dan smiled. "Yes, I'm fine. I'm coming home with Nick and Rhea. Put on some coffee and get out some snacks. We'll explain when we get there. See you soon." He closed the connection.

As Dan climbed on Atlas's back, Atlas turned to the other two dragons. "You follow me. Go directly to Dan's house. No swerving."

"Yes," the two dragons said.

Atlas lifted off with Dan. The other two dragons, humans on their backs, followed.

# CHAPTER 16

Carlos stepped out of their house as the dragons landed. When Dan slid off, Carlos walked over and embraced him. "Thank goodness you're all right. I was getting worried. Where were you?" He released Dan.

Dan nodded toward where the other two dragons had landed. Rhea and Nick were sliding off. "Helping Rhea and Nick." He called to the dragons. "Thank you, Brutus and Henrietta."

"We're happy to help," Brutus said.

"Just ask," Henrietta added.

The two dragons flew off.

Rhea and Nick walked slowly toward them.

"You look as if you've been through hell and back," Carlos said.

"We have," Nick said.

"Remember our telling you about The Terror?" Rhea said.

"Yes," Carlos said.

"It came after us," Rhea said, "and Zinnia and Morran. It killed Zinnia's grandparents right in front of us."

Dan turned to Carlos. "Atlas and I went after it, then we went back to help Rhea, Nick, Zinnia, and Morran."

Carlos's mouth fell open for a moment. He closed it, grabbed Dan by the forearms and shook him slightly. "You went after an entity that killed two dragons? What were you thinking? Do you realize you could have left me without you?"

Atlas swung his head over to Carlos. "We had to go. To find out where The Terror lived. To find out how to stop it from killing us. It killed my parents."

Carlos looked from Dan to Atlas and back to Dan again. He let go of Dan. "I hope it was all worth it."

"It was." Dan nodded to Rhea and Nick. "Our friends need a rest. We can talk inside, around a table and with some cups of coffee."

Dan and Carlos led Rhea and Nick inside. Dan took off his helmet and put it on a table by the door. Rhea and Nick did the same. The two engineers took chairs at the kitchen table, accepted the coffee and snacks, but did not seem to be inclined to talk. Dan and Carlos let them sit in peace. Atlas walked in and settled down close to the threshold.

Carlos waved a hand toward the outside. "The dragons who brought Rhea and Nick back were ones I hadn't seen before. What happened to Zinnia and Morran?"

"Exhausted," Dan said. "Kieran and Thalia are going to escort them to their home. They're uninjured."

"Yes, I read about dragons in the Dragon Appreciation Society newsletter while I was waiting for you to come back," Carlos said. "Apparently even bullets can't penetrate their hides. How in blazes did that Terror kill two dragons?"

Nick took a swig of coffee. "Not just killed … disintegrated."

"Nick and I analyzed the sandglider components," Rhea said. "Even dead, the components are pretty invincible. I don't doubt that consuming a dragon is within the means of a live entity."

"Hell's bells," Carlos said.

"You asked if it was worth it," Dan said, "and it was. We found out The Terror is a swarm of crab-like creatures that live by the ocean. You know those kids' toys that start out as cars and then you can turn them into robots?"

"Yes."

"They're like that. The crabs, the sandgliders, can get together and assemble themselves into swarms, which can go out and fly and consume things. When they're done, the swarm separates into component parts, the parts become sandgliders again, and then they burrow into the sand. Apparently they live underground, like ants or moles."

Carlos rested his chin on a hand, apparently considering. Rhea and Nick continued to sip tea and nibble on snacks.

Dan took a breath and continued, "I think our theory, Carlos, is correct. They consume dragons and dragon eggs—and cows and whatever else they come across for that matter—because a lava flow covered a vast amount of land where their food supply grew. My guess is if we replace that, they'll stop bothering the dragons—and everyone else, too."

"Seems as if I have my work cut out for me," Carlos said.

"I took soil samples," Dan said. "They're in my clinic. I have samples of the lava layer and whatever came out of a sort of mud volcano nearby."

Carlos raised his eyebrows. "Mud volcano. Wow."

Nick leaned forward a little. "I forgot to tell you. I left the ground radar device over by the lava flat. We'll have to get it eventually."

"Will it rust or anything if we leave it there?" Dan asked.

Nick shook his head. "No, but we will need to get it eventually."

"I can go find it," Atlas said.

Nick turned to him. "It shouldn't be hard, Being a human device, it should stand out. It's in the grassland just off the lava flat."

Atlas raised his head. "I can go now."

"We'd be grateful if you could," Dan said. "Just bring it back and leave it outside Rhea and Nick's house. Carlos and I will be taking Rhea and Nick home soon and we can meet you there."

"Yes." Atlas backed out of the entrance and flew off.

Dan turned to Rhea. "By the way, Rhea, before I forget, the shells at the ocean are all right to touch."

Rhea nodded slowly.

Seeing how tired they were, Dan said to Rhea and Nick, "Can you walk home? We can retrieve some carts or your ATV if not."

Rhea and Nick looked at each other. "I can walk as far as home."

"I can, too," Nick said.

Carlos pushed back his chair and stood. "We have ready-to-eat dinners in the refrigerator. Dan and I will bring them over and make supper for you later." He got out a food delivery pack, opened the refrigerator door, and began to fill the pack.

Rhea and Nick got out of their chairs slowly and walked to the door. They picked up their helmets on the way out. Dan and Carlos walked with them, at an easy pace, back to their house.

Once inside their house, Rhea and Nick put their helmets on a shelf.

"Why don't you lie down for a while," Carlos said.

"Good idea," Nick said.

"Nick, can you give me your smartphone? I want to see your video."

"Sure thing." Nick handed the phone to Dan, walked to his bed, kicked off his shoes, and stretched out on the top blanket. Rhea had already removed her shoes and climbed into her bed.

Dan synced the smartphone to the computer so that he and Carlos could watch on the larger screen. He also put the recording on mute.

"That's horrific," Carlos said in a low voice when the recording ended.

Dan nodded.

Carlos put a hand on Dan's shoulder. "Don't ever do that again."

"I don't intend to. If we succeed, no one will have to."

"Did you record the transformation of the cloud into the sandgliders?"

Dan shook his head. "Never occurred to me. I was too focused on pursuing the cloud." He gestured to the screen. "I want to see this again. Slowly, this time. I want to stop and magnify some of the frames."

"I'm with you."

After they analyzed the video a second time, they heard the sound of wings followed by a soft thump outside. Dan and Carlos left the screen and walked out the door. Atlas sat near the radar device.

"I picked it up carefully," Atlas said. "I didn't disturb anything. The Terror didn't follow me."

"It was good of you to be careful," Dan said. "though it would take a thunderous pounding of the ground to bring up The Terror again, I think."

"I flew over Zinnia's home on the way here," Atlas said. "Zinnia and Morran are sleeping. Thalia and Kieran are watching over them."

Carlos gestured to the door. "Rhea and Nick are sleeping, too."

"What do we do now?" Atlas asked.

"We're going to stay here with Rhea and Nick and then eat with them when they wake up," Dan said.

"I'll keep watch here." Atlas settled on his stomach.

"Thanks," Dan said. "We'll call if we need anything."

By the time they had the table set, they heard the cackle of the swimmers coming back to their nests from the lake.

"Do they always do that?" Carlos asked.

"Twice a day," Dan said. "I'm used to it now. I hardly notice it."

"I think I'll keep the noise-cancelling headphones nearby, just in case," Carlos said.

Rhea and Nick began to stir.

"How are you feeling?" Dan called.

Nick sat up at the edge of his bed and rubbed his hair. "Better."

Rhea slowly got out of her bed. "I wonder if we'll have nightmares."

"If you do," Nick said, "come on over and we'll cuddle on the couch. I'll do the same if I have nightmares."

"Do you want us to stay with you overnight?" Carlos asked. "We can bring a futon over here."

Nick waved a hand. "No. I think we'll be fine."

"Remember," Dan said, "we're just a phone call away if you need us."

Rhea peered out the door. "Is that Atlas out there?"

"Yes," Dan said. "He brought back Nick's radar device."

"Where are Morran and Zinnia?" Nick asked.

"Atlas said that they're sleeping," Dan said. "Thalia and Kieran are watching over them."

Rhea walked to the kitchen table and took a seat. "Poor Zinnia. Losing her grandparents like that, right before her very eyes."

Nick took a seat next to Rhea. "They put up quite a fight. Anything besides The Terror would have been killed."

"Yes, we saw the video," Carlos said.

Dan and Carlos put supper on the table and sat next to each other. Everyone ate in silence.

When they were down to coffee and dessert, Nick turned to Carlos. "Think you can grow enough to keep The Terror off our backs?"

Carlos took a deep breath and nodded. "I think so. There are seedlings already. Dan tells me that Atlas said that the wheat-like plants and the fruit pods grow pretty fast."

"If you need our help, let us know," Rhea said.

"We will," Dan said. "But rest up first, for the next couple of days, at least."

When they had cleaned up for Nick and Rhea after dinner, Dan and Carlos walked back outside. The sun was setting and twilight was beginning to descend.

Atlas stirred. "I want to stay with Rhea and Nick. Zinnia and Morran can't, and Kieran and Thalia can't."

Dan nodded. "Carlos and I will be fine. We can call you through your earpiece if we need anything."

Hand-in-hand, Dan and Carlos strolled back to their house. When they reached the clearing, they saw two dragons, one gold, one silver, lying there. Brutus and Henrietta.

Brutus raised his head. "We were flying around and saw Atlas at the home of Rhea and Nick. We saw Zinnia and Morran at their home. We thought we'd stay here with you overnight."

"That's very thoughtful of you," Dan said. "Thank you." He and Carlos went inside their house and slid the door shut.

Carlos turned to Dan. "They have a real sense of community."

"I've noticed that," Dan said. "We're sort of honorary dragons now."

The next morning, after breakfast, Dan texted Rhea.

*How did you sleep?*

*Had a nightmare where a monster was chasing me and I couldn't move,* came the answer. *I'm OK now.*

*How's Nick?*

*Fine. Zinnia and Morran are here. Atlas is going back to your place.*

*Need us for anything?*

*No, but thanks.*

*Text us if you need us.* Dan turned to Carlos. "They're fine."

Carlos looked out one of the windows. "The two dragons that stayed the night have gone."

"Yes, they're going out to hunt."

Carlos slid the door open. "Hi, Atlas."

"Zinnia and Morran came back to Rhea and Nick's house, so I came here."

"Going off to hunt soon?" Carlos asked.

"Yes."

"Can you bring back a swimmer for supper?" Dan asked. "Carlos and I will gather forage for the cows today."

"Yes."

"By the way, can you also get a swimmer egg?" Carlos asked. "A fresh egg? One that's been just laid?"

"I can watch the nests," Atlas said. "Sometimes they lay eggs outside the nests."

"Outside the nests?" Dan asked.

"Yes. The ground birds do that too. Lay eggs outside the nests. They lay a lot of eggs."

"Do the eggs laid outside the nests hatch?" Dan asked.

"Sometimes," Atlas said. "The birds find them and gather them with the other hatchlings."

Carlos nodded. "You only have to get one."

"Two," Dan added. "Can you get two?"

"Yes." Atlas took off.

Carlos turned to Dan. "Eggs outside the nest?"

"Some birds on Earth do that," Dan said, "but yes, it's unusual. We aren't in Kansas anymore."

"That's for sure."

"What were you planning to do with an egg?"

"Make an omelet, of course."

"I thought so. But not until I analyze one. That's why I asked for a second one."

"Of course."

Dan and Carlos cut grasses and fed the cows. They came right up to them and ate right out of their hands. They seemed to like petting, too.

"I brought some RFID tags," Carlos said. "We can put them on the cows and let them out to pasture. If they wander out of sight, we can track them."

Dan peered into the enclosure. "That would minimize the manure in their pen."

"For now," Carlos said, "I can rake that up and add it to the garden."

"I can also try out the pain-killing leaves on them when you put on the tags," Dan said. "I'm still trying to identify and distill the prime ingredients. Arthur just said he swiped the leaves on his skin. One swipe for aches, more swipes for serious pain."

"The RFID tags shouldn't hurt," Carlos said. "I usually just clip them to the ears. The cows don't mind."

"Let me try it anyway," Dan said.

When they came back with the tags, the cows let Dan hold and swipe their ears. Carlos clipped on the tags. The cows showed no sign of distress. The main problem was keeping the cows still; they wanted to nuzzle, maybe expecting more food.

That task done, Dan and Carlos left the enclosure.

"Think you might try to milk Bessie?" Dan asked.

"One thing at a time," Carlos said. "I'm gardening today."

"I'll be in the clinic."

Rhea and Nick came to the clinic door before the dragons returned.

Dan swiveled in his chair. "How are you doing? What's up?"

They walked in. Dan gestured to a couple of empty chairs, and they sat.

"We're doing better," Rhea said.

"We wondered if we could have Atlas fly us to the ocean site," Nick said. "I won't rest easy unless I see that those boulders are secure. I don't want them to fall over and cause another eruption of The Terror."

"As for that," Dan said. "My opinion is that you'd have to have the equivalent of an earthquake or explosion for the sandgliders to come out again in force. Not just a boulder rolling down an incline."

"Still…," Nick said.

"But why Atlas?" Dan asked. "Are Zinnia and Morran ill?"

"No, no, not at all," Rhea said. "But Zinnia doesn't want to go anywhere near the ocean now, and Morran doesn't either."

"I don't blame them," Nick said.

"I don't, either." Dan looked out the door. "Atlas isn't back from the hunt, yet. Brutus and Henrietta were outside the door overnight. If we're going to the ocean, I'd like to take Carlos with me. How was riding on Brutus and Henrietta?"

"Smooth and uneventful," Rhea said.

"No complaints here," Nick said.

"They may come back with Atlas. This brings to mind an idea I had. Zinnia and Morran may take a while to recover from their shock. The golden and silver dragons have expressed a willingness to help us, too. Would it be possible to make up a signaling device that we can put in both the silver and golden dragon places, so that if you need a dragon to fly someplace, you can set it off?"

Rhea and Nick looked at each other, then turned back to Dan.

"I have a couple of extra Bluetooths," Nick said, "but I was hoping to save those."

"But we can set up a system that when we signal it, a light would go on," Rhea said.

Dan heard the sound of wings. "Here they come. Let's see."

When they came outside, Atlas landed near them. He had a dead swimmer in one hand; two eggs in the other.

Carlos came over and took the eggs. "Thank you." He walked inside the clinic.

Dan and Nick took the swimmer and placed it in the clinic.

When they all came back outside, they saw Henrietta and Brutus landing.

Dan approached them. "Rhea and Nick want to go to the ocean. Would you be willing to fly them there?"

"Of course," Henrietta said.

"You said it was safe," Brutus said.

"I was there last night," Atlas added. "Nothing happened."

Dan turned to Carlos. "I want you to come and see the area. We can both go with Atlas..." He turned to Atlas. "...if you think you can carry two of us at once, Atlas."

"Yes," Atlas said.

"Um, I haven't flown with a dragon before," Carlos said.

"It'll be like when we ride a motorcycle together, me in front, you holding on to me in back."

Carlos shrugged. "If you can do it, I can do it."

Dan turned to the other two dragons. "Rhea and Nick want to put a human-made light in each of your homes, if you're willing. Then, if Rhea and Nick need a dragon to fly them somewhere, they'll turn on the light, and if you're willing, you can come. Can you do that?"

"Oh, yes," Henrietta said.

"We'd like that," Brutus said.

"Good. Rhea and Dan need to go back to their homes to get their helmets. Go with them and just fly to the ocean. Atlas, Carlos, and I will come when we can."

Nick motioned to Brutus and Henrietta. "This way." The four of them moved off.

"Let's go get our helmets," Dan said to Carlos.

When they came out, helmets on, Atlas waited patiently while Dan climbed up and then helped Carlos up. The two men had to squeeze together between two of Atlas's back ridges, but they made it work. Carlos put his arms around Dan's waist.

"We're ready. Take off," Dan said.

Atlas leaped into the air and spread his wings.

"Wow!" Carlos said. "This is awesome!"

On the way, Dan pointed out landmarks to Carlos. They could also see Rhea on Henrietta and Nick on Brutus. Atlas closed the gap.

When they reached the ocean, the dragons circled over the area where the boulders had been dropped.

"The first boulder is just sitting in the bed of the lava tube," Nick said through his helmet microphone. "I don't think that's a problem."

"The second is steady but looks as if it could tip over at any moment," Rhea said.

"Should we land?" Dan asked.

"Yes, over on the lava flat," Nick said.

Even though Brutus and Henrietta did not have a Bluetooth on their ears, they still seemed able to hear. All the dragons landed on the lava flat. The humans all slid off.

When Carlos reached the ground, he said, "That was amazing!"

"It is," Dan agreed. "I never get tired of it."

Nick and Rhea walked over to the second boulder, waving at the dragons to stay where they were.

After walking around the boulder, Nick said, "It's stable for now, but I worry that rain could wear away the soil it's on and it'll tumble downhill."

"That shouldn't be a problem," Dan said.

"Still, I'd feel better if it were on more stable ground," Nick said.

Rhea pointed. "How about over there by the river? If we put it there, it would help direct the water down the incline and into the lava tube when the river floods."

"I'm not sure it would be stable there, either," Nick said. "I'd feel better if there was a depression in the ground."

"How about this?" Dan said. "The mud from the mud volcano dries solidly and only breaks up with a lot of water pressure behind it. It should be all right with water flowing beside it."

"Like cement," Rhea said.

Dan nodded. "My analysis shows that it has a lot of elements in common with cement."

"We'll have to go back and get something to scoop it with," Nick said.

Dan turned to the dragons. "How about our friends here? Can you scoop up the mud with your hands and put it over there?"

"Yes, we can do that," Atlas said. The other dragons inclined their heads.

At Rhea and Nick's direction, the dragons placed enough mud to make a base. Then Atlas carefully lifted the boulder and just as carefully set it in the mud. Then Rhea and Nick directed the dragons to pat the mud around it.

"That should work," Nick said. "Thank you."

The dragons took off for the ocean, rinsed their hands, and flew back.

"I have an idea," Rhea said. "Can you direct fire at the mud? That should dry it out and solidify it quickly."

"I'll do it," Atlas said. "The rest of you can stay back."

Everyone else retreated to the lava flat as Atlas flew around the boulder, unleashing fire. Brutus and Henrietta positioned themselves between the humans and Atlas until Atlas stopped and flew back.

Dan turned to the dragons. "Thank you."

Rhea turned to Henrietta and Brutus. "You can take us back home now."

"You'll give us lights?" Brutus asked.

"It'll take a day or two to make them up," Nick said, "but yes, you'll have them eventually."

With that, Rhea and Nick climbed on the dragons. The dragons flew off.

Dan turned to Carlos. "I wanted you to have a chance to look around."

Carlos slowly made a full turn. "Yes, I think we can work with this. The grassland here..." He pointed at the plain next to the lava flat, "...and there..." He pointed to the rise overlooking the ocean, "...look like places we can successfully plant."

Dan gestured. "Let me show you the end of the lava flat." He led Carlos to the layered area. Atlas followed. "See? Sprouts growing out of the layer just underneath the lava flat."

Carlos nodded. "And through the cracks in the lava flat, I noticed."

Dan led the way to the beach. A seaskimmer and what appeared to be two juvenile seaskimmers inched across the sand on their stomachs, using their hands/flippers to help in their progress.

One of the juveniles followed them.

Dan glanced back. "I understand they do that."

"Follow you?" Carlos said. "Yes, I see. Do we feed them or something?"

"They're just curious," Atlas said.

A sandglider skidded across their path.

Dan winced despite himself.

"Is that...?" Carlos said.

"Yes," Dan said.

"Looks harmless as an individual."

"But deadly in a swarm," Dan said.

Carlos stopped, took a breath, stretched, and looked up. "Time to go home?"

"Yes, we can do that," Dan said.

Atlas again patiently waited for them to climb on his back.

# CHAPTER 17

That evening, Dan and Carlos prepared swimmer and purple tubers for dinner. After checking with Rhea and Nick, they came over with covered food carriers and ate dinner together at their place.

"How are the signalers coming?" Dan asked.

"We should have them done some time tomorrow," Nick said.

"Any reaction from Zinnia and Morran when you came back with Henrietta and Brutus?" Dan asked.

"They seemed relieved," Nick said.

"But Zinnia added that she and Morran would still be happy to take us anyplace here," Rhea said. "Just not to the ocean."

"Any objection to having a signal with the silver and golden dragons?" Dan asked.

"Morran said, after they left, that it was about time the other dragons did more work in helping us," Nick said.

"How are you two doing?" Carlos asked.

"I think we're recovering," Rhea said. "I was a little nervous about going back to the ocean, but not seeing The Terror was reassuring."

"Yes, with the boulder issues settled," Nick said, "I'm getting more confident that they won't bother us again unless something drastic happens."

"Or at least until birthing season," Dan said.

"I'm sure we can see some vigorous growth long before then," Carlos said. "That should solve the problem."

"Can't be too soon for me," Nick said.

After cleaning up and parceling out leftovers, Dan and Carlos returned to their house. When the sun had set, Carlos made cocktails with what he brought with him from Earth. He and Dan sat outside the house, side by side, looking at the stars as they sipped.

"Different," Carlos said.

"But still spectacular," Dan said.

"Yes, without the city lights to dim them, the stars are brilliant." Carlos took another sip of his drink and turned to Atlas. The dragon had settled underneath his shelter, swishing his tail back and forth.

"Say, Atlas," Carlos said, "you're a strapping young dragon, ready to mate. Ever think of going out and finding a filly?"

"Filly?" Atlas asked.

"Golden dragon," Dan explained. "Future mate."

Atlas raised his head slightly. "The golden dragons here don't like me much. They think I'm still a hatchling."

"This isn't the only dragon community, is it?" Carlos asked.

"No," Dan said. "The two nearest other dragon communities are over there..." He pointed. "...and over there." He pointed again.

"Then why not visit them?" Carlos said to Atlas. "You'd get a fresh perspective."

"I need to stay here to help you and Dan," Atlas said.

"You don't have to leave permanently," Carlos said. "Just fly over for an afternoon and get acquainted. Dan and I will be fine. We can call Zinnia or Morran if we have an emergency."

"But I'm supposed to stay here and help you."

"You are," Dan said. "But you need to have your own life, too, Atlas. You have to mate with someone. The urge will be too strong. And though Morran isn't always right, he is right about it being smart to find a future mate before mating season, and not leave things to chance. I doubt that Kieran, or Thalia, or Zinnia, or even Morran would think less of you if you went to find a future mate. Carlos and I think you would be helping us if you could find a future mate and be happy."

Atlas raised his head a little more.

"Look at Dan and I," Carlos said. "We're helping, but we're also doing things as mates. You can do both, too."

Atlas raised his head even more. "Yes. I understand."

The next morning, after Atlas left to hunt, Carlos went outside to do his gardening, and Dan kept up his research. The egg analysis showed it was safe to eat, very much like the eggs of Earth, except swimmer eggs were about the size of ostrich eggs.

As he checked again on his leaf analysis, he heard Carlos calling, "Dan! I think your friend is here!"

Dan walked out the clinic door. Win approached, chattering. When he reached Dan's feet, he looked up, chattered, turned around, and walked away while Dan watched. After going a few dozen feet, Win turned again, walked up to Dan, chattered, and walked away again.

Carlos stepped to Dan's side. "I think he wants you to follow."

"Yes, it seems to be a universal animal gesture." Before Dan could move, his phone beeped. He took it out of his pocket. "Hi, Rhea."

"We have the transmitters ready," Rhea said. "Nick and I will go and set them up once Zinnia and Morran come back. Want to join us?"

"Not right now. Win came for a visit and he seems to want me to follow him someplace."

"Oh, wait up," Rhea said. "I want to see this."

"I'm coming, too," Nick said through the phone.

"I'll have Carlos wait for you," Dan said. "I think Win wants me to go now. See you soon." He closed the phone, put it back into his pocket, and turned to Carlos. "Watch to see where I go. I'll walk slowly so you can catch up."

"Will do."

Win did not run, but trotted ahead with determination, taking a straight path. He stopped every so often and looked back to be sure Dan was still following.

Soon, Dan heard the sound of an animal crying. Ahead, he saw a wide, tall tree. Thick, leafy vines wove around it, covering the trunk so well that Dan could hardly see the bark. Near the roots of the tree, tangled in the vines, was one of the kits, squeaking and crying in distress.

Win walked up to Dan again, looked up, and chattered.

Dan looked back at Win. "I see the problem." He saw movement to one side of him and turned to see Carlos, Rhea, and Nick running up.

"The little one is stuck in the tree," Carlos said.

"That must be the clinging vine thing that the dragons talked about," Nick said.

"Morran said he'd show us where they were nearby but never did." Rhea added.

Nick stepped over to the tree and crouched. "If you look closely, you'll see small bones and skulls intermingled with the vines at the base of the tree."

Dan saw a vine move toward Nick. Quickly, he stepped forward and pulled Nick back.

"Nick!" Rhea shouted as the vine retreated.

"Damn! Did you see that?" Carlos looked over the tree. "We ought to call this thing Audrey."

Rhea nodded. "The name of the human-eating plant from the movie."

Nick turned to Dan. "Thanks." He turned back to the kit, still mewling and crying. "Getting the little one out isn't going to be easy."

Win looked up at Dan and chattered again.

"Yes, we'll help, just give us time," Dan said.

"We need to call a dragon." Rhea took out her phone. "I'll call Zinnia." After Rhea touched the controls, she said, "Zinnia. One of the little animals is caught in clutching vines. Can you come?"

"Yes. Did you walk far?"

"Not far, no," Rhea said.

"Then I know where you are. I will be there soon."

Meanwhile, Win walked around Dan, pausing to look up and chatter in agitation.

Dan crouched near him. "We're getting help. Just wait." When he stood, he could see Zinnia, in the sky, flying toward them.

Zinnia landed at the base of the tree. Immediately, Win marched over and began to scold her. Ignoring Win, Zinnia pulled the vines apart.

"Zinnia, watch out!" Carlos said. "There's a vine winding around your leg."

"I'm stronger than the vine." Zinnia reached for the kit, grabbed it, and walked backward. When she did so, the vine snapped.

Zinnia handed the kit to Dan.

Win continued to scold Zinnia, then turned and pooped at her feet.

"Sorry about that," Rhea said.

"I can wash it off or burn it off," Zinnia said. "I need to go before the little animals panic." She flew off.

Win turned his attention to Dan and the kit. Dan set the kit near Win's head. Immediately, the kit scurried near Win. Win craned his neck to check on the kit, and then toddled away, with the kit waddling next to him.

"That is one mean vine," Carlos said.

"Arthur wrote that humans had been trapped by them and died," Dan said.

"What do they do, starve and then the vine consumes them?" Carlos asked.

"Pretty much," Nick said.

"I'll have to read more of Arthur's notes," Carlos said. "I had skimmed the journal and just read the book with the plant and animal information."

"It's on my computer, you can read it whenever you wish," Dan said.

Rhea turned to Dan. "Want to go with Nick and I to set up the transmitters?"

Dan turned to Carlos, who shrugged. He turned back to Rhea. "You and Nick go ahead. But let us know when you're finished, so you can put the signal app on our phones, too."

"Will do." Nick said. He and Rhea walked away.

On the way back to the clinic, Carlos asked, "What's with the pooping?"

"I think I've finally figured it out," Dan said. "I was watching the camera replay and saw a couple of instances where Win or Nona were fending off predators. If scolding doesn't chase a predator away, they kill it by biting the neck. Then they dig a hole, fling the predator in it, cover it with poop, and fling the dirt that they dug with their hind legs. Since their poop has seeds in it, it results in the planting the seeds for future growth."

"Efficient," Carlos said.

Rhea and Nick had the transmitters ready by the time Zinnia and Morran returned from the hunt.

"We want to go to the home of the single golden dragons," Rhea said. "Then we want to go to the home of the bachelors. Would you be willing to go there?"

"Of course," Zinnia said.

When they landed at the home of the golden dragons, Rhea and Nick slid off. Before anyone could say anything, the dragons surrounded Zinnia and Morran and nuzzled them. DeeDee carefully nuzzled Rhea, and Cleo carefully nuzzled Nick.

When they drew back, Henrietta said, "We are sad at the loss of Zinnia's grandparents. We are sad that The Terror pursued you."

"That's very kind of you," Zinnia said.

Henrietta turned to Rhea and Nick. "Do you have the flashing lights you talked about?"

"Yes." Rhea removed a post from her carry bag. The post was about a foot high and an inch thick. There was a spike at one end, a light and a solar collector on the other. Holding it out, she added, "Take this and push the spike at a place where you can all see it but it won't get in the way."

Henrietta grabbed it and walked to the perimeter. She pushed the stake in.

Rhea pulled at the stake and found that it did not move; it was solidly planted. She adjusted the small solar collector at the top and stepped back. "Now watch." She took out her smartphone, opened the app, and activated the signal. The light at the top of the stake flashed.

"Ooooh," several dragons said at once.

"What's this for?" Morran asked.

Nick turned to him. "If we need a dragon for a ride, and you and Zinnia can't take us, this will tell the dragons here to come."

Morran turned to Henrietta. "I thought that at the dragon meeting, before the humans came, you and everyone else said you didn't want the responsibility for humans."

"We're not going to live with them," Astra pointed out. "Just give rides and help in small ways when you and Zinnia can't."

"We didn't want responsibility before the humans came," Henrietta said. "We thought we couldn't help very much at all. But after the humans came, we saw that we could help a little, and maybe fly with them, too."

"Yes," Ora said, "we especially thought if Atlas could do it, so could we."

Rhea and Nick exchanged a look. Nick leaned over toward Rhea. "We're not telling Atlas we heard that," he whispered.

Rhea nodded.

"We are glad that you are willing to help," Zinnia said.

"We're not taking your humans from you," Henrietta said.

"I know," Zinnia said.

Morran turned to Zinnia, Rhea, and Nick. "That is a large change of mind."

"Things do change," Nick said.

Rhea turned to the golden dragons. "Thank you. We'll go over to the bachelor dragons' home and set up a receiver there, too."

The experience with the bachelor dragons was much the same: sympathy, planting the receiver, demonstrating it, taking off again.

Zinnia and Morran flew Rhea and Nick home.

When she and Nick slid off, Rhea said, "Thanks."

"Is there anything else today?" Zinnia asked.

"No, Nick and I just planned to relax today. We're still getting over being chased."

"Yes." Zinnia moved her head closer to Morran. "We are doing things to feel better, too."

"Far away from the ocean," Morran added.

Dan and Carlos returned to the clinic before Atlas came back.

When Atlas landed, he said, "Do you need me for anything?"

"Not today," Carlos said.

"I'm going to work in the clinic," Dan said.

"Then I'll fly over to the dragon homes across the grassland and see if I can find a future mate."

"Good luck," Dan and Carlos said.

They were about to prepare supper when they saw Atlas through the window. Hurrying outside, they met Atlas when he landed.

"I found a future mate!" he said excitedly.

"Hold on," Carlos said. "Let us get some chairs and then you can tell us all about it."

Once Dan and Carlos were settled in front of Atlas—and Atlas had settled on his stomach—Atlas launched into his explanation.

"Her name is Lily. She's very nice, and she's beautiful."

"How did you meet?" Dan asked.

"I was flying to her community when I saw her lying in the grass."

"Was she in a patch of leaves that make you sleep?" Dan asked.

"No. She was just resting. Her eyes were closed. I landed in front of her and rested on my stomach, watching her. I wanted to be sure she didn't need help."

"What happened then?" Carlos said.

"Her eyes were closed. After a time, she said, 'I know you're there.' I said, 'You're so pretty!' She laughed. It was a nice laugh, not a nasty laugh. She opened her eyes and looked at me. She said, 'You're a handsome dragon.' So I lifted myself up like this..." Atlas stood on his hind legs, wings spread, head up, neck extended. "...so she could see me."

"She must have been impressed," Dan said.

Atlas lowered himself to the ground again. "She was. She said she was looking for a future mate. I said I was looking for a future mate, too. She said her father told her to look for a future mate at another dragon community since she didn't think she wanted to mate with anyone in her dragon community. She was on her way here and was resting."

"What happened then?" Carlos asked.

"We flew to her home. I met her parents."

"Ah, meeting the 'rents," Carlos said. "That's serious."

"They were very nice. Her father's human name is Merlin. Her mother's human name is Buttercup. They asked about my parents. I told them that The Terror killed them when I was a hatchling. They said they had heard about that and were very sad about it. They didn't know it was me, though. Then I told them that I was helping the humans to stop The Terror. They said they had heard about that, too, and that was very important work. I told them that I couldn't stay there with Lily before mating season, I would have to come back here. They all said they understood. They said that after we mate, Lily and I could stay there."

"I very much hope that we'll have the problem solved by then," Carlos said.

"Do you want to go and tell Kieran and Thalia?" Dan said.

"No, not now," Atlas said. "I'll tell them later."

"Can we tell Rhea and Nick?" Dan asked. "We're going to make supper and go to their house."

"Yes, you can tell them."

Dan was active in texting Rhea the details as he made supper with Carlos. They packed up the meal and walked to Rhea and Nick's house, with Atlas following. As usual, Atlas rested outside while Carlos and Dan went inside. When they placed the food on the table, they noticed Rhea and Nick watching a computer screen.

"What's this?" Dan asked as he walked over.

"We thought we'd check the camera at Arthur's place," Nick said, "Sure enough, it caught Atlas and Lily meeting."

"They were at a considerable distance away," Rhea added. "We had to zoom in on the image."

Dan glanced at the screen. "Shame on your two. Spying on Atlas...."

Rhea and Nick looked abashed.

"...and not inviting Carlos and I to check it out, too."

Nick smiled and indicated the screen. "It's just as Atlas said."

As Dan watched, Carlos watching next to him, the camera showed a golden dragon stretched out on the grass. Atlas flew toward her and settled down. After a brief time, the camera showed Atlas posing. Then the two dragons lifted off and flew out of camera range.

"That's them, all right," Dan said. "Now, let's eat."

That evening, after Carlos and Dan were in bed, they heard the sound of wings.

Carlos sat up. "Is that a dragon?"

Dan threw back the covers and got out of bed. "Yes. We weren't expecting anyone."

They walked to a window. In the moonlight, they saw a golden dragon flying toward the house.

Carlos turned to Dan. "Could that be Lily?"

"I think it is."

"How did she find us?"

"Atlas probably told her. Besides, where else do you find two houses close together with two tents beside them?"

They watched as the dragon landed and walked toward Atlas's shelter. Dan and Carlos had to move to another window to continue watching as the dragon settled next to Atlas. Atlas stirred and lifted a wing slightly, partly covering her as she snuggled against him.

Carlos turned to Dan and smiled. "Seems as if Lily wanted some boyfriend time."

Dan turned to Carlos. "I can identify with that."

They exchanged a kiss and went back to bed.

The next morning, Rhea received a text from Dan.

*Lily's here with Atlas.*

*Mating already?*

*No, that takes a hormonal surge that's only present during mating season. Courting, yes.*

*Can Nick and I come and see her?*

*We're letting Atlas and Lily have alone time right now. If you can peek and be quiet about it, I guess that would be all right.*

*Thanks.*

*Later.*

Rhea closed the connection and turned to Nick, still at the breakfast table. "Dan says Lily's here."

"Makes sense," Nick said. "After all, Morran and Zinnia are a couple, even though they aren't mated yet."

"Want to go see Lily? Dan says we can if we're quiet about it."

Nick pushed back his chair. "I'm game."

When they walked outside, Zinnia, Morran, Thalia, and Kieran were there, as they usually were before their morning hunt.

"Did you want to test your flashing lights again?" Zinnia asked.

"No," Rhea said. "The silver and golden dragons both said they saw them clearly, so we know they're working."

"We were going to Dan's house," Nick said. "Atlas has a future mate."

"Where did he find a future mate?" Morran said.

"The next dragon community over that way," Rhea pointed.

"That was well done," Thalia said.

"I'm impressed," Morran said.

"His future mate, Lily, came to him last night," Rhea said. "Nick and I were going to take a look. Dan said we could if we were quiet."

"I'd like to see them, too," Thalia said.

"Can you do it without them seeing you?" Nick asked.

The dragons exchanged looks. "We're hunters," Kieran explained. "We sneak up on prey all the time without their seeing us."

"Sorry," Nick said. "I should have remembered."

They crept toward Carlos and Dan's house. For their size, Rhea felt it remarkable that the large dragons made almost no noise. Eventually, they reached a spot where they all could look through the leaves and branches.

Rhea saw Atlas in his shelter, a golden dragon at his side. Both had their eyes closed.

After a minute or so, Lily opened an eye. "I know you're there."

Immediately, Atlas lifted his head, curled his tail around Lily's hindquarters, and leaned protectively toward her.

Nick stepped out of the brush. "Whoa. It's just us, Atlas. We only wanted to meet Lily."

Atlas relaxed as Rhea and Nick walked toward him and Lily but rose to his feet as the other dragons emerged. Lily remained with her stomach on the ground, head up, but looking calm.

"We just wanted to get to know your future mate," Thalia said.

Atlas turned from Dan to Thalia and settled back into a resting position next to Lily.

Lily looked up to Atlas. "Your family?"

"Kieran and Thalia have been my parents since I was a hatchling," Atlas said, gesturing with his head. "My sister dragon, Zinnia, and her future mate, Morran." Atlas turned away from the dragons. "The humans are Rhea and Nick, who are with Zinnia and Morran." He turned again. "This is Dan and Carlos, who are with me."

"I'm Lily," she said.

Thalia dipped her head. "Welcome."

"Yes, you're welcome here," Kieran said.

Atlas rubbed Lily's neck with his. "We're together now."

Lily returned the gesture. "Yes, we will have a home with my father and mother after mating."

"That is well done," Thalia said. "I'm sure your parents are very proud."

Lily nuzzled Atlas. "Atlas is a fine dragon."

"He is that," Kieran said.

"We're happy to meet you, Lily." Rhea said. "I'm Rhea, and this is Nick."

Nick waved. "Pleased to meet you."

Kieran motioned to the other dragons. Rhea thought they were going to fly off, but instead, they turned and began to walk back in the direction of their home. Rhea and Nick followed.

When they were a distance away, Nick turned to Morran. "Well, Morran, I didn't think you had it in you."

"In me what?" Morran asked.

"To stay diplomatically quiet."

"There was nothing to say," Morran said. "Atlas did the smart thing. He found a future mate and secured a future home. That's what dragons should do."

"Another thing dragons should do is hunt," Kieran said, and launched himself into the air.

The other dragons followed.

# CHAPTER 18

When Rhea and Nick left with the other dragons, Dan and Carlos walked toward Atlas and Lily. "Sorry, Atlas. We told Rhea and Nick that Lily was here."

"That is all right," Atlas said. "I was going to introduce Lily to everyone this morning."

Lily turned to Dan and Carlos. "Which one is Dan and which one is Carlos?"

Dan raised a hand. "I'm Dan."

"I'm Carlos," Carlos said.

"Atlas told me about you," Lily said. "He said you and Rhea and Nick are nice humans."

"Thank you," Dan said.

"Lily was a hatchling on a human farm," Atlas said. "Some humans who came to the farm were not nice."

"They tried to hurt me," Lily said, "but they couldn't. The human family on the farm told them to go away. Other humans came and made the bad humans go away."

Dan nodded. "Yes, we know all about bad humans. Some were not nice to Carlos and me, either."

"It's better here," Lily said.

"This place is very nice," Carlos agreed.

Atlas rose on all fours. "Lily and I need to go and hunt."

"Of course," Dan said. He and Carlos backed away to give them room to move out of the shelter and fly away.

Carlos watched them go. "Do you think Lily will stay here or return to her parents' home?"

"I don't know," Dan said. "I'm fine either way."

"So am I," Carlos said.

"You gave me an idea, though." Dan took out his phone and texted Rhea. *Do you have any of those riding straps left? In case Lily wants them?*

*Sure. We'll bring them over.*

Carlos looked at Dan's phone. "Did you have in mind for me to fly with Lily?"

Dan put the phone away. "I was thinking Rhea or Nick to fly with Lily in case Zinnia and Morran weren't available. Did you want to fly with her?"

"The question is, does she want to fly with me?"

"Or does she want to fly with anyone? She might not want the 'decorations.' But I wanted them around in case she does."

When Rhea and Nick came over, Rhea handed the straps to Dan, who quickly stored them in the clinic and came out again.

"What's next for you?" Dan asked.

"Rhea and I were discussing putting a camera by the ocean," Nick said.

"But we're a little nervous about it. We'd have to drive a stake in the ground, and I don't want to disturb the sandgliders."

"I don't think just driving a stake in the ground will do it," Dan said.

"I'm not taking any chances," Nick said.

"Then, why not do what I did with the camera watching the tanklets?" Dan said. "Find a sturdy tree and fasten the camera around the trunk."

Rhea turned to Nick. "That'll work."

"If Zinnia and Morran don't what to go there," Dan said, "you can arrange for other transportation now."

"True," Nick said.

"If you do get a camera set up," Dan said, "can you put the app on my clinic computer so I can monitor it, too?"

"Sure," Nick said.

When Rhea and Nick went back to their home, Carlos turned to Dan. "Could you help me today?"

"Anytime. I thought you wanted to work by yourself?"

"In the beginning, yes. But planting a small garden and planting a field are two different levels of tasks."

"I'm happy to help anytime. You know that."

"I wanted to be sure I wasn't taking you away from your research."

"Oh, that's moving along. I can spare the time. Besides, growing things for The Terror to eat is our first priority, as I see it."

Carlos nodded. He pointed to the field. "I've used the rake to spread out the manure. I need help in pulling out and gathering the seedlings."

"Just let me get my gloves."

Working together, they pulled out and laid the seedlings in rows. They were still doing this when Atlas and Lily returned from the hunt. The dragons landed near them.

"What are you doing?" Lily asked.

Dan looked up. "We're gathering the seedlings to plant."

"You need to separate the pod plants from the grain plants. See?" She picked up a seedling. "This is a pod plant." Putting that down, she picked up a different sprout. "This is a grain plant. They won't grow together."

Carlos straightened up. "You've done some planting?"

"Yes," Lily said. "I was a hatchling on a farm and watched the farmers. Plants are different here. I became tired of flying around in circles around our pod fields, waiting for an opening, then pushing other dragons to get a pod to eat. I thought I would grow some of my own. The other dragons in the community thought I was silly. I did it by myself, anyway."

"I'd be interested in hearing your experiences," Carlos said.

Lily turned to the seedlings. "The grain plants keep the pods from growing. To get pod plants to grow, there has to be a wide open area, and no other grain plants there."

"Do you have to clear the grassland?" Carlos asked.

"Not very much," Lily said. "On your world, farmers always worried about weeds. Here, the grains and pods will crowd out the grasses. Once the pods start growing, they'll multiply fast. The grains will grow back quickly after you eat them. Plants grow fast here."

Carlos rubbed his chin thoughtfully. "Okay. The pods seem to be the plants that were on the lava flats before the lava came. We want to grow those here."

"We can," Lily said. "I made a garden outside our dragon community. Only my parents and I knew where it was. But we could get pods whenever we wanted once I planted them."

"What should we do with the grain seedlings?" Dan said.

"Put them anywhere you want," Lily said. "There are lots of them in the forest. The little animals eat them and when they poop, the grains grow. The tubers do, too, because they eat those and poop those seeds."

"Can you show us your garden?" Carlos said. "I'd like to see how you did it."

"Yes," Lily said. "I have flowers, too."

"Flowers?" Dan said.

"Yes. I told the dragons where I live if they just let the flowers grow a little longer, the flowers would produce seeds and we could have flowers all year. But they said I was silly about that, too. 'Why wait?' they said. I told them they had to wait a year for the next flowers because they would have to grow again from the roots. They still said we can't resist. We want to eat them right away. So I found some small collections of flowers in the forests and grew my own."

"Is your garden very far from here?" Carlos asked.

"Short flight, long walk," Lily said.

"Rhea and Nick dropped off some straps," Dan said. "If you're willing, Lily, you can fly Carlos there while Atlas takes me."

"Yes," Lily said. "I used to give my humans rides on my back when I was on the farm."

"I'll get the straps," Dan said.

Atlas followed Dan. "Dan, shouldn't Rhea or Nick put on the harness?"

"Remember when I showed the bachelor dragons how to build a shelter?"

"Yes."

"It's because I know how to build a tent, too. Same here. Rhea and Nick know how to put on a harness, but Carlos and I also know how to do it. We've done it on Earth many times."

"That's good, then."

Once Dan retrieved the bands, he put them on Lily. When that was accomplished, he put on his own helmet and gave Carlos his.

"When Rhea and Nick come back from setting up a camera," Dan said, "we'll see if they can give Lily a Bluetooth."

"What's that for?" Lily asked.

"It's so we can hear the humans call us from far away," Atlas said.

"That would be useful," Lily said.

When they were in the air, Lily flew ahead. Atlas followed. They flew over alternating areas of grassland and forest. Soon, they reached a clearing. Dan could see from the air that there was a neat, square cultivated area planted with pods and another area close by with flowers.

Lily and Atlas landed just outside the garden area. Dan and Carlos slid off.

Lily sat and gestured with her front hands. "We eat from the back of the area to the front, and then start again at the back."

Carlos walked along the length of the garden. "Yes, I see this row has been recently eaten, and then the pods grow progressively larger down the rows until you get the fully ripe ones at the end."

"Yes," Lily said. "By the time we've finished with a row, the pods we ate earliest have grown back."

"Just like pumpkins," Carlos said. "Grow fast, vines spread, plant themselves, and spread some more."

"All you have to do is start it," Lily said.

"Can I have a pod now?" Atlas asked.

"Yes, there's plenty to eat," Lily said, and devoured one herself.

Carlos walked to the flower section and crouched. "Do the flowers follow a pattern, too?"

Lily walked over. "I wait until the flowers produce seeds. See? These have seeds just about ready to drop off. When they drop off, I eat the flowers and plant the seeds. They're not like the pods. With the pods, all that I need to do is put a little bit of poop with seeds on the ground, and the roots will grow into the ground. With the flowers, I need to dig a little, put the seeds in, and cover them with ground again, like farmers on Earth do."

Carlos stood. "I understand. Can I take some flower seeds with me?"

"Yes," Lily said. "With me gone, my parents will plant the rest."

Rhea and Nick signaled the gold and silver dragons. Henrietta and Brutus responded again, flying them toward the ocean.

"There!" Nick said to Brutus. "Land at the top of the rise overlooking the cove."

The dragons landed there. Looking down, Rhea could see grassland extending to the bottom of the rise. Across the cove, she could see the layered drop-off, the lava flat, and the mud volcano.

Nick looked around. "We ought to be able to find a place to put the camera on one of the trees up here."

After walking around, they found a spire tree. Nick strapped the camera around the trunk and checked the view on his smartphone. Once they had made a few adjustments, they felt satisfied that the camera would remain stable.

Rhea hefted the bucket she brought with her, which they had used to carry the camera. "I want to get some of the mud from the mud volcano."

"Think that will help?" Nick asked.

"Remember that pottery course we took between freshman and sophomore years?"

"Sure. Fun."

"The mud that we put around the boulder and had Atlas solidify by fire must be suitable for pottery. We may be able to do something with it."

"Let's try it."

Henrietta not only flew Rhea to the mud volcano, she handled the bucket, got it filled with mud, and then carried it back to Rhea and Nick's.


When Carlos had finished looking over Lily's garden, they flew back to Dan and Carlos's house. Carlos and Lily had a conference about how best to plant the seedlings in Carlos's garden. Then Atlas and Dan joined them and started spreading seeds as well.

Rhea and Nick walked in while they were working.

"Looks as if you're busy," Nick said.

"Planting, yes," Carlos said. "Lily, there, has a solid working knowledge of the plants on this world."

"Good," Rhea said. "We set up the camera and it's working. We were going to put the app on your computer."

"Please do," Dan said. "And do you have a Bluetooth to spare for Lily?"

"Yes, of course," Nick said. "I see she already has a harness."

When Nick and Dan emerged from the clinic, they joined Rhea, who was surveying the effort.

"You know," Rhea said, "I think that Nick and I could put together some tools to make planting and sorting easier. We got some mud from the mud volcano, and I think that, at least, we could make some clay scoops so we can scoop out sections of manure easier."

"In addition," Nick said, "although we couldn't make heavy-duty powered equipment because we're limited as to what solar cells small enough to put on tools can do, we ought to be able to make some mechanized planters or something."

Carlos waved at them. "Good. I have some ideas of what you might put together for us, too. Come on over and we'll discuss the details."

Some time later, Zinnia, Morran, Thalia, and Kieran walked over to the field. Dan was closest to them and saw them first.

"What are you doing?" Zinnia asked.

Dan nodded in Carlos's direction. "We're planting pod seedlings right now. Carlos will see how they grow here, and then use that knowledge to restore the pods to the grassland by the ocean. We think The Terror will then eat the pods."

While he was talking, Lily walked over and stood in front of Zinnia. "I am glad that you were able to bring humans here to help put a stop to The Terror. I talked to my community about it, but they said I was silly."

"We had to talk a long time here before everyone agreed," Thalia said.

"It helped that I grew up in a human home," Zinnia said.

By this time, Carlos had walked over. "Lily has been doing some gardening herself. This is helping us make a better plan."

"Can we help?" Kieran asked.

"Yes, we'll show you," Carlos said.

The next day, after the dragons went out to hunt, Carlos took a stool and a bucket and walked into the cow pen. Dan went with them. The cows had become familiar enough with Dan and Carlos that they did not shy away when approached. The two men petted them and filled a manger with grasses, which the cows turned to. Carlos patted Bessie's side, put down the stool and bucket, and reached for her udder. Bessie took a moment to look at him, then went back to munching. In that way, Carlos was able to get about a quarter of a bucket of milk.

When he was finished, he patted Bessie's side again and handed the bucket to Dan. "Go ahead and analyze this. Whether you find microbes or not, I'm pasteurizing this before we use it."

"Agreed."

Carlos pointed. "I'm going to do some exploring. I'm thinking of starting a private garden, like Lily did, out of sight of the dragons. In particular, I want to see if I can cultivate more flowers. It'll be a surprise treat for them if it works. Sort of a way of thanking them for helping us."

"I won't tell." Dan turned, hearing a sound in the distance.

*Whee-whoo! Whee-whoo!*

Carlos looked around. "What the hell is that?"

"The ground birds have found us."

"Ground birds?"

"Large quail." Dan gestured. "According to Morran, they migrate. They'll start nesting near the streams in the forest. They lay eggs on the ground, too. If they're smaller, they might be better for cooking than the swimmer eggs."

Carlos nodded. "The swimmer egg was good, fine for an omelet, but too large to use in a recipe."

"Let me know if you see them," Dan said. "Got your phone?"

Carlos took it out of a pocket.

"Good. Don't go too far at first. Call me if you need me."

"Will do."

In the next month, they made substantial progress. All four humans and six dragons helped with the planting. The pods grew rapidly, as Lily had predicted.

Dan kept an eye on the tanklets with his camera, occasionally visiting the nest to refill the platter of water. The kits became too large for all of them to fit in the nest. Nona and Win expanded the shelter of branches at the foot of the tree. The kits slept there, between Win and Nona.

When the next heavy rain came, Dan rushed to the computer screen to watch the camera overlooking the ocean. The view included the river. As he and Rhea and Nick had hoped, the water overflowed on the side of the bend, down into the lava tube, and into the ocean. There was no flood.

Atlas and Lily remained near Dan's and Carlos's house and clinic—sleeping in Atlas's shelter—for the most part, though occasionally, after the hunt, they would go visit Lily's parents. Sometimes Atlas would come back alone before sunset, with Lily joining him the next day, and sometimes Atlas and Lily would come back together.

Rhea and Nick used the time to develop solutions. Their mechanized planter did not work well with planting pods, but Carlos found it useful for working on his private garden. They happily loaned the ATV to Carlos for herding the cows back to the enclosure after a day out grazing and for exploring the area for other species of plants.

Making scoops, however, turned out to be a success. Henrietta, Brutus, and their friends were happy to supply Rhea and Nick with all the mud they needed. Zinnia and Morran helped by firing the mud safely in the fire pit to solidify it, and trying out the various designs until they found one that was a perfect fit for dragon hands. After watching Nick and Rhea at work, Zinnia and Morran tried making the scoops themselves. Their results proved to be even better than Rhea and Nick's. At that point, the dragons—not only Zinnia and Morran, but other dragons as well—took over production until they felt they had enough.

One evening, when Dan and Carlos came over for dinner, Rhea said, "I was thinking about our discussion earlier about not being colonizers."

"I don't think we have been," Dan said.

"Agreed," Carlos said.

"Yes," Rhea said, "but we've just taught the dragons how to make pottery, something they wouldn't have known if we hadn't come here."

"I'm not so sure," Carlos said. "Lily reasoned out gardening, if not agriculture, all by herself."

"We haven't tried to teach them anything they haven't shown any interest in," Nick said, "and we haven't invented anything that isn't in service of fulfilling our job description."

"There's rerouting the flood waters," Rhea said.

"That's on me," Dan said. "Still, even though I'm not a geologist, I think the flooding was caused by changes in the terrain from the lava flat, and we simply restored the flow to what it was before."

"As we are restoring the growth that the lava flat destroyed," Carlos added.

"I see your point," Rhea said.

"It never would have been that the dragon communities would have been unaffected by us being here," Dan said. "What I mentioned before still stands: we can only leave as small a footprint as possible."

"They've already been affected by humans, with so many dragons growing up on Earth, and remembering what they saw," Carlos said.

"And they've been doing that for over a century," Nick said.

Rhea nodded. "You're right about that."

When Carlos and Lily felt that the pods they had planted first had fully ripened, Carlos picked one, took a knife, and opened it up.

"Looks good," Dan said.

"Can we have a bite?" Nick asked.

"Sure." Carlos cut pieces for each of them and passed them around.

Meanwhile, the dragons each plucked a ripe pod and munched on it.

"Yes, they're ripe," Lily said after swallowing.

Carlos took a deep breath. "Good. Next step. We need to call a meeting of the dragons."

"What help do you need?" Kieran asked.

"We need to ask as many dragons who are willing to do so to go to the ocean and poop in the grassland next to the lava flow," Carlos said. "If we can get enough dragons, we also need for them to poop on the rise overlooking the ocean. When the seedlings start to spout, we need to start scooping them up and spreading them around."

"Atlas and I will show them how," Lily said.

"Kieran and I will help," Thalia said.

"We have enough tools suitable for dragons as well as humans," Rhea added.

"I'll talk to the dragon assembly," Zinnia said, "but Morran and I aren't ready to go back to the ocean yet."

"You won't have to," Dan said. "We should have enough volunteers from the dragon community, based on the help we've had so far."

"Once the dragons know how to plant the pod seedlings," Carlos said, "we need ambassadors among the dragons to go to other dragon communities and tell them how to do it."

"The sandgliders are everywhere dragons are, I presume," Dan said, "since you all lay eggs back on Earth."

"That is true," Kieran said.

"What Carlos and I were thinking," Dan said, "is to send one set of dragon ambassadors due east, and the other set due west. That way, the ambassadors only have to cover half of the world and they'll get the word out faster. Hopefully, everyone will have pods planted and sprouting before birthing season."

"The dragons we send out will have to be past the age of mating," Kieran said. "Or else they'll have to settle down."

"We'll tell the assembly that," Morran said.

"How long does it take for a dragon to go around the globe?" Rhea asked.

"From the dragons who have visited in the past," Kieran said. "They should be able to reach half the globe well before birthing season."

"How soon can you call an assembly?" Dan asked.

"How about now?" Kieran said.

"If you'll think they'll come," Dan said.

"They'll come," Thalia said. "Everyone wants to see an end to The Terror killing us."

Kieran raised his head and trilled. The other dragons joined them. Dan heard answering trills in the distance.

Kieran and Thalia led the way to a large, flat, bare area. Dan saw dragons flying in, landing, and gathering in an orderly manner. The humans stood with their dragon family at the edge of the flat. The entering dragons faced them.

After dragons stopped flying in, Thalia and Zinnia stepped forward.

"We need your help in planting food for the sandgliders—The Terror—by the ocean," Thalia said.

"This will stop The Terror from preying on us." Zinnia turned. "Carlos, Dan's mate, and Lily, Atlas's future mate, will tell us what we need to do."

Carlos and Lily stepped forward and explained the plan.

"How many dragons do you need to poop over there?" Brutus asked.

"We don't need all dragons there, but it will be better if we have many dragons helping," Carlos said. "Lily and I will be there after the hunt tomorrow and direct you."

"Then after that, you need us to plant?" Henrietta said.

"Once the seeds start sprouting, yes," Carlos said.

Zinnia gestured to her dragon family. "We have all been helping the humans plant near the house of Dan and Carlos. We can show you how to do it."

"After that," Zinnia said, "we'll need dragons who are not mating and have learned how to plant to visit the other dragon communities and tell them what to do. The humans say if one dragon goes east and the other west, we can visit all of the dragon communities before birthing season."

Duchess and Rock moved to the front. "We will go in one direction," Duchess said. "They will listen to senior dragons."

Titan also stepped forward. "I feel rested after emerging from hibernation. I will go in the other direction."

Icarus lifted his head. "I can go with Titan."

"Good," Zinnia said. "Remember to poop by the ocean tomorrow, and we will call when we need you to start planting."

"Are you sure you're ready to go to the ocean again?" Henrietta asked.

"Morran and I won't be going to the ocean," Zinnia said, "not yet. But we will continue to help the humans here and spread the word to you. No dragon who wants to stay away from the ocean has to go. The humans and the rest of my family can direct everyone who wants to go at the ocean."

"That is a good plan," Titan said.

Dan heard trills that seemed to be sounds of agreement among the dragons. "Thank you for your help," he said when the assembly was quiet again.

"We thank all of you humans for helping us," Icarus said.

Kieran said, "Remember, tomorrow," and flew away. The other dragons seemed to take that as a dismissal and took off.

The next day, when Lily and Atlas returned from the hunt, Lily approached Carlos. "Atlas and I already dropped our poop. Carlos can come with me. The sky will be crowded. It will be better if Atlas and Dan stay here."

"Of course," Dan said as Carlos climbed up on Lily's back.

After Lily and Carlos left, Dan turned to Atlas. "I can watch through the camera in the clinic house. You can see the computer picture through the door, can't you?"

"Yes," Atlas said, "but I can get a better view if I just perch on the cliffs overlooking the ocean."

"You mean at the top of the waterfall there?"

"Yes."

"I'll see you later, then."

Atlas flew away.

As Dan worked through the day, he watched as Lily directed traffic. By dinnertime, the grassland next to the lava flat and the hills overlooking the ocean cove were dotted with dragon manure.

Dan had supper started when Lily and Atlas landed. He went outside and met them as Carlos slid off.

"Step one complete," Carlos said.

# CHAPTER 19

A few days later, the seeds began to sprout. Zinnia trilled a call for dragon volunteers. This time, at the ocean site, Atlas and Dan, Lily and Carlos, Thalia and Kieran, as well as Nick and Rhea, each demonstrated to a group of dragons how to scoop the seedlings and set them on the ground for planting, using either their hands, or the tools that Rhea and Nick had made and adapted for dragon use.

Again, by evening, the area had been satisfactorily planted.

When Atlas, Lily, Dan, and Carlos returned home, Carlos said, "Step two complete. Now we wait and see how much of it grows."

Another month went by. The humans became entirely self-sufficient. The cow provided enough milk for them to have milk, butter, and cheese. Carlos had planted grain separately from the pod field, providing enough flour for bread and other baked goods. Sometimes they followed Arthur's recipes, other times Carlos's culinary experiments produced tasty results. The tubers and pods were good vegetables and fruits. The ground birds proved to be good egg providers; the humans left sufficient eggs for them to hatch offspring. Swimmers and occasional ground bird, or, rarely, the alpacas or cattle, were sources for meat.

They all kept an eye on the pod growth. Zinnia and Morran still stayed away from the ocean, but Atlas and Lily went there regularly, as did other dragons. Carlos and Dan frequently checked their camera view; Rhea and Nick did the same.

Rhea used this quieter interval to spend more personal time with Nick. Neither humans nor dragons worked nonstop; they took frequent breaks with their various tasks. At times, Rhea and Nick would walk hand-in-hand through the grasslands or the forest. Zinnia and Morran pointed out safe areas or flew above them as they walked in case they encountered hazards.

In addition, Rhea also had the opportunity to spend more time with Zinnia. She had wanted to comfort Zinnia on the loss of her grandparents and deepen their friendship. They conversed extensively with Zinnia lying on the ground and Rhea leaning back against Zinnia's side. On these occasions, Nick and Morran went off by themselves; Nick told Rhea that he wanted to explore the dragon world more extensively.

One day, Nick took Rhea by the hand. "I want to show you something."

"What is it?" Rhea asked.

Nick smiled. "You'll see."

He led her through the forest. Zinnia and Morran walked a discreet distance behind him.

Looking ahead, Rhea saw something glittering through the trees and leaves.

She pointed. "Do you see that? It looks like the trees are sparkling."

"Yes, that's what I wanted to show you."

They emerged into a clearing. Dan and Carlos stood at the edge of the glade with Atlas and Lily.

Directing her gaze up and around, Rhea saw that the trees had been decorated with gold chains and jeweled necklaces. Sunlight glistened on the curved gold and faceted stones.

"How beautiful," Rhea said, as she slowly turned around a second time. "Is this Minerva's work?"

She looked down to see Nick kneeling at her feet. He raised a hand toward her.

"Rhea, you are the light of my world and I want to be with you for the rest of my life. Will you marry me?" He held up a ring.

Rhea smiled, laughed merrily, put her hands to her mouth, and nodded her head. Lowering her hands, she said, "Yes, of course I'll marry you, Nick."

Nick stood and took Rhea's hand. He slid the ring on her finger. "I bought this on Earth and brought it with me just in case."

Rhea raised the ring to look at the details. She saw a gold serpentine dragon whose head met the tail. Two sapphires had been set at the eyes. "It's lovely, thank you."

Nick rose and gazed intently into her eyes. "I love you, Rhea."

Rhea moved her hands to Nick's waist. She returned his gaze. "I love you, too, Nick."

They sealed their promise with a kiss.

When they parted, Dan and Carlos hurried over. They patted Nick on the back and shook Rhea's hand.

"Congratulations, Nick," Dan said. "Best wishes, Rhea."

"Yes, congratulations and best wishes, you two," Carlos said.

"Did we do it right?" Atlas asked.

Nick turned to him. "Yes, you all did it right." He turned back to Rhea. "Minerva was more than cooperative in lending us decorations from the hoard. Carlos, Dan, and the dragons helped adorn the trees."

Rhea looked up again and nodded. "It's stunning. I love it."

Dan held up his smartphone. "Take a picture?"

"Yes," Rhea said.

She and Nick posed for photos, by themselves and with the dragons.

"It's good that you have pleased your future mate, Nick," Morran said, "but it seems a lot of work just to ask a question."

Zinnia turned to him. "Humans like to play when they do important things. It's fun."

Nick faced Morran. "Just humans doing human things, Morran. Just as dragons do dragon things."

"We are always happy to help," Morran said.


A few weeks later, after checking the ocean view, Dan said to Carlos, "The pods by the ocean are looking ripe. I want to go over there and see if we can tempt a sandglider with one."

"Good idea," Carlos said. "I want to check on the growth, too."

After the hunt that morning, Atlas and Lily were willing to take Dan and Carlos to the lava flat. What they found, from the air, was that the pod vines had spread out and grown over the lava flat, leaving little clearing space for the dragons to land.

"Set down in the sand near the lava flat," Dan suggested.

The dragons did so. Dan and Carlos slid off and started walking along the length of the flat, stepping carefully over the vines.

"The pods at the end of the vine are hanging down toward the sand," Carlos said.

"That's good, isn't it?" Dan said.

Carlos nodded and crouched. "Look here. The vines are putting down roots in the cracks along the lava flat."

"Also good, right?" Dan said.

Carlos stood. "Right. Anchoring on the lava flat just spreads the pods wider." He slowly made a 360 degree turn. "Yes. The grassland next to the flat, and the rise overlooking the cove, are amply covered with vines and ripening pods."

Dan took out a pocket knife, bent over, and cut a pod from a vine. "Let's see if we can tempt a sandglider."

After they joined the dragons back on the sand, Dan turned from side to side. He spotted a sandglider on its way from the shore to the nesting area and placed a pod in its path.

The sandglider scuttled around it.

"It didn't even pause," Carlos said.

"Maybe not hungry right now?" Dan said. "Ate a fish that washed up on the shore?"

"Well, we can keep watch at home," Carlos said.

They turned to Atlas and Lily, who were facing upwards.

Four dragons approached and landed near them: Roc, Duchess, Titan, and Icarus.

"We were talking," Titan said. "We think we should go soon."

"Yes," Duchess said, "we know how to plant now."

"Several dragons have made their own gardens," Icarus said. "There is less pushing and shoving now on the mountainsides to get the pods."

"Dragons have asked me to show them how to make gardens near their homes," Lily added. "They're leaving the pods here to grow for the sandgliders."

"Rhea, Nick, Zinnia, and Morran showed us how to make scoops," Roc said.

Dan nodded. "Yes, you can start anytime." He turned to the pod on the sand. "We aren't going to disrupt the sandgliders just to make a test, but I was hoping that I'd see one come for a pod."

"They're already nibbling on the pods here." Titan said.

"They are?" Carlos said.

Titan walked toward the lava flat and then closer to the sandglider nesting area. Titan pulled back the vines at the edge. "See?"

Dan and Carlos moved closer. They saw mostly-eaten pods, whose remains still clung to the vines.

Dan turned to Titan. "You're right."

Atlas pointed. "See over there."

Dan leaned so he could see around Titan, gasped, and winced. Three sandgliders had settled next to the pod on the sand, using their pincers to rip off pieces of pod and stuff them into their mouths.

Carlos grabbed Dan by the upper arm. "You okay?"

"Yeah." Dan took a deep breath. "It's just that seeing sandgliders together reminds me of the cloud."

"You said there was no danger unless their nest was disturbed?" Titan queried.

"Dragons have been coming here for days and days without seeing The Terror," Duchess added.

Dan nodded. "That's true. It's just that the memory of seeing the cloud is very strong."

"Some dragons feel the same way," Duchess said.

"That is why we feel we need to go and waste no time," Titan said.

"Of course," Dan said. "Go whenever you feel ready."

The next day, after the hunt, Atlas and Lily approached Dan and Carlos.

"Come fly with us," Atlas said. "It's time to say goodbye to the dragon ambassadors."

Once in the air, Dan could see what seemed to be the whole community of dragons circling the area. He also saw Rhea with Zinnia and Nick with Morran in the distance.

The dragons trilled what seemed to Dan to be a hopeful tune. Probably "good luck" or "bon voyage" he guessed. Then he saw Roc and Duchess head off in one direction, and Titan and Icarus fly off in the opposite direction.

"Step three accomplished," Carlos said.

With the dragon ambassadors gone, and the pods showing healthy growth, all they needed to do was wait for mating season, which was approaching. Checking the camera on the tanklet nest, Dan saw that the kits had grown almost to the size of Win and Nona. The single golden and silver dragons on the verge of mating seemed to be flirting? Courting? Checking out who among the prospective mates would be the best match, Dan guessed. Atlas and Lily, as well as Zinnia and Morran, spent more time snuggling and flying together.

One day, after the hunt, Lily stood at the edge of the garden with Dan and Carlos. The pods were growing very large, and Carlos wanted to check them to be sure they were not becoming overripe or rotting. Atlas had been sent to the ocean to bring back a large pod from there.

Cutting one open, Carlos said, "Still looks good, looks fresh."

"We usually eat them before they get to that size," Lily said.

A huge sonic boom coming from the ocean thundered in the distance.

"That's Atlas," Lily said, and unfolded her wings.

"Wait!" Dan said. "Let me check the camera first."

"Not The Terror again?" Carlos said.

Dan ran in and watched the ocean camera view. He saw Atlas right away, with a smaller dragon who seemed to be struggling to fly, trapped in a net. And...?

"Humans?" Dan said.

Lily looked inside the clinic at the screen. "A dragon has come from Earth. Humans have come with it. They've brought human things with them."

"They must have used the net so they could come with the dragon," Carlos said.

"They have guns, and backpacks, and a dirt bike." Dan activated his Bluetooth. "Atlas, what's going on?"

"Humans came with a dragon," Atlas said. "The dragon is trying to get away but is tangled in a net. I'm taking it off."

"They're shooting at Atlas," Carlos said.

"They can't hurt him," Dan said.

"They can't," Lily agreed. "Humans tried to hurt me on Earth with those."

"Atlas," Dan said. "Grab the things in the humans' hands and toss them into the volcano."

"I have to protect the young dragon first," Atlas said.

"Help is on the way." Dan rushed out of the clinic. "Lily, can you take us both?"

"Henrietta can take one," Lily said.

Looking up, Dan saw a number of dragons in the air, rushing toward the ocean. Zinnia with Rhea, and Morran with Nick, were among them. Henrietta landed near them.

Dan called Rhea and Nick on the Bluetooth. "Humans with guns. Tell Zinnia and Morran to stay out of firing range. They can't hurt the dragons, but they can hurt us."

"Will do," Rhea said.

"I'll go with Lily, if that's all right," Dan said to Carlos.

"Come with me," Henrietta said to Carlos.

Once in the air, Lily and Henrietta flew toward the ocean quickly.

Rhea and Nick stood near the fire pit where Zinnia and Morran fired their latest pottery experiments.

They heard a dragon's roar and turned in that direction.

"Young dragon in trouble," Zinnia said. "We have to go."

"That's in the direction of the ocean," Rhea said.

"I know," Zinnia said, "but we have to help the young dragon."

Rhea and Nick quickly climbed on Zinnia's and Morran's backs. The dragons took off. Other dragons joined them, flying in the same direction.

Rhea put a hand to her helmet, listening to Dan's message. "There are humans with guns," she said to the dragons. "You need to keep us away from them. They can hurt us."

"That should be easy," Morran said. "We want to take the young dragon away as fast as possible. That should keep us away from the other humans."

"Those dragons over there," Zinnia said, pointing with her head, "must be the young one's parents."

Rhea looked and saw one large golden and one large silver dragon taking the lead, with Kieran and Thalia flying close by.

The ocean came into view. Five humans stood on shore, guns in their hands.

"Can you tell the other dragons to take the things in their hands away and toss them into the volcano?" Rhea said.

Zinnia and Morran let out loud trills.

Rhea could see the young dragon, tangled in a net. Atlas burned it off and wedged himself underneath the youngster, helping the smaller dragon get into the air. Once in the air, the parents flew straight toward their offspring, escorting the newcomer away.

Meanwhile, the humans with guns, putting distance between themselves and fire-breathing Atlas, took aim at the airborne dragons and started firing. Zinnia and Morran flew out of the line of fire. The closer dragons, undaunted by the bullets, landed right in front of the humans, wrenched the guns away, and flew straight to the volcano, dropping the weapons into the lava.

Two of the shooters reached into a large pack and removed a cylinder.

When they took it out, Rhea said to Nick. "What's that? A bazooka?"

"Either that or a grenade launcher?" Nick said. "A missile launcher?"

"Where the hell did they get those?" Rhea said.

"Morran and Zinnia," Nick said. "Tell the dragons to watch for the humans firing something out of the cylinder and to get out of the way."

The two dragons trilled.

Dan's voice came through the Bluetooth. "All dragons! Fly as high as you can!"

A projectile emerged from the cylinder, going directly toward a hovering dragon, who swerved out of the way and flew upward. The missile landed near the lava flat and exploded with a boom, shaking the ground. Rhea could feel the edge of the shock wave.

As Zinnia and Morran ascended, Rhea saw Lily and Atlas, directed by Dan, hit the attacking humans from behind, knocking them to the ground. Atlas grabbed the cylinder and flew to the volcano.

Rhea heard a buzzing sound and looked around.

"Rhea, it's The Terror!" Nick yelled.

Rhea turned to the sand flat, where a cloud of sandgliders had assembled. They rose from the beach. Rhea expected them to chase the fleeing dragons, or head toward the humans on the shore, but instead, the cloud dipped and spread over the field of pods. Perhaps it was her imagination, but Rhea felt she could almost hear a crunching sound as pods were consumed. The Terror ate its way through the pods in the grassland, lifted again—Rhea winced in anticipation of an attack—then moved in an arc back to the sands, disassembled into sandglider opponents, dove back into the sand and disappeared.

"Success!" Rhea heard Carlos say through the Bluetooth.

Meanwhile, the humans on the beach, oblivious to the danger, reorganized. One started the dirt bike and headed toward the dragon community. The four others ran across the grassland, in the direction of the forest.

"We'll get the guy on the dirt bike," Nick said. "Dan, you and Carlos go after the others."

"Will do," Dan said.

"Morran and Zinnia," Nick said, "follow the bike."

The two dragons turned. By the time they descended, the bike and its rider had disappeared into the forest. Fortunately, however, the engine made a lot of noise. They closed the distance.

"I see the human," Zinnia said. "He's a big one, with hair on his face."

"We can't go down and grab him," Morran said. "Too many trees in the way."

"Just follow," Nick said. "He'll have to come into a clearing some time."

They followed the bike for miles, flying over the machine and matching its pace. Turning to the side, Rhea saw other dragons flanking them. If they needed help, they would have it.

"Do you think he knows he's headed toward the lake?" Nick asked Rhea.

"No, I just think he's just taking whatever easy path he sees in front of him, hoping he can outrun us."

"Ha!" Nick said. "The engine will stall before the dragons tire."

The forest eventually gave way to softer ground near the lake. The bike skidded, and the rider fell flat on the ground. Nearby, the swimmers, apparently panicked by the noise, rushed to the shore and, like a stampeding herd, ran toward their nests. As the rider slowly rose to stand, the loudly cackling swimmers knocked him over. He fell to the ground, covering his head, while the edge of the herd passed by and over his legs.

When the swimmers had gone, Rhea and Nick directed the dragons to land. They did so, in front of the rider, who struggled to his feet.

Nick stepped forward. "You okay?"

The bedraggled man faced Nick squarely but said nothing.

"What's your name, buddy?" Nick asked.

"Not telling you," he said angrily.

"Well, NotTellingYou," Nick said, "you're going back to where you came from."

"Says who?"

Nick jerked his thumb up and backwards. "Me, my girlfriend, and my dragon friends."

"I'm not afraid of you." He drew out a gun.

Zinnia's tail lashed out and knocked it from his hand.

Skipper, who had landed nearby, picked it up. "Throw it in the volcano?"

"Yes," Nick said. Skipper took off.

"That cost a lot of money," the man said.

"Too bad," Nick said. "You should have thought of that before you came."

"So sue us." Rhea snapped her fingers. "Oh, that's right. Earth courts have no jurisdiction here."

The man turned and began to run. Brutus caught and held him.

"We'd better blindfold him before going back," Rhea said.

"Why?" Nick asked.

"Tell you later." She took out a scarf from a pocket and tied it around the man's eyes. "Can you carry him back to the ocean?" she asked Brutus.

"Yes."

Rhea spotted Hunter nearby and pointed to the dirt bike. "Can you take the bike?"

"Yes."

"Let's go, then," Rhea said.

Two of the four humans ran faster than the others. Henrietta and Lily caught up with the ones lagging behind and grabbed them.

Dan and Carlos slid off their backs and turned to Atlas, who had landed nearby.

"Atlas," Dan said, "can you go over and bring some of those vines without pods?"

"Yes."

When Atlas returned, Dan and Carlos tied up the two men and made them sit in the sand.

"What are you going to do to us?" one asked.

"You're going back home, once we catch up to your friends," Dan said.

"We aren't going back without the treasure," another said.

"We'll share it with you," said the first man.

Dan threw back his head and laughed.

"No, there really is treasure," the first man said.

"Everyone knows dragons have treasure," the second man said.

"Who says we're interested?" Carlos said.

"Then what are you doing here?" the first man said.

"What are your names?" Dan asked.

"I'm Forrest." The first man nodded to the second. "And this is Andy."

"Well, Forrest and Andy," Dan said, "we're here because we're scientists, and all the treasure we want is knowledge."

"Bull," Andy said.

"Think what you want," Carlos said. "We're going after your other two friends."

Leaving Forrest and Andy under the watchful eye of DeeDee, Dan climbed up on Atlas and Carlos climbed up on Lily. When they took to the air, Henrietta and Gus followed them.

"Fly low and as slowly as you can," Dan said. "They can't have gone far."

As Dan predicted, they had not gone very far until they heard cries of help. They landed near a grove of trees.

After Dan and Carlos slid off the dragons, they found themselves face-to-face with two men entangled in clutching vines.

"Get us outta here!" one said.

"We'll share the treasure with you," the other said.

Carlos chuckled, then took a breath and faced Dan. "Sorry."

Dan smiled. "It is funny, isn't it?"

"Not funny!" the first man called. "Get us outta here."

"The vines grabbed us and pulled us in and we can't break free," said the other.

"What are your names?" Dan asked.

"I'm Elmer and he's Fred," Elmer said.

"Well, Fred and Elmer," Dan said, "the dragons here are going to pull you out. Then they'll grab you—gently—and take you back to your friends. I suggest you keep quiet and don't try to get away."

Elmer and Fred looked warily at Henrietta and Gus as they parted the vines and then pulled them out. They made surprised noises as the dragons flew them back to the shore. Atlas and Lily, with Dan and Carlos, followed.

When they arrived, Dan pointed at Fred and Elmer. "Sit."

They sat next to Forrest and Andy, still tied up.

"Where's Hiram?" Forrest asked.

"If that's your remaining friend," Dan said, "he should be here shortly."

Carlos looked up and pointed. "There they are."

Zinnia and Morran arrived with Rhea and Nick. Their dragon escort set down the dirt bike on the sand, and Hiram next to Fred and Elmer. Rhea dismounted and took the blindfold from Hiram.

Dan crossed his arms in front of him. "Good. Now that you're all here, let me tell you what happens next. The dragons are going to take you back to Earth. Don't even think of coming back. The four humans you see here..." He pointed to himself, Carlos, Rhea, and Nick, "...are the only humans here. The only humans who have lasted more than a few days here are humans who have dragons watching out for them. That's us. That's emphatically not you."

"What about the treasure?" Elmer said.

"What treasure?" Nick asked.

"The treasure that's supposed to be here," Fred said.

"Who told you there was treasure here?" Carlos asked.

"The book," Andy said.

"What book?" Carlos asked.

"The Arthur book," Andy said. "Everyone's talking about it."

"Oh, my gosh, they must have published it," Rhea said.

Dan rubbed his forehead. "Yes. The university press. From the copy the history department has." He put his hand down. "Look, guys, as you've already seen, this place isn't brimming with treasure. If you don't know where the stashes are, you'll probably die before you find it. Besides, the dragons aren't going to let you get it. So you might as well go home."

"We ain't leaving," Elmer said.

"Oh, yes, you are," Rhea said.

"See all these dragons around you? They're making sure you aren't going anyplace else but back to Earth." When Dan finished speaking, he heard the sound of wings and saw a great golden dragon landing behind him.

"One of the little one's parents," Rhea said softly.

"Aurora," Zinnia added.

"What about our guns?" Hiram said.

"The dragons have determined that you were using them in aggression against the members of their community, confiscated them, and destroyed them," Dan said. "They're the law here. I suggest you be happy that you're returning in one piece."

Rhea pointed behind her. "Did you see that swarm that looked like black bees over there a while ago?"

"Yes," Forrest said. "So what?"

"That swarm could have killed you in seconds had we not diverted them," Nick said. "We've seen that swarm kill before. It isn't pretty."

"Not to mention all the other dangers here, like those vines Fred and Elmer were caught in," Carlos added.

"I presume you noticed the pile of bones at the bottom of the tree," Dan said.

"Step back," Atlas said.

Dan could see that Atlas was addressing him and the other humans. They moved aside.

Aurora approached the five humans and glared at them. Dan had not seen a dragon glare before and was glad he was not the object of her attention.

"You used my offspring," she said in a low voice that sounded like the rumble of distant thunder.

"We didn't mean to," Elmer said.

"Don't let it eat us," Forrest pleaded.

Zinnia moved next to Aurora. "We aren't going to eat you, silly humans. But we are taking you back, and Aurora is going to lead us because she knows the place where her offspring was."

Dan approached Forrest and Andy and cut the vines binding them. He took a step back. "Bye!"

With that, five dragons each grabbed a human, a sixth grabbed the dirt bike, and they huddled next to Aurora. They disappeared.

"How long will they be gone?" Dan asked Atlas.

"Not long," Atlas said.

Nick turned to Rhea. "Now I know why you wanted to blindfold that guy. He could have seen Minerva's hoard through the air."

Rhea nodded. "Not that it would have made any difference anyway, since they know about Arthur's book."

All seven dragons reappeared.

Aurora faced the humans and other dragons. "We need to call a dragon meeting. We need to bring back all the hatchlings from Earth. Now."

# CHAPTER 20

Aurora lifted her head and let out a trill. The other dragons joined her. Soon, they could see dragons flying toward them, settling on the sand.

When they were assembled, Aurora raised her head. "We know from Minerva that humans have come here before, holding dragons who have gone to Earth briefly and then returned here. We know that humans have held on to our hatchlings before. We just take them back. But this is different. This time humans have used our hatchlings to try to destroy our home. We cannot allow this to continue. We must bring back our hatchlings now." Aurora turned to Dan, Carlos, Rhea, and Nick. "They would be safe here now. We saw that The Terror did not attack us when they could have."

Dan raised a hand. "What Aurora said is true. Humans will try to come back. There are humans who want to protect dragons on Earth. But there are also humans who will try to use the hatchings to get here and steal."

Carlos said. "I need to get in the air to take a look at what The Terror did before I can say anything. Lily?"

Lily stepped toward Carlos.

Carlos climbed on her back. "This will not take long."

They flew up into the air, hovered for maybe a minute, then landed.

Carlos slid off. "Yes. The Terror consumed maybe a quarter of the pods in the area, maybe a third. They'll grow back quickly. We have pods still in the process of ripening. There will be plenty come birthing season, but we can't have violent humans coming back here and constantly disturbing the sandgliders, or they'll exhaust our supply. More to the point, the other dragon areas don't have pods planted yet. If destructive humans come there, they won't have any defenses yet."

Kieran raised his head. "We have to send dragons out again."

"We just sent dragons out," Brutus said.

"Those were for showing dragons how to plant," Zinnia said. "We need other dragons to tell parents to bring back their hatchlings as soon as they can. The four we sent out will have to linger at communities to show them what to do. Our next ambassadors will have to tell them to bring back their hatchlings and move on. They will be quicker."

"Yes, we must do that," Minerva said.

"I'll go," said a large golden dragon.

"I'll go in the opposite direction," said a large silver dragon. "I'm past mating, too."

"We only need two, and we're grateful for your help," Kieran said.

"Start now," Aurora said.

The two volunteers took off.

"The parents among us must retrieve their hatchlings, today," Aurora said. "Don't wait."

More dragons disappeared.

"We need to go back to Earth and spread the word there," Dan said. "There are already protections for dragons, that's why Lily's humans were able to get help for her there so quickly. But more must be done. I'm sure once I get in touch with the Dragon Appreciation Society, there will be humans all over Earth watching hatchlings to be sure they're not taken advantage of."

"We still would like you here," Thalia said. "At least through birthing season. To be sure The Terror no longer preys on us."

"You are nice humans," Minerva said. "We would miss you if you were gone."

Dan heard what seemed to be sounds of agreement.

"Thank you," Dan said. "We like you, too. But I should go back to Earth, tomorrow if possible, to spread the word to leave the hatchlings alone."

"How does this sound?" Carlos said. "We humans need to talk about what we have to do, and we'll talk to the dragons around us about what you need us to do and work out a plan."

Again, they heard sounds of agreement.

In the air above them, pairs of dragons, with juvenile dragons between them, began to appear.

The dragons on the ground crooned sounds of welcome.

\* \* \*

At dinner that evening, the four humans sat around a table at Rhea and Nick's house.

"It's going to get boisterous around here," Dan said. "Hatchlings are bundles of energy who constantly want to play."

"I didn't notice that with Zinnia," Rhea said. "She was generally relaxed. In fact, she slept a lot."

Dan nodded. "Because she was growing. The young hatchlings do, too, but when they're awake, they're a handful. Zinnia wasn't because she was about your age, seven years, when she came to your house."

"The terrible twos," Carlos said with a smile.

"That's probably why the dragon parents want them to stay on Earth until they grow wings," Dan said. "The hatchlings would be prone to wander off exploring, just like human toddlers do, and go to places where The Terror would find them during birthing season."

"Any idea why The Terror is out during birthing season?" Carlos said.

"It's probably their birthing season, too, and they need the energy to reproduce," Dan said. "Just eating random fish washed up on the beach just isn't enough."

"I think we've fulfilled our employment contract," Nick said.

"Yes, it's time to talk about phase two," Dan said.

"Nick and I want to make wedding arrangements," Rhea said. "Even for just family—which includes you two, of course—that would take around ten days. We'd like a honeymoon in New Zealand, which would be another seven to ten days."

"We can stay for mating season, which I understand is in the next couple of days," Nick said. "Then birthing season is a whole season after that, maybe two to three months?"

Dan nodded. "That's my understanding, as well."

"So we could get married in the interval," Rhea said.

"We don't know what we're going to do after birthing season," Nick said. "Rhea and I have talked about having six months on, six months off, depending on what the dragons want."

"It is nice here," Rhea said. "I don't have to keep my keys in my hand when I walk alone or watch for someone who might be stalking me."

"I know exactly what you mean," Carlos said. "Dan and I haven't had anyone tell us to go back to where we came from or tell us we speak good English."

"Or tell us we're going to hell," Dan added.

"We haven't made any definite plans, either," Carlos said. "My land reclamation assignment is over, and I don't have another job lined up."

"I put in my notice at the university's veterinary clinic before coming here," Dan said. "They'd probably take me back at any time, but I'm not in a hurry to do so."

"In any case, other than Dan going back for an afternoon to spread the word about the hatchlings," Carlos said, "we thought we'd stay through birthing season, and then talk about where we go from there."

Nick nodded. "That's probably what we'll do, too."

After the hunt the next day, Dan and Rhea asked the dragons to pose with them for pictures. They told the dragons it would help them get assistance for the hatchlings. Since the engagement pictures showed items from the hoard, the humans felt it was better to take pictures of dragons without that in the background. Nick took photos of Dan and Carlos with Atlas and Lily. Carlos took photos of Rhea and Nick with Zinnia, Morran, Kieran, and Thalia.

Rhea and Dan then left promptly for Earth with Zinnia. Zinnia returned by herself to await their signal.

When Dan and Rhea returned with Zinnia, they found the other dragons waiting with Nick and Carlos.

"Just in time for dinner," Nick said.

"Did you succeed in telling the humans to leave the hatchlings alone?" Thalia asked.

"Yes," Dan said. "The Dragon Appreciation Society sent an alert to its members worldwide. They'll keep watch on the hatchlings until their parents come for them."

After they sat down to dinner, Carlos said, "I was wondering why the dragons here couldn't gather all the hatchings on Earth to return them to their parents. Kieran and Thalia said dragons could locate only those on Earth they had a connection to.

Without that connection, they'd only appear at a random place on Earth."

"So, dragon parents could only find their own hatchlings," Nick said.

Dan nodded.

"Was it very difficult to get their attention?" Nick asked.

"No, we contacted the Dragon Appreciation Society right away and they wanted to talk to us," Rhea said. "Seems that the would-be treasure hunters put out a story of mean old dragons that nearly killed them and they barely escaped with their lives. The Dragon Society members were skeptical and eager to hear our side of the story."

"We even got on television," Dan said. "The segment went viral very quickly."

"Dan and I emphasized that it is true that it's dangerous here for humans," Rhea said, "but that it's not the dragons that would do us harm."

"Yes, I think we got the point across that no one should even think of coming here without an invitation," Dan said.

"The Dragon Appreciation Society quickly put together a 'Save the Hatchlings' campaign," Rhea said. "So in addition to the Dragon Appreciation Society watching out for them, local law enforcement and animal protection societies will be on alert, too."

The next day, Dan got up before Carlos and fixed breakfast. When Carlos joined him, he said, "Did you hear swimmers this morning?"

"Come to think of it, no," Dan said.

"It's awfully quiet." Carlos swung around in his chair and looked out the windows. "No animal noises whatsoever."

Dan slid back his seat and stood. "No sign of Atlas or Lily, either."

The two of them left the breakfast table and walked outside. Strolling around the grounds, they saw the cow and calf in the enclosure, peacefully munching fodder. Atlas and Lily were nowhere to be seen.

"Let me check the clinic's cameras," Dan said.

When they looked at the camera view of the tanklet nest, they saw no tanklets.

"Maybe they left for the stream early?" Carlos said.

"Nothing on the ocean view, either," Dan said. "No sandgliders, no seaskimmers, not even the local sea urchins or starfish."

Dan took out his smartphone and texted Rhea. *Heard from Zinnia or Morran today?*

*No. Kieran and Thalia came over and asked if we needed anything. When we said we didn't, they said it was mating season and we wouldn't see Zinnia or Morran today or tomorrow. Nick and I are just going to hang out together and talk about wedding plans.*

*Thanks and good luck.* Dan closed the phone and turned to Carlos. "We're on our own today."

Carlos busied himself with the cows, the large garden, and his private garden, which he told Dan was coming along nicely, though Dan had not seen it yet.

Dan spent the day in the clinic, analyzing data and outlining a paper he hoped to take back to Earth for publication in veterinary journals.

After dinner, Carlos and Dan sat outside, watching the stars, and drank cocktails. It was still breathtakingly quiet.

Soon after they turned in, they were awakened by a cacophonous racket. Squawking. Quacking. Trumpeting. Growling. Roaring. Crowing. Bellowing. Other sounds Dan could not even identify. The windows in the house vibrated from the clamor.

Carlos sat up in bed and reached for the noise-cancelling headphones. "What the hell is that?" he shouted.

Dan shouted back, "Is every animal on the planet mating at once?" He reached for his own set of headphones.

"Sounds that way." Carlos put on the headphones and snuggled under the blankets again.

Dan made sure his own headphones were secure before placing his head back on the pillow.

In the morning, Dan carefully pulled aside one of the headphones. Quiet again.

After breakfast, Carlos and Dan checked the clinic cameras.

"Nothing on the ocean view," Dan said. "But look. Nona is sleeping in the nest for a change. Win is digging."

Carlos bent toward the screen as Win came up with a purple tuber and dropped it near the nest. "Only the finest of tubers for his bride."

Dan smiled.

They heard the sound of wings. Both men peered out the window.

"It's Atlas," Dan said.

They hurried outside just as Atlas landed.

"Well, how did the mating go?" Dan asked.

Atlas smiled. "It was wonderful! We are so happy together!"

"Mating should be a happy occasion," Carlos said.

"She's sleeping," Atlas said.

"At her home?" Carlos asked.

"Yes," Atlas said.

"Well, Atlas," Dan said. "You know what this means, don't you?"

"Yes! Lily and I will be mates forever."

"That's true," Dan said, "but it means something else, too."

Atlas seemed puzzled. "Something else?"

"Yes," Dan said. "You had a successful mating. There's going to be an egg. You're going to be a father."

Atlas dipped his head. "I don't know anything about being a father."

"No one is born knowing how to be a father," Carlos said. "You learn on the job."

"Atlas, even though you haven't been a father," Dan said, "you know how Kieran raised you. Kieran was a good father to you, wasn't he?"

"Yes."

"Then do what he did," Dan said.

"Besides," Carlos said. "You're going to live with Lily's parents, as I understand it. Merlin will be there to help you."

"Grandparents are very good at that," Dan said.

Atlas seemed to be thinking it over.

Carlos waved at Atlas. "Stay there for a moment. I'm going to get you something." He walked away.

"I have to get back to Lily," Atlas said. "I just came here to tell you."

"I'm glad you came to tell us," Dan said. "But Carlos will be back shortly. We know that you want to be back with Lily as soon as you can." After a moment, he added, "You and Lily will be great parents. When you love, take care of, and play with your hatchling, your little one will think that you are the greatest parents in the world."

Atlas smiled and nodded. "Yes, Lily and I will do all of that."

Dan smiled back. "Then you'll do fine."

It was not long before Carlos appeared again, holding two bouquets of flowers. He held out one bouquet to Atlas. "This is for you and Lily. I've been cultivating them in my own garden just for the occasion."

Atlas took the bouquet. "These are wonderful!"

Dan put an arm around Carlos. "We're very happy for you and Lily. We hope we'll see you again."

"We'll come back," Atlas said. "We just need to be with each other for a while."

"As it should be," Carlos said.

Atlas left with the bouquet.

Dan released Carlos and turned to him. "The other flowers are for Zinnia and Morran?"

"That's what I had in mind, yes."

"Let's go off and see if we can present it, then."

Before they reached Rhea and Nick's, a tanklet intercepted him.

"Win?" Carlos asked.

"No, it's one of the kits," Dan said. "I privately named this one Rascal."

"You named the kits?" Carlos said.

"In my imagination, yes," Dan said.

Rascal turned and walked ahead, then turned back and walked to Dan and Carlos, then turned and walked away again.

"He wants us to follow," Dan said.

"Let's see where he's going," Carlos said.

Rascal led them to a clearing, where, in a nest similar to Win and Nona's, a female tanklet slept. He turned, walked up to Dan, faced upward, and chattered.

"Does he want the flowers?" Carlos asked.

"I doubt it," Dan said.

"He wants something," Carlos said.

"I have an idea," Dan said, and started back to their house, Carlos following, Rascal trailing behind.

"Rhea and Nick gave us a couple of pottery platters," Dan said. "I was thinking of taking one and setting it near their nest and filling it with water, as I did for Win and Nona."

"We have tubers in storage, too," Carlos said. "Win kept us supplied."

Rascal waited as Dan retrieved the platter and filled up the water pitcher. Carlos held on to the flowers but picked up a tuber from storage. When Rascal saw they were returning to his nest, he trotted in front and led the way.

At the nest, Carlos put down the tuber and Dan set the platter on the ground. Before Dan could fill it with water, Rascal grasped the platter with his teeth and moved it.

"Rascal seems to be arranging the furniture," Carlos said with a smile.

"Well, one does what one must for one's mate." Dan grinned in turn and poured in the water.

Rascal chattered at him, and then turned to drink.

Carlos turned to Dan. "Seems we got another couple off to a good start."

They continued to Rhea and Nick's. Just as Dan and Carlos approached the doorway, Rhea and Nick walked out.

"Morning," Dan said. "Sleep well?"

Rhea and Nick each raised their eyebrows. "Yes, why do you ask?" Rhea said.

"All that noise last night," Carlos said.

"What noise?" Nick asked.

"Surely you heard all those animal noises," Dan said.

"Mating," Carlos added.

"Oh," Rhea said. "Nick and I wore our stereo headphones to bed last night. We wanted to listen to music."

"I guess we missed something then," Nick asked. "Was it loud?"

"Incredibly," Carlos said.

Dan smiled and changed the subject. "Have you seen Zinnia or Morran?"

"No," Rhea said. "We were just about to see if we could find Kieran and Thalia and ask about them."

At that moment, they saw Kieran and Thalia approach.

"How are Zinnia and Morran?" Rhea asked.

"Good," Thalia said. "Zinnia is sleeping. Morran is snuggling with her."

"He's an attentive mate," Kieran added.

"Sounds like an excellent match." Carlos held out the bouquet. "We have flowers for them. Is there any way we can get the flowers to them without disturbing them?"

Thalia reached for the flowers. "We'll see that they get them."

Carlos handed over the flowers. "If you and Kieran want some flowers, come over to Dan's and my house later. We have more."

"Lily showed us how to plant flowers for ourselves," Kieran said. "She said they should bloom soon, so we will have them then."

"When Zinnia is ready," Rhea said. "Tell her that Nick and I are ready to go back to Earth to arrange for our union."

"You will return here?" Kieran said.

"Of course. After our honeymoon." When the dragons looked confused, Rhea added, "Our first mating time."

"Of course," Thalia said.

When Thalia and Kieran left, Dan turned to Nick and Rhea. "Before you leave, I want to do something for Arthur."

"Arthur?" Nick asked.

"Yes," Dan said. "I want to at least return the journals to his house. Carlos and I have been talking, and Carlos wants to plant flowers at his gravesite. We wondered if you could use your pottery skills to make a headstone?"

Rhea turned to Nick. "I think we can do that."

After the two dragon couples returned from their honeymoons, their human friends asked if they would fly to Arthur and Rex's place. They readily consented.

Lily, Carlos, and Dan had not been to the site before, so Rhea and Nick gave them a tour. Rhea reverently placed Arthur's journals back on the desk where they found them.

Outside, they gathered around the rectangular pile of rocks, Arthur's final resting place. Rhea directed Zinnia to plant the headstone at one end of the cairn. The inscription simply said, "Arthur Johnson 1890-1956." Carlos reached for his gardening tools and planted flower seeds and seedlings.

When that was done, the humans stood back and remained in respectful silence for a few minutes. The dragons watched curiously.

Dan turned to the dragons. "This is one way humans honor those who have died."

"It's nice," Atlas said.

Rhea turned to the dragons. "Yes, without Arthur helping us, and Rex helping him, and all of you helping us, we would never have done as well."

"We would have not found a way to stop The Terror without you humans," Zinnia said.

Rhea nodded. "We are grateful for each other. That's what friends do."

Back at Rhea and Nick's place, they discussed their wedding plans with Dan and Carlos over dinner.

"It's going to be a small, brief wedding," Rhea said. "Besides Nick and me, it'll be just you two, my parents and sister, Nick's Uncle Jack, the officiant, and six dragons."

"Are the dragons willing to go?" Carlos said.

"Yes, I've discussed it with them," Nick said. "I said it would be similar to the engagement gathering. At first they were politely curious, but after I told them we'd have an abundance of flowers for them to eat as part of the celebration, they became more interested."

Dan chuckled.

Rhea smiled. "We'll tell the florist not to put any preservatives on the flowers."

"Have you ordered anything yet?" Dan asked.

"When Dan and I were on Earth talking about the hatchlings," Rhea said, "I took the time to order my dress. It's a short-sleeved white dress with a design of a dragon sewn in sequins. A craft site has been selling them to members of the Dragon Appreciation Society for weddings."

Dan turned to Carlos before addressing Nick. "Do we need to retrieve our formals?"

Nick shook his head. "I'm just going to wear a suit. Uncle Jack never dresses up. He'll probably just wear a knit shirt and pants."

"Where are you having the wedding?" Carlos asked.

"Uncle Jack's country estate. There's plenty of room for the dragons on the grounds."

"What's your timeline?" Dan asked.

Rhea turned to Nick briefly before answering. "I thought we'd ask Zinnia to take us to Earth tomorrow. We still need to make some arrangements, especially for the honeymoon."

"Give us about three days," Nick said. "I've put together a timer app that we can share. It will give a countdown that we can see on our smartphones on Earth and you can see on your computer here."

"What if you have unexpected delays?" Carlos asked.

"Then the dragons will have to take you back until another time," Nick said.

"I'll talk to Zinnia about it." Rhea turned to Dan. "It won't hurt her to go back and forth, will it?"

Dan shook his head. "No, I think she'll be fine. As will Lily."

Carlos faced Dan. "Why would it be a problem?"

Dan smiled. "They're both pregnant. Or, more precisely, 'with egg.'"

Carlos nodded. "I see."

As it happened, the wedding took place on schedule. When the timer showed zero, Dan and Carlos gathered with the dragons.

"I see Rhea signaling," Zinnia said.

Once they all appeared on Earth, Dan looked around. Flowers were everywhere, arranged in garlands and on frames fashioned from sturdy vines. Nick and Rhea stood under an arch festooned with flowers, with a middle-aged man wearing a suit who smiled at them.

Nick and Rhea made introductions, and the humans sat in chairs behind the arch for the ceremony.

Nick's Uncle Jack, sitting next to Dan, leaned toward him and said in a low voice, "The officiant, Bruce, is a member of the Dragon Appreciation Society."

Dan nodded and glanced back to see six dragons sitting behind them, watching curiously. He had coached them beforehand not to say anything until he raised a hand to signal that the ceremony was over.

Bruce started promptly and the vows took only a few minutes. After Rhea and Nick exchanged a ceremonial kiss, the humans surrounded them, giving and receiving hugs, handshakes, and warm wishes. Some took pictures with their smartphones.

Dan raised his hand and waved to the dragons.

Rhea and Nick approached the dragons.

"Thank you for coming. Go ahead and eat the flowers," Rhea said, and the dragons headed for the displays.

Dan waved at a table. "I presume the cake is for us?"

"Yes," Nick said.

The humans all gathered around the cake table and made friendly conversation as it was served.

After the cake, Nick and Rhea signed the marriage license with Bruce. He shyly asked if he could get closer to the dragons. Rhea called Zinnia over, explained that the man was a member of the Dragon Appreciation Society, and asked it would be all right if he touched her. Zinnia lowered her head and the officiant stroked it.

"Thank you, you made my day," Bruce said.

"I'm always happy to meet a human who is a friend to dragons," Zinnia said.

Nick handed Bruce a thick envelope. "Thank you."

"Yes, thank you," Rhea said.

"The pleasure was all mine," Bruce said. "My best wishes for your future happiness. I'll take these papers to the courthouse and file them." Nodding and waving to the others, he left.

"Rhea and I will get going, too," Nick said to the others.

"We'll signal Zinnia in about ten days," Rhea said. "I've already discussed our plans with her."

"We'll be waiting for you in the dragon world," Dan said.

After Rhea and Nick left, Morran approached Carlos and Dan. "They've gone to mate?"

"Yes, that's what usually happens after a wedding," Dan said.

"Good. It is good to have a mate," Morran said.

"We definitely agree," Dan said. He turned to Carlos, and they exchanged a kiss.

On the last day of their honeymoon, Rhea and Nick strolled side by side along an oceanside beach. The moon was full, and even though it was midnight, there was plenty of light to see by.

"This has been a wonderful honeymoon, Nick," Rhea said. "Thank you."

"Anytime with you is a good time," Nick said.

Rhea stopped and leaned toward him. They kissed while the ocean breezes played with their hair.

When their lips parted, Nick said, "We can stay longer, if you like."

"No, I think I want to go back home now," Rhea said.

"I take it 'home' now means with the dragons?"

"I hadn't thought of it that way," Rhea said. "The dragons, yes."

Nick smiled. "I thought so. I'm sort of missing them myself. Even Morran, though he can be an asshole at times."

Rhea chuckled. "That can be said of just about anyone."

Nick paused a moment before answering. "True."

Rhea stopped and looked Nick in the eye. "Do you mind going back to the dragon world?"

"No, I realized here that I've come to think of the dragon world as home, too. Besides, I remember that all through college, every day you'd look up in the sky hoping that Zinnia would come back for you. I have the feeling that you'd do the same if we stayed here on Earth. I saw how happy you were in the dragon world, and that made me happy, too."

"We did talk about six months on Earth and six months on the dragon world."

Nick nodded. "Yes, we did. But I know now that I'd wonder what Zinnia and Morran and Atlas and Lily were up to if we stayed here, not to mention Dan and Carlos."

"Have they said anything to you about staying on the dragon world for the long term?" Rhea asked.

"No, but Carlos has his agricultural research and Dan is deeply involved with his animal research. Dan still wants to find out what the mysterious organ he found does, as well as distilling and testing those medicinal plants. And remember before he came, how it seemed that Dan wanted more than anything to live with dragons? I don't think they're planning to leave anytime soon."

A young man ran up to them.

"Are you the lady I saw on social media talking about dragons?" he asked Rhea.

"Yes," Rhea said.

"I'm a member of the Dragon Appreciation Society." He reached into a pocket and bought out a pen and his wallet.

Taking out a card, he offered it and the pen to Rhea. "Would you autograph my membership card?"

"Sure." Rhea signed the back and returned the card to the young man.

He smiled and waved a farewell. "Save the hatchings!" he said as he ran off.

Nick turned to Rhea. "Have you kept track of how many people have asked for your autograph here?"

Rhea smiled. "No, but it's nice that there are a lot of them."

Nick put his arm back around Rhea and gave her a squeeze. "Ready to signal Zinnia?"

"Anytime," Rhea said.

They had their bags packed. After returning to the hotel, they checked out and enlisted a cab to drive them to a remote park. Rhea signaled to Zinnia. She appeared almost immediately, and escorted them back the dragon world, where it was still afternoon.

Zinnia's family, as well as Dan, Carlos, Atlas, and Lily, were waiting.

"Welcome back!" Dan said.

"How was the honeymoon?" Carlos asked.

"Excellent," Nick said.

"Wonderful." Rhea turned to Zinnia and put a hand on Zinnia's face, looking into her eyes. "I'm home now, Zinnia."

Zinnia trilled happily. The other dragons joined in.

THE END

Would you like to read the story where Rhea and Zinnia met? Find information about *Wondry Dragon Finds a Home* at https://ftlpublications.com.

# About the Author

Joan Marie Verba is an autistic author, publisher, and web developer with a bachelor's degree in physics. She was an associate instructor of astronomy for one year. She has worked as a computer programmer, web developer, editor, publisher, and social media manager. An experienced writer, she is the author of fiction and nonfiction books plus numerous short stories and articles. Her novels have received the Mom's Choice Award® and the Scribe Award. She is a member of the Science Fiction and Fantasy Writers Association and the International Association of Media Tie-in Writers.

To find out more about Joan's books, subscribe to her newsletter at: https://joanmarieverba.com/

# Acknowledgments

I wish to extend my sincere thanks to the members of my critique group, Elizabeth Rowan Keith, Eleanor Dorn, Ted Schoep, and P.C. Hodgell, for their valuable advice and encouragement as I wrote this novel.

www.ingramcontent.com/pod-product-compliance
Lightning Source LLC
Chambersburg PA
CBHW060548260626
47161CB00003B/1104

* 9 7 8 1 9 3 6 8 8 1 7 4 1 *